Th
Cam

But the city was not uninhabited.

Shadows of creatures that had once been the Bright Folk of Fairy slunk through its streets, hungering for human prey. Mab had created monsters in Mordred's honor, monsters enough to haunt the dreams of children for a thousand years.

The golden stone of Camelot had already begun to crumble, and black weeds had grown up through the blocks of stone. From this place Mab would spread the blackest of her magic, slaying what she could not subvert, until she had destroyed all of mortalkind on the Isle of Britain.

Unless someone stopped her.

ALSO BY JAMES MALLORY

Merlin: *The Old Magic*
Merlin: *The King's Wizard*

HALLMARK ENTERTAINMENT PRESENTS
SAM NEILL   HELENA BONHAM CARTER
JOHN GIELGUD   DUTGER HAUER
JAMES EARL JONES   MIRANDA RICHARDSON
ISABELLA ROSSELLINI   MARTIN SHORT
"MERLIN"
LEGEND ADVISOR LOREN BOOTHBY
MUSIC BY TREVOR JONES
CREATURE EFFECTS BY JIM HENSON'S CREATURE SHOP
EXECUTIVE PRODUCER ROBERT HALMI, SR
PRODUCED BY DYSON LOVELL
TELEPLAY BY DAVID STEVENS AND PETER BARNES
STORY BY EDWARD KHMARA
DIRECTED BY STEVE BARRON

ORIGINAL SOUNDTRACK AVAILABLE ON VARÈSE SARABANDE COMPACT DISCS

Voyager

Merlin:
The End of Magic

JAMES MALLORY

HarperCollins*Publishers*

Voyager
An imprint of HarperCollins*Publishers*
77–85 Fulham Palace Road,
Hammersmith, London W6 8JB

www.voyager-books.com

A Paperback Original 2000
1 3 5 7 9 10 8 6 4 2

A catalogue record for this book
is available from the British Library

ISBN 0 00 651291 7

Set in Times

Printed and bound in Great Britain by
Caledonian International Book Manufacturing Ltd, Glasgow

For Betsy, Jane, Fiona, and Russ,
for all their help and support,
and to MJ, for the usual.

Contents

Chapter One
The Battle of Honor 5

Chapter Two
The Battle of Loyalty 35

Chapter Three
The Battle of Sorrow 67

Chapter Four
The Battle of Shadows 105

Chapter Five
The Battle of Mirrors 135

Chapter Six
The Battle of Cruelty 167

Chapter Seven
The Battle of Deception 197

Chapter Eight
The Battle of the Forest 225

Chapter Nine
The Battle of Magic 255

Appendix A
The Camelot Comet 277

Appendix B
The Matter of Britain 281

Merlin:
The End of Magic

WHAT HAS
GONE BEFORE

At a time when the wicked King Vortigern rules
England, Mab, Fairy Queen of the Old Ways, cre-
ates Merlin to become a great wizard who can lead
Britain away from the New Religion and back to the Old
Ways. She trains him to be a wizard, but Mab's thought-
lessness and cruelty soon cause Merlin to despise all that
she stands for. When Mab kills Merlin's foster mother,
Ambrosia, Merlin vows that he will never use his powers
except to defeat her.

Undaunted, Mab arranges for Merlin to come to the
attention of King Vortigern, and makes Vortigern believe
that he must sacrifice Merlin so that the fortress he is
building will stand. Merlin prophecies a great battle between two dragons, which will end with the destruction
of the white dragon, Vortigern's totem. Furious, the King
orders Merlin imprisoned. While imprisoned, Merlin

once more encounters Princess Nimue, whom he had loved many years before.

Mab, still seeking to force Merlin to use his magic in her cause, arranges for both him and Nimue to be offered as a sacrifice to the Great Dragon. Merlin uses his magic to defeat the dragon, but not before Nimue is hideously injured. Fearing for her life, Merlin takes Nimue to Avalon Abbey to recover. Though Nimue will live, she is permanently scarred.

Realizing that he must strike out against both Mab and Vortigern, Merlin goes to the Lady of the Lake for help. She gives him the sword Excalibur, which can only be used by a good man in a good cause. Merlin takes Excalibur to Uther and promises him victory over Vortigern if Uther will take Merlin's advice. In a great battle fought on a frozen lake, Merlin destroys Vortigern and makes Uther King. But Uther is greedy and lusts after Igraine, the wife of Duke Gorlois of Cornwall. Angered, Merlin takes back Excalibur and seals it in a rock from which only a good man can withdraw it. He leaves Uther's court to return to Nimue, but many months later he returns, fearful that Uther's war will destroy the kingdom he has labored so long to protect. Realizing that the child that will be born of Uther and Igraine's night of passion— Arthur—will grow up to be the great and good King that Britain so desperately needs, Merlin agrees to use his magic to help Uther. But Uther tricks him, killing Gorlois and leaving Igraine a widow. When Arthur is born, Merlin gives him to Sir Hector to raise. Merlin becomes young Arthur's tutor, and Arthur grows up in ignorance of his heritage.

When Uther dies, Merlin makes the young Arthur king, but Lot, the father of Gawain and Guinevere, disputes his claim to the throne. Arthur manages to make peace between his army and Lord Lot's, but in the celebration that follows, a mysterious stranger comes to visit Arthur.

She is Morgan le Fay, his half sister and Mab's pawn. Morgan wants to rule England, and tricks Arthur into begetting a son, Mordred. When Merlin explains to Arthur what he has done, the young King is devastated with guilt, and vows to go on a quest for the Holy Grail. While Arthur—now married to Guinevere—prepares for his journey, Merlin seeks out a champion to hold Britain while the King is gone, and finds him at Joyous Gard. Sir Lancelot defeats all of Arthur's knights at the Easter tourney, and Arthur feels confident about leaving the kingdom in Lancelot's hands as Arthur rides off in search of the Grail.

But Mab, scheming to destroy Arthur out of her hatred for Merlin, has caused Lancelot and Guinevere to fall in love. . . .

The Battle of Honor

Jt was spring again, and Merlin was always most restless in the spring. The spring breeze ruffled the feathers that trimmed his long cloak, and sunlight flashed off the crystal ball embedded in the head of his wizard's staff. It was as if the green life of the earth called to him, wooing him to walk through the tall grass and shadowed forest paths. In his soul, he longed to give in to the blandishments of the daffodils and bright butterflies that he could see beyond the castle walls and follow their trackless path. Somewhere out there was the forest hut in which he had been born, the forest in which he had spent so many happy, innocent years before Mab came to claim him as her champion. Later, he had returned to Barnstable Forest to live a simple life as the child Arthur grew to manhood in the home of Sir Hector, safe and loved and secure.

But there is nothing in life as constant as change, and just as Merlin's life had been torn apart years before by the revelation of his true parentage, so Arthur's life had been similarly rent asunder when the time had come for Merlin to tell him that he was not a simple country lad but a prince, King Uther's son. Arthur had taken the news well, but unfortunately for Arthur, he had possessed a mother as well as a father, and therein lay the seeds of Merlin's greatest failure to protect his young charge.

Arthur had not been the unfortunate Lady Igraine's only child, and Arthur's half sister, Morgan le Fay, was rotted through with ambition. Morgan had wanted the crown, but couldn't have it while Arthur lived, so she had schemed to become the power behind the throne. Morgan's lust for power had caused her to ally herself with Queen Mab, using fairy magic to trick Arthur into lying with her.

Now Arthur had a son, Mordred, begotten in sin and raised in malice, a boy who lived for the day when he would tear down all that Arthur and Merlin had painstakingly built together, destroying Camelot and Britain.

Merlin's gaze traveled toward Tintagel and the west as the breeze ruffled his untidy light brown hair. How old was Mordred now, and what was he doing? It had been nearly seven years since Merlin had last seen him, and even then the boy had been growing unnaturally fast. Seven years ago the King had not yet been married, had not yet declared his intention to go on this disastrous quest for the Holy Grail.

But Mordred was surely still a child. There would be years in which to decide how best to deal with his menace. And today, Merlin faced other problems. He sighed, resting his weight on his staff. The stone walls of Camelot that he lived within so much of the time seemed to cut off all light and air—even when, as now, he stood upon the highest battlements, gazing toward the northern horizon and feeling the warm spring sun soak into his bones.

Old bones, and older every year, Merlin thought ruefully. *I was a grown man when Arthur was born, and now Arthur is a man grown in his turn. Where is he today, I wonder?*

The letters that came from Arthur and the little band of knights that he had taken with him upon his quest to find the Grail were few and far between. One had come to Camelot three months before, written three months before that, so the freshest news was six months old now. Six months ago Arthur had still been in France; who knew where he might be now? *Wherever he is, I fear he is no closer than before to what he seeks. The Grail seems always to elude him, glimmering just out of reach like a will-o'-the-wisp. And he has sought it for so many years. . . .*

As always, thoughts of the Grail led Merlin to thoughts of Avalon, and Nimue.

He had loved her from the moment he had first seen her, more than half his lifetime ago. He loved her still, though he had not so much as spoken to her since that night many years ago when he had learned of Arthur's disastrous liaison with Morgan le Fay. While Mab schemed to destroy Merlin and all he loved, even a letter between the lovers might be too dangerous.

For a moment Merlin's shoulders drooped with weariness. All he had ever asked of the world was bound up in Nimue's smile, but Merlin was not an ordinary man who could allow himself ordinary joys. He had been created by the Queen of the Old Ways to be her champion, to destroy the rule of the New Religion in Britain, and to return Queen Mab to supreme power. Half human, half fay, caught between both worlds and never at home in either, for most of his life Merlin had battled toward a goal that daily seemed to be slipping farther out of reach: freedom for Britain from the tyranny of the Old Ways, and peace and happiness for her under the reign of a good King.

He had held such high hopes of Arthur, and Arthur was a truly good man. But somehow Merlin's dream had slipped away with Arthur's decision to quest for the Holy Grail. For centuries, Christendom's great treasure had reposed at Avalon Abbey, but it had vanished on the night that Merlin was conceived, and had not been seen since. Arthur believed that Britain could not truly begin to heal from the carnage and treachery of three bad kings until the Grail was restored to Britain, but the king's abrupt departure left his new-wed queen, Guinevere, alone to rule the country in his absence.

Guinevere was barely a bride when Arthur's quest began, and he had never lain with her to make her his wife in more than name. There was trouble brewing in that corner, for Guinevere was of royal blood, raised as a princess of the Iceni and only lately converted to the New Religion that Arthur followed. She could not understand Arthur's motives in searching for the Grail and leaving Britain behind.

What she *could* understand was that she was left alone in Camelot year after year while the memory of Arthur grew ever more distant in her mind.

Merlin sighed tiredly, and somehow the sunlight seemed less warm and inviting than it had when he'd climbed all the way to the top of this tower to enjoy the solitude and the view. He could not blame the young Queen for her increasing attachment to her Champion, Lancelot of the Lake, but no good could come of it. And with Mab hatching her plots in Tintagel, raising up Arthur's bastard son Mordred to be her willing accomplice in damnation, they must all be eternally vigilant.

Merlin did not know if Arthur had confided to his Queen the exact nature of the transgression that caused him to seek the Grail so passionately, but he suspected she was unaware of what it was. Should he warn Guinevere of Mordred's existence? Merlin hesitated. Arthur's conscience had long since passed out of his keeping. If Arthur had not told his wife, it was not Merlin's place to reveal so painful a secret. And perhaps the Queen need never know at all. . . .

The ravens who lived in the tower took to the air, cawing and complaining. Someone had entered below, and Merlin suspected who it was, and on what errand she was bound. Drawing his cloak around him and clutching his staff tighter, Merlin descended the long winding stair that led to the ground floor of the White Tower.

Guinevere, Princess of the Iceni and Queen of Britain, stood on the ground floor, peering up toward the light that spilled down from the windows above. The years had ripened Arthur's child-bride into a magnificent

woman, strong-willed and regal. She had never quite lost
her distrust of Merlin, a pagan wizard at a Christian court,
but she had come to accept his presence, and sometimes
she even took his advice. But Merlin knew that to Guinevere he would always remain half-unreal, a creature out
of fable. A Wizard of the Old Ways in a land that was
rapidly forgetting that Magic had ever existed at all.

She did not come here looking for me, Merlin reflected, and when the Queen recognized him, his guess
was confirmed.

"Oh," Guinevere said. "I was just . . . good morning,
Master Merlin. I did not expect to see you here."

Her cheeks were flushed and she would not meet his
gaze. Merlin thought he could well guess who the Queen
had come here alone so early hoping to meet.

Lancelot.

Lancelot of the Lake had been Merlin's own choice
to guard the Queen while Arthur was gone. Mab's sister,
the Lady of the Lake, had sent Merlin to Joyous Gard to
find a champion to preserve Camelot in Arthur's absence,
and there Merlin had found the best knight in the world—
Lancelot. When Lancelot had returned to Camelot with
Merlin, he had easily defeated all of Arthur's knights on
the field of honor and been named the Queen's Champion. In the few weeks they had known each other,
Lancelot and Arthur had become fast friends, and Arthur
had willingly entrusted his dream of Camelot, a shining
city of peace and charity, to his friend.

Merlin knew that Lancelot had only the highest
ideals and the most honorable intentions, but sometimes
it seemed to Merlin that all those principles weren't quite

in Camelot's best interest. The city should have been finished years ago, but Lancelot was forever tearing things down, redrafting Arthur's plans, trying to force Camelot to match a perfection that was simply inhuman. It never occurred to the knight of Joyous Gard that some dreams were not meant to become real.

"Were you looking for someone, my lady?" Merlin asked Guinevere. "I fear I am the only one here." *Did you ask Lancelot to meet you here? Was he wise enough to refuse? My children, what am I to do with you?*

"No, of course not," the Queen answered, a little too sharply. Bright color flamed in her cheeks. "I was only . . . looking around."

"You should go back to your women," Merlin told her as gently as he could.

"I shall," Guinevere replied, with a haughty jerk of her chin. She swirled her heavy skirts about her and walked quickly away, the silk making a hissing sound against the stone.

Merlin sighed quietly as he watched her go. Her distrust of him made her temperamental; for all that it had been seven years since her wedding day, the Queen was still very young. But perhaps it was wrong of him to still treat her as a child. For better or for worse, in Arthur's absence, Guinevere ruled Britain, and her word was law here. If the choices she made sometimes seemed foolish to him, then it was no more than her right to choose her own path.

Merlin leaned upon his staff, drawing what solace he could from the smooth surface of the gnarled wood. They would all endure somehow—he, Guinevere, Lancelot, Britain. And Arthur would return.

Someday.

The Queen strode out of the tower and into the bustling streets of the town. She blinked at the brightness of the sunlight after the dimness of the tower, but stumbled determinedly back to where she had left her attendants. It had been a foolish notion really, to go off looking for Lancelot like that. He would not thank her for interrupting his morning's work for a bit of inconsequential chatter. Lancelot was a busy man, and despite all his efforts, the building of Camelot went more slowly every year. Sometimes she thought that Arthur might even be back before it was finished.

As always, thoughts of the King—even after seven years, Guinevere found it hard to think of him as her husband—brought an unhappy, guilty twinge. How could Arthur have chosen to leave if she hadn't failed him somehow? Would he have felt such a need to gain the Grail if she'd been a better person?

What did you want from me, Arthur-the-King? Why wasn't I good enough—or just enough *for you, damn you?*

She'd repeated the unanswerable questions to herself so often down the years that separated sixteen from twenty-three that they'd almost become a litany, but the answer was always the same. Silence, from her heart and in his letters. Though he wrote of his many adventures and always sent his love, there was never any hint in his letters of a longing to return—to Camelot or to her. There were times when Guinevere could not imagine why Arthur had married her at all. He seemed to have no earthly need for a wife or a Queen.

But no matter how little Arthur needed her, there were others who did. Lancelot needed her. She could see it in his eyes.

"Your Highness! There you are!" Dame Linnet cried with relief. Dame Linnet was a plump young woman who favored blue gowns, and her timidity often frustrated Guinevere nearly to tears. Today, however, Guinevere was almost grateful to see her.

"Yes," Guinevere answered composedly. "I went to look at the tower, but it was too dark inside to see much."

"Oh, but that was because the shutters for the upper windows are still closed. When the glass for the windows arrives from Flanders, it will be bright enough inside to read at midday! Sir Lancelot was just telling us how it would be."

Dame Linnet gestured back toward the others, who were gathered about a familiar figure.

His bronze hair gleamed in the pale sunlight, and he wore a bright blue cloak that Guinevere had embroidered with her own hands, for with Arthur absent she had no one else to lavish her needlework upon. Beneath the cloak he wore a simple linen tunic, but no sword, for Lancelot was a civilized man, from a country so unlike Guinevere's war-torn Britain as to seem almost mythical. He smiled when he saw her, and Guinevere smiled back, all the shadows and doubts of a moment before gone like morning mist. Nothing bad could happen while Lancelot was with her.

"Your Grace," Lancelot said, bowing to her. "I was just explaining how this section of the wall would look once the buildings along the street are finished."

"As beautiful as the castle, I trust," Guinevere answered in a steady voice. Camelot Castle had finally been finished two years before, the second structure to be completed in the Golden City after the great Cathedral.

"More so," Lancelot answered. "Providing the architect does what I tell him. And now, ladies—and Your Highness—if you would care to accompany me, I will show you the new marketplace."

He held out his arm to Guinevere, and she placed her hand upon it. She could feel the roughness of the sun-warmed linen beneath her fingers, and she fancied she felt the warmth of the flesh beneath as well. Her heart beat faster, and for a brief instant she wished that Arthur had never been born.

Merlin watched them go from the doorway of the tower. He shook his head sadly. He did not need his wizard's gift of prophecy to see what was happening between the Queen and Sir Lancelot. And what he could now see, others would soon see. He did not doubt that—for the moment—the friendship was innocent, born of loneliness on the Queen's part and sympathy on Sir Lancelot's. Both Lancelot and Guinevere were too proud to casually betray their ideals to gratify a momentary whim—and Lancelot, at least, was so convinced of his moral superiority that he felt himself beyond the earthly temptations of illicit love. Such confidence could be fatal—no one knew that better than Merlin.

Oh Nimue, Nimue—if you were here, could you stop what I fear is going to happen? Lend me your wisdom to gaze into the workings of the human heart, for there magic is powerless and even the greatest wizard is blind!

But for Merlin, as for Guinevere, there was no answer, and slowly the wizard turned away and walked slowly through the open gates of the city.

Oh, Arthur, where are you? You need the Grail, but your people need you more. . . .

In the wilds of Cornwall a great keep stood upon the coast, its back to the land. Grey sea-mist veiled it day and night, and the ways to its gates were twisted ones. The gruff fisherfolk who took their living from the grudging ocean swore that Tintagel was only a myth, and that to see the castle looming out of the fog was a promise of dire misfortune. Who had lived in Tintagel, and what had happened to them, was something the fishermen did not know. Their King lived in Camelot, and they had no other lord.

And that was just the way Queen Mab wanted it. There would be time enough to gain the love of the people when Mordred ruled in Camelot . . . and Arthur was dead.

The Queen of the Old Ways gazed out the window at the shifting weave of mist. Once she had ruled all this land and the Land of Magic as well. Now her earthly domain was confined to this one small headland, cloaked and saturated with magic.

She could no longer remember the day upon which her fight for survival had begun, so long had it endured.

Nor could she remember what life had been like before the New Religion had come to Britain, to steal all that was rightfully hers. Once Mab would have mourned the loss of her past, but generations of fighting had burned that softness from her. She did not know when she had stopped believing in a victory that would erase all her defeats, but she no longer cared that the Old Ways—the very thing that gave her life through her worshipers' belief in her—had been changed irrevocably by the New Religion. Making things the way they once had been no longer mattered to her, so long as she could have victory—and revenge.

Against Merlin. Against Arthur. Against everyone who had betrayed her, thwarted her plans, destroyed her shrines and her worshipers, *changed* her by the very way they thought of her, through curses where there had once been prayers. They had made her what she was, and they would pay the terrible price.

She would give them *Mordred,* whose very name meant "the fear of death."

She had learned from her failures, for this time Mab would not leave the raising of her champion in someone else's hands. She would mold her child—her Mordred—from his first breath to the moment he fulfilled the destiny she had decreed for him: ruler of Britain, destroyer of Arthur, Camelot, and the New Religion.

And Merlin would be there to experience every moment of her triumph. Mab smiled, telling over her dreams of the future the way a miser might gloat over his hoarded wealth. Killing Merlin was no part of her plan. She wanted him to suffer, to agonize, to yearn for what he had lost. She did not mean him to escape that.

But Mordred was still a young man, untutored in the Old Ways, and Arthur was still far away from Britain. Even Mab could not quite see how to take a throne away from someone who didn't currently have it. Defeating the Queen alone would be no sport. Let Guinevere destroy herself with Lancelot first; her betrayal would soften up the people until they were *happy* to welcome Mordred as their rightful King.

But for the moment Mab truly did not have any interest in what went on in Britain. She had her dreams of future glory, and she had Mordred. She walked away from the window and took her place at the long table in the great hall of Tintagel.

Unlike Arthur's Round Table, this table had a definite head and foot, and Mab was seated near the head. As five of the castle servitors shuffled into the room, their eyes rolling with terror, Mab's brow wrinkled as she tried to remember what they'd originally been before Frik had transformed them with his magic. Mice, she thought, or perhaps rabbits. They certainly looked like scared rabbits at the moment, but no matter how terrifying his forms of amusement, no one in Tintagel was brave enough to rebel against Mordred.

As the years had passed, Mab and Frik spent more and more of their time at Tintagel, until the castle was nearly as magical as the Land Under Hill. Mab lavished all of her care and attention on Mordred. She had erred in leaving Merlin's raising to Ambrosia, and the old priestess had corrupted him with soft human emotions. Mab would not make the same mistake twice. She would burn all the softness from Mordred's heart, leaving it as hard and crystalline as her own. Every game, every gift that she gave him was aimed toward this, toward the day when he, her perfect instrument, would take his rightful place as King and sweep the New Religion and all its works from the face of Britain.

She glanced around the Great Hall at Tintagel, and even the sight of Frik in his ridiculous swashbuckler's disguise billing and cooing with the enchantingly beautiful Morgan le Fay could not irritate her today. She was on the verge of her ultimate victory. She could feel it.

"Show Auntie what you've learned, Mordred," Mab cooed coaxingly.

Mordred stepped from the shadows at the far end of the hall into a beam of light.

Arthur's son had grown into a compellingly beautiful young man. He wore his hair down past his shoulders; through the years it had darkened to a shade of red that was almost black. His eyes were a pale grey, brilliant as mirrors. He dressed all in black, saying it was the only color left unused after Morgan's brilliant extravagances, and today he wore a tunic of black suede trimmed in matching doeskin, with a double row of silver buttons running down the placket. At his hip he wore a box-quiver filled with silver-tipped arrows cut from black hawthorn, and he carried a large double-curved horn bow that Mab had brought him all the way from Khitai.

Across the breadth of the hall, the servants in their dun-colored tunics each quiveringly set an apple atop their heads. They stood along the wall behind Morgan's chair, almost too terrified to breathe.

"If you five gentlemen don't stop trembling, I might miss and kill you all," Mordred called out to them mockingly.

Their terror increased, but Mordred gave no hint that he noticed it. With inhuman speed he drew and fired, drew and fired, over Morgan's head, sending the next arrow on its way before the previous one had found its target. Their impact was one long *thrum* of sound, as the five apples fell to the ground.

But only four of them had been pierced. The fifth servant reeled back with a cry of pain, Mordred's arrow protruding from his right shoulder.

"Ah, less than perfect," Mab said. It was important that Mordred always be aware of his shortcomings, she felt.

Mordred's eyes flared at the rebuke, and his anger, never far below the surface, exploded into rage. He nocked another arrow and loosed it at Mab—who caught it unruffledly and dropped it to the floor—and then one at Frik, who was lounging in the corner conversing with Morgan. Frik yelped in surprise and seized it only a bare inch from his throat. But Mordred wasn't done. He had nocked a third arrow, and was aiming at his mother . . . and that arrow would find its target.

"That's enough, Mordred," Morgan said sharply, without the faintest trace of fear. Mordred hesitated, his face still white and furious. After a long moment he lowered his bow and smiled without any trace of surrender.

The years since his birth—few though they'd been as

the World of Men reckoned time—had been more than kind to Morgan le Fay. Though it was a gnomish illusion, she still possessed the dazzling beauty that had allowed her to bespell a king, and through Frik's magic, Morgan lived a life filled with every form of luxury. Today she wore a jade-green gown in the Roman style that Frik preferred, with a massive gold necklace with three long pendant plaques around her neck.

She watched Mab with her son with a faint flame of jealousy burning in the back of her glorious hazel eyes, for avarice had always been the defining principle of Morgan's nature, and though he was her own son, Morgan resented the gifts that Mab lavished on Mordred.

"You mustn't get carried away, my sweet," Mab said. If the murder attempt had fazed her at all, the Queen of the Old Ways didn't show it. "It shows a lack of control."

Mordred tossed his bow aside and walked toward the foot of the table, ignoring the further rebuke.

"And why fire at Auntie Mab and Uncle Frik?" Morgan added, anxious to seize control of the conversation.

"I do hope the boy was just having fun and it wasn't personal," Frik said, coming toward Morgan's side. He was holding the arrow very much as if he expected it to turn into a poisonous snake at any moment—which was not completely unlikely—and he still sounded breathless and flustered.

"Of course it wasn't personal. He likes you," Morgan reassured him. She took his hand and turned her head to the side to kiss it.

"I often wonder what he'd do if he *didn't* like me,"

Frik muttered under his breath, staring directly at Mordred.

Mordred gazed back expressionlessly. As always, Frik irritated him, but Mordred knew better than to challenge the gnome openly. There would be time enough for that, when Auntie Mab stopped stalling and granted him the power he needed to take the crown. Until then, he had to restrain himself and be nice to the people who mattered.

"Oh, stop fussing, Mother," he snapped. "Auntie Mab understands. Don't you, Auntie Mab?" he appealed, looking toward her.

"Of course I do," Mab cooed in her graveyard voice. "You were testing yourself. Now come sit by me."

The avidity in her voice was plain to hear, and it soothed Mordred's wounded feelings. He swaggered over to her, seating himself at the head of the table. Mab, seated in a chair behind him, reached out to stroke his cherry-black hair.

"You know you're my favorite, Mordred," she said wheedlingly. "But you must learn to channel your aggression."

"Against Arthur," Mordred said promptly. That had been the first and most constant lesson of his life: Arthur was the enemy, Arthur must be destroyed.

"Yes, always Arthur—and Merlin," Mab added, smoothing Mordred's hair as though she could not get enough of touching him. Mordred was her future—a future in which the Old Ways would be restored and all those who had dared to challenge her would be punished.

"You're looking pale, Mordred. You're not eating enough."

There was a flash of lightning, and suddenly the whole length of the table was covered with trays of savory delicacies in dishes of gold and silver, plucked from other lands and other feasts through the power of the Old Ways. Morgan sat forward with an expression of greedy interest, inspecting the treats closest to her as if she actually intended to eat something.

Mordred picked up a morsel of sweet-and-sour chicken and glared at it as if it were a personal enemy. "I already have the strength of ten men," he said pettishly. He regarded the banquet that lay before him without favor.

"Listen to your aunt," Morgan said from the foot of the table. "And please do something about your hair."

Mordred glanced over his shoulder at his patron. She nodded, indicating he was to agree. Mordred knew that his Auntie Mab liked his hair just the way it was. But Mother was jealous and spiteful—Mordred could recognize his own best qualities in another without regret—and yet did not dare to go against the power of the Old Ways. So she sniped at him, and he criticized her, and round and round they went on the Wheel of Years, waiting for the day when each of them might come into their power.

But Morgan's day was past, Mordred knew. And his was yet to come.

"Very well, Mother," Mordred said reluctantly. He popped the chicken into his mouth and bit down on it savagely, wishing it were her finger. At the other end of the table, Frik was using Mordred's silver-tipped arrow to offer Morgan a choice dainty, and Morgan had always been easily distracted by her gnomish cavalier.

She'd never loved him. Only Mab loved him. And then only if he did what she wanted.

"There's a good boy," Morgan said obliviously, the matter already forgotten.

Mordred sneered once he was sure she wasn't looking. He wasn't good, and he was fast leaving his boyhood behind. As soon as he proved himself ready, Auntie Mab would take him to the Land of Magic, and give him the fairy gifts that would make him unstoppable.

And then . . .

Mordred was not entirely sure what came next, but he had his dreams. Smash Camelot, smash Avalon, kill Arthur and every one of his knights who followed the New Religion. Drench the land in blood until all that was left was a void and the howling of old night and chaos come again. He would smash and destroy until there was no one anywhere who had anything that he didn't have: not love, not light, not family, not hope.

When Mordred was finished, there would be nothing left.

He smiled and sat back, humming a tuneless little song under his breath.

The future was bright.

It has been seven years since they came here. Nimue gazed at the empty altar before her. *Where have they gone?*

She knew she should be keeping vigil, clearing her

mind of earthly distractions in preparation for the great blessing she was about to receive. After so many years, she was about to enter her novitiate, taking one more step away from the world and one step closer to God. Nimue had longed for this day down through all the years when she had wondered if she was worthy of it.

Seven, and seven, and seven again. My life runs on sevens.

The beads of her amber rosary were cool against her fingers. Instead of praying, Nimue used them to count the years.

Seven years from the day she first met Merlin to the day she saw him being carried unconscious into Vortigern's dungeons. Seven weeks of joy to spend with him under the shadow of the old tyrant, until Mab's plotting sent them both to the maw of the Great Dragon. Then Merlin had brought her back here to Avalon, the place where she had grown up sheltered from Vortigern's evil, and she had never been able to bring herself to leave again.

Seven days passed from the day she entered these gates until Vortigern faced Uther upon the field of battle and died so that Uther could regain his throne. Seven days more, and Uther was crowned.

And seven months after that, all Britain knew their King for a mad and venal man. By autumn of that year Cornwall was dead, and Igraine disgraced. Nine months later Arthur was born—spoiling her count a little—then seven, and seven, and seven again while Merlin raised him in secret on Sir Hector's estate in the Forest Sauvage.

Those had been the best years of all, Nimue reflected, for in them she and Merlin had often written back and forth to share their joys and cares, hoping for the day when Arthur would take the throne and the two of them could be together once more, because Mab's ambitions would be defeated and Britain would no longer have any need of a wizard.

Then Uther died, and Merlin made Arthur King. And in the aftermath of Arthur's great battle with Lord Lot, Merlin had come at last to Avalon to take her away with him, and Nimue had wept for joy that the two of them could finally be together.

Only it was not to be. Mab's treachery had intervened once more, and Merlin had left in the night. After that there were no more letters, only silence. Weeks later, Nimue had learned the news through the gossip of nuns and messengers, of Arthur's wedding, his vow. . . . If Arthur was going away, then Merlin was not free. He would have to stay at Camelot to protect Britain while Arthur was gone.

And then one day she had seen Arthur himself.

He had come riding into Avalon at the head of a band of knights, and asked for the Father Abbot. Gossip ran swiftly through the little community, and soon everyone in Avalon knew that Arthur had come to Avalon to pray for a blessing on his quest to seek the Grail. He had knelt in the Grail Chapel just where she was kneeling now, surrounded by his knights. The chapel had been filled with candles and incense, and Arthur had seemed as if he were formed of gold to Nimue's dazzled eyes.

But only her eyes were dazzled. Her heart told her that the young king's quest meant disaster for Britain, no matter how much joy the religious at Avalon greeted it with. Nimue had spent enough years at Vortigern's court to know that a King must be on his throne, ruling his land, not gallivanting where he pleased in search of a dream, no matter how holy.

But in those days she had been only a lowly postulant, and she knew from bleak experience that no one would listen to her anyway. She was doomed to know the truth but never dare to speak it, a marred Cassandra, unable either to warn or to guide.

She knew that for as long as Arthur wandered, Merlin would remain at Camelot, helping to guide Arthur's young Queen to rule the land. And so every morning and evening for the last seven years Nimue had added her own special prayers to those of the Abbey, praying for Arthur's speedy and safe return.

But if God had heard her prayers, He had not granted them. Perhaps her faith was too weak to compel His attention, and she must strengthen it through further vows.

Nimue hung her head, listening to the holy silence all around her. Was that the reason behind her decision to join the novitiate? To make a vassal of God?

Or did she do this in the hopes of erecting a further barrier between herself and Queen Mab? On the night after Merlin had left her, she had gone walking in the herb garden to calm her soul—and there Queen Mab had found her.

Though Nimue had heard tales of the wicked Queen Mab all her life, it had been the first time she had ever seen the Queen of the Old Ways. She had been wary, and rightfully so, for the Queen of Magic had come to offer her a devil's bargain: *"I'll restore your beauty if you take Merlin away to a place I've created for you. You can live with him there to the end of your days."*

Nimue had refused, but Mab had not withdrawn her offer. *"If you change your mind, just call my name. Out loud."*

And so the matter had lain between them for the last seven years. Was it any wonder that Nimue, weary with the unequal battle between her mind and her heart, sought to put the temptation as far away from her as she could?

To be whole—to be with Merlin—there was nothing more Nimue could imagine wanting. But all Mab's promises led to selfish and wicked ends. Britain needed Merlin more than she did, so long as Arthur was away. And so Nimue turned to God to protect her from her own heart.

Come back to us, King Arthur! Nimue prayed angrily, clutching her fists against her chest. *Come back to us! Your people need you!*

And I need Merlin. . . .

The woods were bright with the leaves of spring, a dappled canopy of green and gold between the knights below and the sky above. Arthur gazed up at the sunlight, sighing disconsolately. The beauty of springtime was eternal, but even that could not buoy his spirits at this moment. His quest had never been closer to failure than it was now, nor Arthur closer to despair.

When they had ridden out through the gates of Camelot seven years before, they had been four-and-forty of the most puissant knights in Christendom. In seven years their travels had led them through Gallacia, Allemagne, and the kingdom of the Rus, all in fruitless search for the Grail. They had seen marvels and wonders—serpents made of living fire, giants taller than trees, peasant huts that walked on chicken legs—but they had received only tantalizing rumors of the Grail. The years that had passed had winnowed their numbers. Some had died, some had been taken hostage by foreign kings, some had succumbed to magic and enchantments. Only a scant two dozen of them remained, and Arthur feared that by nightfall their numbers would be thinned further.

A narrow path led through the woods down to the banks of the river. Across that river lay the road to Rome, and Arthur had hopes that the Eternal City would at last hold the answers he and his men had sought so diligently. Surely Roma Magnus, once the center of the world, held news of the whereabouts of the treasure they so eagerly sought? They had been following the banks of the river for three days, looking for a place that was shallow and slow enough that the armored knights could cross safely.

But finding a ford hadn't solved their problems. The one they had found was guarded by a party of stranger knights who refused to let them cross. The party had already tried to cross once, several hours earlier, and the knights had beaten them back with almost contemptuous ease. Arthur could not bear for more of his comrades to die senselessly. Kay had been wounded, and Arthur had retreated to consider what to do next.

I wish that Merlin were here, Arthur thought despondently. His old tutor had always had some wise counsel for him when his plans became hopelessly muddled, and, though Arthur followed the New Religion, he did have to admit that there were times when Merlin's magic would come in very handy.

Like now.

He glanced down the hill to where the party of stranger knights stood, blocking his men's access to the ford. Their armor gleamed brightly in the sun, perfect and polished, and Arthur felt the ragged condition of his own knights keenly. The years of questing had battered away all their ornamental aspects, leaving only the warrior beneath the gilding.

"Let me go down and talk to them," he said to his companions. "Perhaps they will be reasonable."

"By my beard!" his foster-brother Kay swore. "We have already had a taste of their reason, have we not?"

The others grumbled their agreement—even Gawain, who had been unfailingly cheerful even in the face of disasters that had claimed his three brothers one by one.

"Sure and there must be some other way across this foul river," Sir Balan said.

"Perhaps," Arthur said. "And I swear to you, Sir Balan, we shall seek it in haste if I cannot reason my way across this ford."

"Reason!" Kay snorted. "The only reason they'll understand has a sword blade." He cradled his helmet in the crook of one arm and rubbed gingerly at the large purplish welt over his right eye.

"I'd expect you to say such a thing, since you fight so much better than you can think," Sir Bedivere shot back. Kay turned on him, his hand going to his sword hilt, and Arthur stepped quickly between them.

"Gawain, stop these hotheads from killing each other. I'm going to go see if they'll parley. I won't be long," Arthur said tiredly.

He mounted Boukephalous and rode slowly down the wooded slope toward the ford where the three-and-thirty stranger knights waited. Their leader wore a red surcoat with a black minotaur embroidered upon it, and his gleaming helm was ornamented with a pair of painted and gilded bull's horns.

"We wish to cross the ford," Arthur said.

"No one crosses this ford and lives," the horned knight rumbled. "We slay all who dare."

"It must get tedious for you," Arthur commented politely. He wished Merlin were here. Merlin had so much experience of the world. Surely he would know what to do.

"It does," the horned knight answered unexpectedly. "And so we will give you a choice, Arthur of Britain. Seek another path to your goal, or answer my riddle."

"What is your riddle?" Arthur asked. The other knights stood still and unmoving. Not even their armor creaked.

"It is a simple one," the horned knight said, and now he sounded amused. "All you need to pass this ford unscathed with all your men is the answer to the question: what is it that women desire most?"

"That isn't a riddle," Arthur said indignantly. "It's a question."

"If it is a question, then answer it, Arthur of Britain," the horned knight said reasonably.

"Have I leave to consult with my men?" Arthur asked quickly.

The horned knight bowed his acquiescence, and Arthur rode quickly back up the hill.

"Well?" Gawain asked eagerly.

"He's set us a riddle. If any of us can answer it, we may pass unmolested."

"I say we fight them!" Kay said.

"Are we surprised?" Bedivere answered. Kay lunged for him.

Gawain pulled them apart with a clatter of armor. "What is the riddle, Arthur?"

"It seems to me to be more of a question," Arthur answered, swinging down off his horse. "We have to tell him what women desire most."

"Ah, that's easy enough. Love-talking and pretty clothes," Balan's brother Balin said.

"Castles."

"Titles."

"A handsome husband."

"Jewels."

"Tourneys fought in her honor."

"To be always young and beautiful."

Each of the knights made his suggestion, and Arthur listened to them all, but in his heart he knew the answer couldn't be as simple as this. The suggestions came slower and slower, and at last there was silence.

"Gentlemen, this is getting us nowhere," Arthur said. "There can be only one right answer to such a question."

Then Bradamante cleared her throat pointedly. The woman warrior was armed and armored just as her male companions were, for she was under a vow not to assume women's dress until Jerusalem had been freed. She had come to Britain to ride in Arthur's tourney, and had stayed to join in his quest. Alone of Arthur's band, she had not offered an answer to the question the knights of the ford had put.

The others all stared at her, until at last Arthur realized what she meant. He blushed. Painfully. In all their months of traveling, he sometimes forgot what Bradamante was.

"My lady knight," Arthur said humbly. "You are a woman. Can you answer this riddle?"

"It seems too simple to be a proper riddle, Your Majesty," Bradamante said. "Women want what men want, and what men desire most is their own way. That is your answer."

"Preposterous!" Bedivere scoffed. Bradamante glared.

"But women want dresses, and jewels, and fine castles," Kay protested. "While men want horses, and armor, and tourneys. The answer cannot be the same for both."

"Am I so different from you?" Bradamante demanded. "I bleed as you do, Sir Kay—and fight much better."

Bedivere made a rude noise. Kay scowled.

"My lords," Arthur said hastily. "And lady. I think Dame Bradamante's answer is worth offering. I shall ride back down and try it, for the hour grows late and I should not like to spend the night here in this desolate wilderness."

"I will go, Sire," Gawain said. "If they do not like the

answer, better that I face their wrath than that Britain should be without her King."

Arthur smiled tiredly. "She is without her King *now,* Gawain. I will not give them any reason to call me a coward. I asked the question and I will deliver the answer. If necessary, Excalibur will protect me."

He touched the sword at his hip. This was the sword that the Lady of the Lake had given to Merlin, the sword that had defeated the tyrant Vortigern. Arthur had pulled it from the grasp of the Old Man of the Mountain to become king, and it was filled with magic. The true kings of Britain had carried it in an unbroken cycle stretching back into the mists of history. It would not fail him.

He rode back to the water's edge.

"Well, King of Britain?" the horned knight asked.

"I have the answer to your question. What women desire most is what men desire most: their own way."

The horned knight's horse reared, and the man within the ornate armor howled. His companions, standing in a double row on each side of the ford, wailed and clashed their swords against their shields. The sound increased until Arthur was deafened, until it seemed to blot out the very sun. A whirlwind rose up, blowing dust and leaves into his eyes. Arthur raised his arm, as if it could shield him from whatever necromancy was occurring. He could feel the ground shake as his compatriots rode to join him, but even if they had wished to, there was nothing here for them to fight.

A moment later the wind dropped and Arthur could

see again. The ford was empty. The stranger knights were gone. He looked at Gawain.

"So we cross, then?" Gawain said pragmatically.

Later that night, when they had made camp, Arthur took the time to pen a rare letter to Guinevere. They would be in Rome soon, if all went well. He could find a messenger there who would take his message to Camelot.

But what was there to say? Honesty warred with the desire to spare his wife distress. There were so many things he wanted to say to her, and as always, words came hard to him.

"We are no nearer finding the Holy Grail than when we left," Arthur wrote with painful honesty. *"We hear rumors that it is housed in the next town . . . and the next, and the next, and each town takes us further away from you and Camelot."* He set down his pen and sighed. No news there. Only the eternal unwavering truth. *I need the Grail and I need you, my love and my Queen.*

The Battle of Loyalty

Master Wancallant had been Camelot's architect from the very beginning. He was a dignified white-haired old gentleman dressed in the robes of a professional builder, wearing the golden chain of office that King Arthur had bestowed upon him with his own hands. Together he and Arthur had planned every street and stone to turn Camelot from a dream to a tangible reality.

But sometimes it seemed to Master Wancallant that Sir Lancelot was intent upon undoing all of his and Arthur's careful work. Hardly a day had passed since Arthur rode away that did not see some new improvement to his designs suggested by the Queen's Champion. Usually these were small changes—and, Wancallant had to admit, generally for the better—but lately the changes to Camelot that Sir Lancelot had asked for had grown more sweeping and contradictory. His last suggestion had required pulling down half the curtain wall of the castle in order to fit in the new courtyard!

"The work's going much too slowly," Lancelot said now, frowning down at him sternly as they strode through the new building.

"You keep changing your mind, Sir Lancelot," Wancallant said pleadingly. He had to half-run to keep up with Lancelot's long strides as the knight inspected yesterday's work in the new section of the castle, ducking under timber balks and around piles of brick. The architect did not remember when he had first started to dread these morning meetings with Lancelot of the Lake, but he did. His stomach hurt and he had a pounding headache. *Count yourself lucky you aren't working for Vortigern. Now* there *was a man who was hard on his staff!*

"First this, then that . . . I'm doing my best, Sire," he protested.

"Well, you've got to do better than that," Lancelot shot back without breaking stride.

"How can I do better than my best?" Wancallant demanded, coming to a stop in confusion. It was a good question, but he was fated not to receive an answer, for Lancelot had seen the Queen and was hurrying toward her.

Wancallant's lip lifted in a sneer. They had forgotten his presence, just as they had forgotten that other eyes might be watching as well, here among the builders and the castle servants. Lancelot flew to the Queen like a bee to a honeycomb—and who knew what intimacies she permitted him? It wasn't right, and if the King were here, he'd send the meddling Sir Lancelot packing and make

Queen Guinevere mend her trifling ways. That was as sure as Church on Sunday!

Wancallant sighed, and his shoulders drooped. But Arthur *wasn't* here, and who knew when he'd return? The King had been gone for a very long time, and things were starting to fall apart in Camelot.

That, too, was certain.

Lancelot hurried to where Guinevere waited for him in the center of the little courtyard, certain that no one else had remarked the Queen's presence. She was dressed in red, her pleated straight gown covered with a golden brocade *pallia*, her dark hair captured in two flowing braids. She watched him advance with a small secret smile meant for him alone. Lancelot's heart lifted at the sight of that smile, even though he knew his happiness was sinful. Lancelot was a good Christian, and he knew that adultery was a sin—and to Lancelot, sin was simply another opponent to be defeated in battle. As Lancelot was invincible, he had always assumed that temptation could be vanquished just as any terrestrial antagonist could.

But who could have dreamed that this sweet wickedness would be the one opponent he could not defeat? He had not seen the trap until it was too late, and it had not been Guinevere who had set it, but his own heart. Even now, he did not know what he could have done differently.

He had come to Camelot as a great knight, Master of Joyous Gard, husband of Elaine of Astolat, father of Galahad. Invincible in war, mighty in peace, Lancelot had never been afraid in his entire life. Certainly he had never feared to be close to the Queen. Serene in his spiritual invulnerability, Lancelot had not seen his defeat until it was too late.

Until he found himself in love with the Queen, sin though it was.

"Are you alone, my lady?" he asked in a low voice.

She took a step toward him, looking up at him through her lashes. "Merlin is my faithful shadow," she whispered.

"That's right and proper," Lancelot said painfully.

Love had led him into sin and betrayal, but he could not find the strength to regret it. Destroying what he felt for Guinevere would be like destroying himself. And so he burned with love for her, yearned for the sight of her, and knew with every beat of his heart that he was further damned.

"Why not you?" Guinevere said, glancing away. "You're my champion." If she had not loved him, Lancelot could have set aside his own feelings. But Guinevere loved him as he did her, loved him with a yearning as great as that of the soul for God, and against Love Sir Lancelot had no defense.

"Because when I'm near you I can't control my heart," Lancelot answered. He could see no escape. To deny their love was surely as great a sin as to give in to it.

"You're near me now," she answered.

She moved closer, as if she would embrace him there, in front of everyone.

"It's dangerous," he whispered, warning her with the last of his strength. Her fingers sought his, and clung.

"Yes," Guinevere whispered.

Her face was turned toward him like a flower to the sun, and in that moment nothing mattered as much to Sir Lancelot as answering that unspoken longing. Her fingers trembled in his clasp and he could smell the faint soft scent of roses from her hair.

"My lady? My lady?" Merlin's voice, calling from the other chamber, cut between them like Excalibur's un-yielding blade.

"Perhaps we should be grateful for my shadow," Guinevere said sadly. She stepped reluctantly away from Lancelot.

He watched her go, knowing that he loved her as he had loved no other woman in all his life, even his wife. Knowing that there was nothing he could do about his love except pray for the strength not to fall further, not to succumb to the appeal that shone from Guinevere's beautiful eyes.

And this battle, too, Lancelot was destined to lose.

Merlin watched Guinevere walk toward him. He knew it was useless to try, but he felt he had to save Lancelot and Guinevere from themselves—and the horror they could bring down on the kingdom.

They were truly in love. That was the saddest part of all. Lancelot loved his wife and son, but they were far away. And more than he loved either of them, Merlin knew, Lancelot loved being *needed*.

And Guinevere . . . she had married Arthur for honor, and duty, but he had left before she could grow to love him. In the years Arthur had been gone, Guinevere had grown from a gawky child into a loving woman, and her love sought an outlet just as spring flowers sought the sun. Lancelot was worthy of her love, and loved her in return. If only each of them were not married to someone else!

Merlin must find some way to warn Guinevere that others saw what he did, that she favored Lancelot too much. But she was the queen—Merlin could not call her to account as though she were an errant waiting-maid. The Queen would resent that, and rightly so. He must be subtle, and amuse Guinevere as well as making her think.

He was a wizard, after all.

When Guinevere reached him, Merlin was leaning against the wall, his ear pressed to its painted surface and an intent expression upon his face. She regarded him with curiosity mixed with a hint of her usual wariness.

"What's wrong, Merlin?" she asked.

Merlin regarded her mysteriously. "The walls are whispering, Guinevere. Can't you hear them?"

A proper daughter of the New Religion would have shied away from the mere suggestion of such animistic practices, but the Queen had only converted when her father and brothers had, after the Battle of Badon Hill. She was intrigued rather than scandalized, and pressed her ear against the painted plaster, curiosity overcoming her distrust of Merlin. But she heard nothing.

"No," she answered. She straightened and looked at him expectantly. "What do they say?" she asked, smiling.

"That you're too friendly with Sir Lancelot."

Guinevere's smile turned hard. "Do you believe such whispers, Merlin?"

She knew as well as he did that there were those who were jealous of her place as Queen. There had been gossip since before she'd married Arthur, all of it unfounded.

Until now?

"No," Merlin said placatingly. "But I've seen you two look at each other." *And what I have seen, others can see also. Beware, my lady!*

She took a deep breath and fixed Merlin with a challenging stare. "I don't care what others think. I'm the Queen." She nodded to herself, as if to indicate that the matter was settled and no more could be said.

She was so young, so painfully conscious of her Queenly dignity!

"That is why you must take special care," Merlin said imploringly. He closed the distance between them. "I can't protect you in this matter." He stood over her, staring down into her eyes, willing her to heed his warning. *I will not lie for you, or connive with you to hide your crimes. I did that for Uther and caused the death of many good men. Never again!*

Guinevere looked away, her jaw set into a stubborn and inflexible line. Merlin walked on, leaving her standing there. There was nothing else he could do. He could not order her to listen to him. She was the Queen. She was ruled by her pride.

Pride, always pride. Arthur's, in thinking he must be the one to achieve the Grail; Guinevere's, in thinking that no matter what her actions are, they cannot be condemned; mine, in thinking there is anything I can do to save those I love. What will be, is. It is written in the Book of Fate, and no mortal hand may change what is written there. . . .

Guinevere watched Merlin go, her eyes angry and troubled. Part of her was filled with fury at the way Merlin dared to upbraid her as though he were the King, and she but a lowly subject.

Another part of her was angry because she knew he was right. She was the Queen. She did not rule in her own right, but as Arthur's consort. Her actions must always be above reproach. To take the Royal Champion as her lover would be to betray her husband, and to lower herself in the esteem of all their people.

But she loved Lancelot. He made her feel strong and self-assured for the first time in her entire life. Without him she was not whole. To reject her feelings for him was to betray herself. How could that be better than betraying Arthur? The King was far away and might never return. How could what she did matter to him when he was so far away?

There was no simple answer.

All Merlin does is tell me to "beware"—he does not tell me what I should do, or how I should find the strength to do it. How can he know what it is to burn with love? He is a wizard; he has never loved!

Behind her, Guinevere heard Lancelot lecturing Master Wancallant. She turned and walked toward the sound of his voice.

If I sin, let it be in doing, rather than in doing nothing. I was not born to be a nun, and wall myself up within a holy place, raising my voice in prayer.

* * *

Anoeth was a land of grey mist and the blackened stumps of stark, twisted trees that reached out of the mist like hands from the grave. This was the land of Death and Winter, ruled over by its own grim and terrifying king, Idath.

Once, long ago, Idath had been the darkness to balance Mab's light. When the Wheel of the Year turned, spinning the seasons from summer to winter, Idath was there to take up the weak who fell to winter's cruel sharpness, and convey them to his own realm to await rebirth into the world once more.

But as the years had passed, bringing the New Religion to Britain to erode the power of the Old Ways, Mab's own nature had darkened, until Lord Idath seemed less to be her dark counterpart than a faint reflection of her own desolation. Once this grey wasteland had seemed alien to her. Now it only seemed to be a fitting backdrop to her battle.

We have all changed, and been changed. How can we fight to regain what is rightfully ours when even the true memory of it has passed away? she wondered bleakly.

Far ahead she could see Idath's ring-shaped castle, its eight tall towers surrounding the octagonal center courtyard. Within its walls was that which she sought. Mist coiled about her, rising up from the edges of the path. Mab quickened her pace as she walked the ghost road that led to Idath's stronghold. Soon she stood before the high walls of the eight-sided castle nestled among the Mountains of the Moon. Two gates pierced its walls.

They were carved in elaborate knots and spirals and whorls, until even Mab grew dizzy following all the convolutions of the tangle. One set was the translucent golden color of horn, the other the glistening cream of ivory. Mab chose the ivory gate and hammered on it with her small fists.

"Let me in!" Mab shouted.

"Who summons me?" Lord Idath demanded, as the gate swung wide. He was tall and gaunt, dressed all in grey and wearing a heavy bronze helmet crowned with branching antlers. His eyes glowed a feral red. He was the Lord of the Wild Hunt, and even though the people turned to the New Religion, Idath would not be forgotten so long as Mankind feared the shadow at midnight.

"I summon you, Lord of Winter," Mab answered boldly.

"It has been many years since you sought me out," Idath said in his slow deep voice. "Vortigern . . . Merlin . . . your champions have failed you, one by one."

"I have a new champion who will not fail," Mab said proudly. "I will ensure it. I will give him Caliban. Now let me pass."

"You dare much, Madame," Idath said, stepping back to allow her to pass into his domain. "Caliban was forged at the beginning of time to be a match for Excalibur. Each warrior who has wielded it has brought an end to an age in blood and fire. Is that what you want? This is the last boon you may ever ask of me, Queen of the Old Ways. Choose well."

"I want *victory!*" Mab hissed. "And I will pay any price to get it. Show me the sword!"

Idath regarded her for a long moment, then turned away, his dark cloak swirling around him like shadows. Mab followed him as he walked across the courtyard and into the eight-sided castle. The labyrinthine corridors were dim and twisted, but Idath navigated them without difficulty, and Mab hurried to keep up with him.

At last he stopped before a door made of black iron, inlaid with a design of untarnishing silver.

"Behind this door lies what you seek, Queen Mab," Idath said.

She put her hand on the door. "It's locked," Mab said accusingly.

Idath held out his hand. On his gloved palm lay a key, its metal green with age and neglect. "Take this, and do what you will, Mab. It will link my domain and yours, so that you may come and go here as you will."

"And Caliban is here?" Mab demanded.

"In its fashion," Idath answered, and then before her eyes he slowly faded away, until he was one with the shadows of his stronghold. "Have a care what you do, Queen of the Old Ways. . . ." His voice echoed through the corridor like the howling of the winter wind.

Mab turned away with a hiss of impatience. Let others pretend that the Old Laws must still be observed! She knew better. All that mattered was victory. And armed with Caliban, Mordred would be invincible.

She touched the key to the door, and it swung open.

A lake of fire filled all the space beyond the doorway. Bright and ever-burning, it rippled and surged, its soft hissing making a dull cushion of sound. The brightness of it hurt even Mab's eyes. The smoke of its burning cast a dark pall over the sky above, the flames reflected from the smoke turning the whole world red.

Mab peered into the brightness. Somewhere out there in the distance was a glimmer that was not fire.

Caliban.

Mab stepped out into the flames. The uprush of heated air blew her gossamer draperies back from her body, giving them the appearance of great filmy wings. But no matter how insubstantial her robes or her frail body, Mab did not burn. She was an elemental force, as unchanging as the stones and the stars. Only the thoughts of Men could affect her.

As she passed through the veils of flame, she at last saw what she sought. In the center of the lake of fire at the heart of Idath's domain, there was a pillar of ice. It jutted up out of the lake, unmelting. Cold radiated from the ice as heat did from the fire, and the pillar was surrounded by mist where the two elements met. Moisture beaded on the surface of the ice for a few moments before becoming steam, but though the ice was surrounded by a turbulent fog, it was not consumed.

When Mab reached the ice-pillar she placed a hand on its frosty surface. The film of water on the surface of the ice made it slicker than glass, but Mab held her hand steadily against the pillar. Deep inside, she could see Caliban.

Where Excalibur was bright and shining, the surface of Caliban's blade was pitted and dull, the ugly grey of ash. Its black hilt was starkly plain, its only adornment a depiction of a comet cut crudely into the hilt. Beyond that, it bore nothing that might hint where its allegiance lay, for Caliban had only one purpose. It was the destroyer of ages, and when it was carried into battle, an epoch would pass away.

Soon you will be free, my pretty. What a toy you will make for my Mordred. He so enjoys it when I bring him toys. . . .

Mab gazed upon the black sword for a moment longer before turning away and crossing the lake of fire once more. She reached the corridor and carefully locked the door behind her. When she turned, she was in her own palace in the Land of Magic. Just as Idath had promised her, the key gave her the ability to come and go as she wished in that part of Idath's domain.

Soon the time would come when Mordred would be ready to receive this gift.

Then Camelot would fall.

In fact, Camelot was falling *now*.

Merlin lay in his narrow bed in his cottage at the edge of the village and writhed in uneasy sleep. He dreamed of dragons. Not the symbolic dragons, red and white, that had once held Britain's future between them, nor the fearsome beast of flesh and magic that had nearly ended Nimue's life before he had slain it so many years ago.

No, the dragon that he dreamed of now was a creature of shadows, a dragon born out of the darkness of the eclipse. Its eyes were the color of mirrors, and where it breathed its deadly exhalations, the grass crumbled to dust and the trees to ash, leaving nothing behind but a wasteland.

Beware, Merlin of Britain! Beware . . . beware . . .

He heard a boy's mocking laughter, and saw again the figure he had glimpsed in previous visions: a bat-winged knight who bore upon his chest the sign of the eclipse.

I'm coming for you, Merlin, it seemed to say. *I will destroy all that you have given your life to create. Tonight is your last chance to stop me—if you only knew what to do. But you don't. Once again you have failed your trust. It's happening right now. Here. In Camelot. And you don't know what to do. . . .*

The Knight of the Eclipse raised his sword in salute. It was black and pitted, as if with centuries of corrosion, and as he lifted it the blade began to shimmer, to flow and to change, and the bat-winged knight's form flowed and changed as well, becoming a dragon of shadows in a lake of fire.

Merlin sat up with a gasp, looking wildly into the darkness. His heart beat wildly, and it seemed almost as if he could taste the evil of the figure in his vision. Never had one of his visions carried with it such a weight of fear.

Merlin ran his hands through his hair. He reached for his staff and got stiffly to his feet, gazing out his window in the direction of Camelot. All was hushed, silent, and dark, yet Merlin still feared. He was wizard and prophet, and his dreams never lied. There was danger abroad in the peaceful night, danger to Arthur and to Britain both.

Merlin peered into the darkness until his eyes ached, yet he saw nothing. He did not need more proof that sometimes a wizard was as powerless as an ordinary mortal.

Merlin rubbed his eyes tiredly. Whatever danger Britain faced tonight, Merlin was powerless to avert it. He could only hope to recognize its aftermath, and do what he could to set things right.

But sometimes it seemed that he could do so very little.

It was late on a warm spring night, and the castle and town of Camelot were silent. The Queen lay abed but not asleep.

Guinevere was waiting, just as she had waited all the days of her life, for the moment that would transform her, give her a purpose and a place in the world, make her *real*. Once she had looked to her marriage to provide that, but she knew now that this had been a foolish hope. Arthur did not care for her. All he cared about was the Grail. He had forsaken her.

Restless, she threw back the covers and got to her feet. A small vigil light burned before a statue of the Blessed Virgin in the corner of her bedchamber. Guinevere turned toward the icon and tried to pray, but in her thoughts the words of the Litany were brushed aside by older, darker prayers.

To Epona, mother of mares, guardian of the Iceni. To Melusine All-Mother, who watched over the women of Britain. Goddesses of fruitfulness, of love, of children.

Help me . . .

Since the first day she had seen him at the tourney, Lancelot's presence had brought Guinevere a peace and joy she had never believed could exist. How could it be right for them to be forced apart when she longed for him as much as he desired her? Arthur's love was a pale and distant thing in comparison. Arthur was the perfect golden savior of Britain. What need could such a man have for a wife?

But Lancelot was human, and flawed, and because of that, she loved him. Guinevere cherished each of his faults—his impatience, his pride—for they made him all the more human, and dearer to her for his simple humanity.

But she could not have him. She was the King's wife, her chastity an offering to the New Religion. To love outside her marriage bonds was a great sin, an offense against God.

I do not care! Where was God when I was betrothed to Arthur, when Arthur left me for the Grail? If Arthur prefers God to me, then he has broken his oaths first, and I am free. . . .

There was a sound behind her, from the doorway. Guinevere turned, and saw what she had somehow expected to see. Lancelot was standing there in the doorway.

He wore a white linen tunic embroidered in dark blue and the plain leather belt of his knighthood.

"You look . . . beautiful," he said.

Guinevere turned away. No one had ever loved her as Lancelot did, she knew that in her soul. She knew what would happen if she did not send him away at once. She longed for it to happen, even as she knew it was wrong, that it would cause nothing but suffering and disaster. She was the Queen. She was held to a higher standard than ordinary mortals. What could be excused in them could not be excused in her.

"I should jump," she said in a trembling voice. "Throw myself from the battlements."

"Then I'll jump, too," Lancelot said, close behind her. He put his arms around her and buried his face in her hair. She could feel the tremors in his body as they passed from his flesh to hers. "I can't live without you," he whispered.

She had no choice. As a drowning swimmer reaches for air, Guinevere turned and took Lancelot in her arms.

In her Sanctum Sanctorum in the Land of Magic, deep in the heart of the earth, Mab sat upon her dark throne gazing into the magic mirror she held in her hand. Its border and handle were a braid of intertwined serpents, and its silver back was a Gorgon's head with diamond eyes.

Even though it meant that she had to be without Mordred, sometimes she could not resist retreating to her subterranean palace to be among her own kind, for Mab was not as fond of the human world as Frik was. Frik was a fool, always playing his gnomish games and parading his ridiculous disguises! One might almost think he'd grown fond of Morgan le Fay, he spent so much time fawning upon her.

Mab did not waste her time with such childishness. Everything she did was for a purpose. Only Mordred was important . . . Mordred, and the destruction of Camelot.

And she was here to take another step toward that destruction tonight.

Mab gazed into the mirror that she held. It was a potent tool of illusion, and sometimes of more than that, for tonight the truth would be crueler than Mab's most subtle illusion.

She made a small gesture, and the image in the mirror flickered. It no longer showed Mab's reflection, but the Queen's bed in the Royal Bedchamber in Camelot. On the bed, Guinevere and Lancelot lay as entwined as the serpents of Mab's mirror.

"Now to be sure that the one this will hurt most will see it . . ." Mab crooned to herself.

In Joyous Gard, a place both miles and years away from Britain and Camelot, Elaine of Astolat sat before her mirror, brushing out her hair before going to bed. Her bedroom mirror was one such as Morgan or Guinevere could only dream of, a large square sheet of silvered glass that cast a reflection both sharp and true.

Elaine was lonely, though her pride in her husband never faltered. It had been many years since Lancelot had sailed away with the wizard Merlin. Little Galahad had grown so much that his father would not recognize him. Soon he would be ready to assume the mantle of knighthood.

Elaine dreaded the day when Galahad, too, would leave her to seek out a life of danger and adventure. Why couldn't he be content at Joyous Gard? Why couldn't Lancelot have been content to stay here, with her?

Elaine shook her head sadly, sighing with downcast eyes as she unhooked her heavy necklace. She knew it was Lancelot's nature to seek adventure, and Joyous Gard was a peaceful place, unworthy of his great warrior skills. She could not deny what he was, or deny him the right to do what he did best.

Looking down at her jewels, Elaine did not see Mab's image fill her mirror. Mab's black-painted eyes inspected Lancelot's lovely wife with birdlike malice, but when Elaine looked up again, Mab was gone, retreating with inhuman speed.

Another image filled Elaine's mirror now. She stared in horror.

"I don't believe it," she whispered brokenly. She glanced quickly around to make sure that Galahad had not come into the room in the last few seconds, then looked back at the mirror, tears of outrage welling up in her eyes. Her own grief gagged her, making a hard lump in her throat.

"Lancelot would never . . . ," she protested, as if her words could be a shield.

But she did believe it. Elaine's own father had been a great sorcerer, and she had some small magics of her own. Instinctively she reached out with them, and to her desolation they told her what her heart already knew: that this was a true vision. What she saw in the mirror was truly happening, just as she saw it.

Suddenly unable to bear the sight a moment longer, Elaine flung her shawl up over the mirror to blot out the spectacle of the radiant lovers. She did not know who the woman was. It did not matter. She knew the sight of her own husband. Lancelot had betrayed her. He had forgotten her as she waited patiently here in her lonely tower, and found someone new to love. As if she, Elaine, had never existed, had never loved him, had never borne him a son.

It isn't true! It isn't! How could Lancelot, so careful always to do only what was right, betray her so?

As if compelled, Elaine pulled the scarf away from the mirror again, shuddering with tears, hoping the scene would be gone.

But it wasn't. She could see them both so clearly, could almost imagine that it was she in Lancelot's arms and not this wanton stranger. She could almost hear the tender words of love they exchanged, Lancelot and his unknown love.

She could not bear it.

Elaine of Astolat put her face in her hands and sobbed.

It was a quiet evening at home in Tintagel Keep. Frik and Morgan le Fay were playing at cards—he always made sure that he lost, just to please her—and Mordred was lounging in a chair with his back to them, catching insects and slowly pulling them to pieces. He'd switched to insects after Morgan had complained about the mess he made with the mice, and Frik was just as glad. The squealing had been quite unnerving.

But then, everything about Mordred was unnerving. The way he stared at you and didn't blink, for example. Morgan assured him that Mordred was fond of him, but personally, Frik doubted it. He didn't think Mordred was fond of anybody, except perhaps Mab. He was quite a little horror, that lad was. Queen Mab ought to be perfectly delighted with him.

Thoughts of Mab always made Frik's stomach hurt these days. She was the Queen of Air and Darkness, but there had used to be something more to her than petty spite—a dark majesty, the tragic queenliness of a monarch in exile.

No more. That majesty had dwindled away during the years of her battle and her many defeats. Now Mab thought of nothing but small-minded revenge, catering shamelessly to Mordred as the instrument of it.

Frik was just as glad she'd decided to be elsewhere this evening. When Mab was absent, he didn't have to worry that some chance remark of Morgan's would draw Mab's wrath down upon her. Under the guise of studying his cards—all bad—Frik gazed at Morgan.

She was as beautiful as the day he'd transformed her from her bucktoothed, squint-eyed, hopelessly plain self into a creature of loveliness; still as sweetly self-centered and oblivious as she had been when she demanded that he get her the crown of Britain. Mordred's monstrousness couldn't touch her, because Morgan simply didn't see it. She paid little attention to anything outside of Frik and her own comfort, and since Frik was the source of that comfort, she adored him with uncomplicated single-mindedness. And Frik found that he adored her in return, his crabby old gnome's heart growing and softening until sometimes Frik felt, well, quite human as a matter of fact.

In fact, if not for Morgan, the last several years would have been quite unbearable, Frik thought. Unbearable, and lonely. He *liked* being a dashing golden swashbuckler. He liked being appreciated, for that matter.

Appreciation wasn't something you could expect from Mab, and certainly not from Mordred.

"Gin!" Morgan crowed triumphantly, flinging down her cards. Frik smiled at her, shutting out Mordred's tuneless humming as he vivisected his latest prey.

"As always, my lady, you are more than a match for me," Frik answered gallantly.

At the moment he spoke, he felt a shiver in the air, the sharp electrical tang that indicated that Mab had just arrived from the Land of Magic.

Frik froze, like a rabbit beneath the hungry gaze of a hawk. He could see Mab out of the corner of his eye, poised behind one of the great standing braziers that warmed the hall. The flames turned her skin to copper and her hair to blood. She gazed silently down into the fire as though she could see wonders there—or horrors.

Frik made a mental note to ignore Mab as long as possible, but others were less circumspect. Mordred had tired of his games. Brushing the last of the flies from his hands, he got to his feet and went toward her.

"Auntie, you look extraordinarily pleased with yourself. What have you done? Is it terrible?" Mordred asked hopefully. "Do tell. I'm sure it's *perfect. . . .*"

Mab smiled proudly. "I've made sure that Elaine knows Lancelot and Guinevere are lovers," she whispered smugly, confident of his praise.

Mordred did not disappoint her. "How absolutely delicious," he cooed.

It was more than Frik could bear, to see her seeking approval from the monster she'd created. *Bearing tales like a child out of school, she who once commanded the winds and the storms!* "Isn't that . . . rather unworthy of us?" he asked unthinkingly.

In the sudden silence, Frik knew that he had gone too far.

"Unworthy?" Mordred asked in astonishment. He turned to Morgan. "What does that mean, Mother?"

Frik was frozen with terror, staring toward Mab. But oddly, in that moment of crisis, the gnome's fear was not for himself. If Mab blasted him out of existence, who would protect Morgan from the others?

Morgan frowned, thinking very hard about Mordred's question before giving up. "Oh, I've forgotten! What does it mean?" she asked, turning toward Frik.

"Yes, it is unworthy," Mab said, ignoring Morgan and concentrating on Frik. If he had hoped that their centuries of association would count for anything with her, he was doomed to disappointment. Mab smiled at him, a faint, almost fond smile.

"But I don't like to be told, Frik."

She made no gesture, but suddenly Frik went flying backward to crash into the wall with bruising force. As he slid to the floor he heard Mordred chuckle with delight—the suffering of others could always make Mordred laugh.

Morgan rushed over to Frik, crying his name. He forced himself to smile at her reassuringly, but his eyes were on Mab, awaiting his further punishment.

But Frik had nothing more to fear from Mab tonight. The Queen of the Old Ways gazed dotingly at her protégé, while Mordred's delighted laughter filled the Great Hall of Tintagel.

*   *   *

All wizards lived in towers, so the folk belief ran, and Merlin was not unhappy to acquiesce to this view of his needs, as it had gained him a spacious room at the top of the highest tower of the castle, where he could look down on the rooftops and out over the walls. He spent as much time here as he did in his little hut outside the castle walls, for here, high in the sky, with the shutters open to the winds that tumbled through his tower, Merlin felt as though he were living among clouds, not stones. His beloved books filled the shelves, and his desk was filled with letters from correspondents in many lands, as well as copies of the dispatches sent to the Queen. These days, Merlin was the only one who read them, for the Queen had let the reins of government fall from her hands as she concentrated upon other matters.

Like Lancelot.

Lancelot and the Queen were lovers. For all Merlin's watchful care, matters had trickled through his fingers like a handful of springwater, leaving Merlin in control of nothing. As the hours turned to days and then to weeks, and spring to summer's heat, they made no secret of their liaison. Though they had once welcomed Lancelot with open arms, the people of Camelot did not love the Queen's Champion now. If they did not resent Lancelot for his part in the Queen's adultery, they resented him for his tacit assumption of Arthur's rightful place. It seemed to them as if Lancelot wished to reign in Camelot, but the common people still loved their king, and daily hoped for his return.

If he had any sense, Merlin reflected broodingly,

he'd find where the boy had gotten to, and go and fetch Arthur back. It was the least he could do to mend matters after having been the one who brought Lancelot to Camelot in the first place.

But as much as the adventure tempted him, he dared not leave Camelot.

Mordred was coming. Merlin knew it. The winds told him. The trees, the hearthfire, the whole natural world reverberated with the foreknowledge of Mordred's arrival. If not this year, then soon, very soon. . . .

Merlin had hoped to have a natural lifetime to prepare, as Mordred grew from child to man, but it was not to be. He had forgotten that Morgan's child grew with magical speed. Mordred would be a grown man seven years after his birth—in fact, he must be nearly grown even now. And once he had come into whatever dark power Mab intended to gift him with, he would be a formidable foe of all that was good.

The very walls rebuked Merlin's willful blindness. Here he'd sat, year after year, hoping for the best but unwilling to meddle magically in human lives the way his great enemy was so fond of doing, and now it had all come down to this. The Queen an adulteress, her Champion a joke, the King's bastard son coming long before anyone expected that he would, Arthur lost somewhere in the lands to the East.

All muddled, all gone awry, and no way for him to mend even those problems within reach. Guinevere would not see him. She'd made it clear that she wanted no wizard's counsel, and Merlin could not find it in his heart to blame her. He'd brought her Lancelot, after all. Was it any wonder she no longer trusted him?

Merlin left the castle, hoping a walk in the evening air would clear his thoughts. He made his way slowly through the town. Though many turned away from him, making the sign against ill-fortune and magic, there were as many more who greeted him cheerfully, glad of a link with the Old Ways. There were fewer of them this year than last, and soon there would be none at all. Mab's power was waning as the people forgot her.

Did she know it?

Merlin was certain that she did. There was little that transpired in Britain that the Queen of the Old Ways did not know about these days. Being forgotten was her greatest fear. Merlin was sure she knew exactly how the tides of belief ran across the land. Who was winning. Who was losing.

What would she do?

He didn't know. Though he was a wizard, Merlin had little taste for magic at the best of times. When he had steeled himself to spy upon Mab with his magic, he'd had little luck. Tintagel was hidden from him behind a shroud of magical mist, and even Merlin could not see into the Land of Magic. He could only guess, from what he knew of Mab, that she would be plotting some elaborate revenge upon all who had disappointed her, and that Mordred must be a part of it.

Despite his broodings, Merlin's feet had brought him to the shore of the lake below Camelot. It was a perfect jewel, nearly as beautiful as the Lake of Magic itself. The River Astolat came from the far north to fill its deep basin, and from it drained three other rivers that nourished the whole of Britain with their waters. The lakeshore was a beautiful, peaceful setting, and the sight of it calmed Merlin.

He told himself that the strength of his anxiety came as much from living within stone walls as from any action of the Queen's. It was only the childish fear of imprisonment, first triggered when he'd journeyed to the subterranean Land of Magic as a boy, then intensified by his near-fatal captivity in Vortigern's dungeons, that turned his thoughts and mood so dark. It was not too late to change the events he dreaded. The matter of the Queen's lover could still be mended. He would send Lancelot home to Joyous Gard—to his wife—and in his absence the people would forgive their Queen. And once matters had been so settled and Camelot was at peace again, he would go in search of Arthur and bring him home. Let others search for the Grail. A king's place was with his people, no matter what his heart told him. And with Arthur and Excalibur at Camelot, what real harm could Mordred do?

Then Merlin could return to his beloved forest, away from the stone walls and roofs that so oppressed his spirit. Perhaps his aversion was linked in some way to his magic, but though Merlin would gladly cast off his magic, he would never be willing to give up his beloved wild places.

They were still there, he told himself. He drew a deep breath, trying to draw strength from that knowledge. The great trees of Britain, the magnificent forests, could not be harmed by the petty intrigues of the Queen and court. They awaited him still. And he would rejoin them soon.

Merlin felt the aura of gloom that had possessed him ever since the spring begin to lift, and as it did, far out across the water, Merlin saw a spark of light.

It was dim at first. He was not sure what he saw. But as the sun set and the blue shadows lengthened across the water, the small sparks in the distance became more distinct. A boat.

It was a barge, really, carved of a dark silvery wood like none found anywhere in Britain. Torches burned within it, and Merlin could see the bulky shape of its cargo, but no human figure sitting or standing within it. The craft was redolent of magic, and without wanting to, Merlin suddenly knew where it had come from and what cargo it bore.

And a moment ago, he had thought things would turn out all right.

Merlin turned and ran toward the castle, toward the Queen's chambers, as if in his flight he could outpace this new knowledge, could outrun both it and its dire tragic consequences. Breathless, he reached the doors of Guinevere's rooms and flung them open.

As he had known would be the case, there was no one in the room but the Queen and her Champion. The two of them stood close together, their heads bowed over their clasped hands, oblivious to anything outside themselves.

"I warned you—but you wouldn't listen!" Merlin cried in frustration and anger.

The lovers looked up in surprise at his unruly entrance, but even now they did not move away from one another. It was as if it did not matter to them who saw them together.

"What's happened?" Lancelot said finally.

"Did you think your reckless folly harmed no one?" Merlin said furiously. "Come and see the price another has paid for your actions, Sir Lancelot!"

The Queen followed Lancelot and Merlin down to the shore of the twilit lake. The funeral barge had drifted closer to the shore. Its curled prow was painted gold, and the hull had been filled with flowers. In their midst, on a raised dais draped with rich fabrics, a woman lay as if asleep. She wore a golden tiara and was dressed in queenly robes. Lighted candles flickered at each side of her head, to light her way into the land of Death.

"Elaine," Lancelot whispered, as if he had only just remembered his wife's existence.

Merlin waded out into the shallows to intercept the ship, and Lancelot followed him. Between them they pulled it toward the shore, where it rested quietly in the reeds.

"How did she die?" Lancelot asked, standing in the water looking down at the still face of his wife.

There was a golden plaque inset into the surface of the bier at Elaine's head: *"Here lies the Lady Elaine of Astolat, whose kind and generous heart was wounded to breaking by the indifference of one she loved."*

"She died of a broken heart," Merlin said softly. He had met the Lady Elaine only once, but surely she deserved better of knowing him than this? Was everything he did so doomed, that Elaine, like the Lady Igraine before her, should die just because he had come into her life? The thought was terrifying. He was Mab's creation—did that mean that everything he did was to be tainted with her evil?

"It was because of you," Merlin said, more harshly than he wished to. *It is your fault, Sir Lancelot, not mine. Yours the sin, and yours the blame. Not mine—not mine!*

Lancelot groaned aloud, staggering away from the boat and the sight of his dead wife as though he'd been dealt a mortal wound. He slogged toward the shore, only to stop short at the sight of Guinevere.

He raised a hand and let it fall again without touching her. "I'm sorry," he whispered. Then he lowered his head and strode past her, shutting her out of his life.

Guinevere stared after him, only slowly realizing that Lancelot intended to leave her with no more word than that. She turned back to Merlin, her eyes narrow with fury.

"Well, wizard?" she said angrily. "Happy now? You must despise love, if the sight of it causes you so much pain that you must always destroy it!" She gathered up her skirts and followed after Lancelot.

Merlin stood in the water beside the boat, his sodden robes chilling him and weighing him down, though not as much as his own thoughts. He gazed after the lovers. *I judged them too harshly,* he thought. *The guilt is mine as well—I picked Lancelot, after all. I wish I had told them that instead of shouting at them. It might have made this easier.*

The lake was cold, and the last rays of twilight were fading. Merlin shook his head sadly as he waded to shore. A flick of his fingers sent magic to guide Elaine's funeral barge on its interrupted journey again. He stood on the shore and watched after it until it had disappeared into the evening mist, then began to walk slowly along the shore, toward his little hut at the edge of the village. His wet robes flapped around his legs, but he hardly noticed. *Oh, Arthur! Come back to us, I beg you! Without you we are truly lost.*

Standing unseen and invisible in a corner of the courtyard, her eldritch finery covered by a cloak woven of black cobwebs, Queen Mab watched as ostlers saddled Black Bayard, Lancelot's destrier. Lancelot was leaving Camelot, and the Queen.

Mab was pleased with the way matters had turned out. Elaine's death was an unexpected stroke of good fortune—all Mab had dared to hope for was a tearful letter, or perhaps an angry visit. But Elaine was dead, and now his guilt and complicity would drive Lancelot mad. Certainly his guilty conscience would destroy any vestige of good sense he possessed.

Lancelot, fully dressed in his armor and sword, came across the stableyard toward his stallion. If she listened now, Mab could hear his thoughts. They were all of Galahad, his son, deserted and orphaned by Lancelot's actions. All he thought of now was getting home to the boy.

Let him hope in vain.

Mab spread her hands and fingers, and for a moment a blue tangle of energy seemed to stream between them.

With a quick gesture she flung the intangible cat's-cradle toward Lancelot. It settled over his head and shoulders as he mounted Black Bayard, but he gave no sign of having noticed it.

Now, Lancelot, you will seek Joyous Gard in vain, condemned to wander forever across the face of the Earth, until you stop loving Arthur's Queen . . . Mab gloated.

Lancelot swung into Bayard's saddle and urged the horse at a gentle trot through the gates of Camelot. No one but the stableboys was there to see him go.

Mab laughed soundlessly as she disappeared.

The Battle of Sorrow

 fter much hardship, Arthur and his band of knights
had reached Rome. It was not the city that he
had studied as a boy, learning his Latin and Greek at his
tutor Merlin's knee. Rome was no longer the center of
the far-flung empire that had ruled Britain in his great-
grandfather's day, nor in fact of any empire. Imperial
Rome had held the greatest empire the world had ever
seen, but empires, like men, have lifespans, and Rome
had grown old and senile, lapsing into decay and factions
as it lost its hold over the lands it had once ruled. Justin-
ian ruled what remained of the Roman Empire from his
new city of Constantinople in the East, and what had
once been the Western Empire had become the prey of
Goths and Vandals who had brought chaos, destruction,
and ruin in their wake.

But though the mantle of the empire had departed

and Rome was only a shadow of what she had been, the glorious city herself was eternal, though dressed now in a gypsy's rags.

By now less than half remained of the party of forty-four valiant handpicked knights that had set out with Arthur from Camelot so many years before. Time and hardship and magic had winnowed their numbers until this small band was all that remained of the pride of Britain.

When they had reached the city, Arthur's knights had, as was their custom, sought out a monastery in which to find lodging. They had taken humble lodgings in its guest house outside the city gates, while Arthur and Gawain went in search of allies who might aid Arthur's quest for the Grail.

Sir Kay had grumbled mightily about being left behind, but he was still injured from their battle with the Knights of the Ford, and in any event, diplomacy was not Kay's strong suit.

"Stay here, brother," Arthur had said. "Rest. Gawain and I will return soon—with what I hope will be good news."

"We could use some of that, for a great change," Sir Bedivere muttered.

Afoot and dressed in the finest clothing remaining to them after their many adventures, Arthur and Gawain walked through the city toward Vatican Hill, trying hard not to marvel at what was, even though in ruins now, the greatest city the world had ever seen. Its streets were still choked with marvels—and none of them, Arthur knew, owed anything to the Old Ways. All were the product of mortal ingenuity.

At last the two men reached their goal, the Holy See itself.

When Pagan Rome had ruled the world, this hill had held the *collegium* of the Vestal Virgins who kept watch over the sacred flame of the Eternal City. When the New Religion had defeated the Old Ways, it had become the stronghold instead of the flame of faith, and the center of all that remained of goodness and learning in these dark times.

"Who goes there?"

The pikemen who challenged Arthur and Gawain did not even wear armor, so civilized was this city. On their doublets they wore the crossed keys of the Papal insignia, and long curling feathers in their soft black hats.

"King Arthur of the Britons, and his liegeman Gawain," Gawain answered, before Arthur could speak. "We seek an audience with His Holiness."

"The Holy Father does not see many travelers," one of the guards said cautiously.

"He will see me," Arthur said, with more confidence than he felt. "Tell him it is about the Holy Grail."

One of the guards left to bear a message, and soon a priest appeared, wearing long plain robes of cardinal red, and a small round skullcap in the same color.

"If you will come with me, travelers?" he said.

The Cardinal admitted Arthur and Gawain to the papal palace itself, and conducted them to an antechamber while the Holy Father was notified of their arrival.

"This is a grand sight," Gawain said once they were alone. "Won't Jenny love to hear about it?"

"You'll have to tell her, Gawain," Arthur said. "You've a poet's way with words. I just don't have the knack."

"And it would take a poet to do justice to this place," Gawain agreed, gazing around himself in admiration.

The air was balmy and scented with jasmine and oranges, for Italy was a much warmer country than cool, misty Britain. Arthur felt overdressed and provincial in his good wool tunic and gartered breeches, his cloak pinned at the shoulders by twin round brooches of beaten gold. He smoothed the beard he had grown in his travels with a hint of nervousness. He'd thought it made him look more kingly, but perhaps it only marked him as a provincial barbarian. The beauty he saw on every hand—of statues, paintings, and finely-wrought furnishings—shamed him. He had once thought to make Camelot a city more splendid than any in the ancient world, but he saw now that such dreams had been foolish. Cities already existed that—even in decay—were far more splendid than he could have ever imagined when he began his quest, and there was no way for Camelot to begin to equal them.

His grand dreams had all been foolish, unattainable. All of them.

"His Holiness will see you now," a slender man dressed all in red announced, entering the antechamber. He held the doors open as Arthur and Gawain passed through them into the audience chamber itself. It was the most enormous room either man had ever seen, and the most lavish.

The ceiling of the audience chamber was the deep blue of lapis lazuli, studded with golden stars, and the walls were covered with gilding and painted with images from the Holy Book. The air was thick with incense, and the heat of an Italian summer was made more sultry by the beeswax candles that stood in enormous golden candelabra along the walls of the room. As Arthur watched, a single teardrop of wax fell from one of the chandeliers above to spatter on the floor of inlaid marble.

At the far end of the enormous chamber, the Papal throne was set at the top of three steps of black and white marble. The throne glittered with gilding and bright enamel. There was a canopy above it, of blue velvet embroidered with golden stars, and curtains of white samite hung down on either side. On each side of the throne stood men in ornate Roman armor, staring straight ahead and holding javelins. Rome had bowed to the Church centuries before, and all that remained of its temporal might had been placed in her service.

The magnificence of the throne made its wizened occupant look even smaller by contrast. Virgilius was an old man, whose holy office and privileges had been worried like a bone between the Eastern Emperor and the greedy North African bishops. He had been deposed, excommunicated, and jailed during his years upon the throne, but had always survived and triumphed. Now, though he was at the height of his power, Virgilius was a very old man indeed, though the ravages of Time were mostly concealed by the sumptuousness of his pontifical robes. These were stiff with gold embroidery and jewels, and his gloved hands were covered with heavy rings. On his head

Virgilius wore the Papal crown, and its gold-encrusted lappets lay upon his chest. He looked like a carven doll. Only his ancient eyes were alive.

Arthur tried to feel the reverence that he thought he ought to at this auspicious moment, for in looking at Virgilius he was seeing Christ's Vicar on Earth, the anointed shepherd of the New Religion. But at the moment, all Arthur could think of was that he had seen beggars in the streets of the city, and that all this pomp and temporal display could have been sold to feed them. Camelot might never be as grand as Rome, but there at least no one would ever go hungry. As he thought of that, he felt a little better.

"Who is this?" Virgilius asked in a thin wavery voice. One of the cardinals near him was poised to reply, but Arthur spoke first.

"I am Arthur of Britain, King in that land, come with Sir Gawain to pay my respects and to seek aid in my quest."

"And what is this quest?" Virgilius asked. "Come closer, come closer, Arthur of Britain. I can barely see you."

Arthur and Gawain advanced the length of the audience chamber until they were standing at the foot of the Papal throne among the cardinals and bishops and other courtiers and ambassadors to the Holy See. Arthur disliked having to look so far up to see Virgilius, but he said nothing of that. He was here to ask a favor, after all.

"I come seeking the Holy Grail, the cup from which Our Lord drank at the Last Supper. I have sworn a vow to bring it to Camelot, to show before the people."

"The Holy Grail?" Virgilius said in disbelief. There was a chorus of whispers as the princes of the Church began to gossip among themselves excitedly. "But surely . . . tell us what you know of this Grail, Arthur of Britain."

Arthur glanced toward Gawain before replying. He had expected the Vatican Palace to be like Avalon Abbey, only larger, but this place, with its splendor and intrigue, reminded him more of the tales he'd heard of Uther's court. Nevertheless, he answered courteously.

"I know that Joseph of Arimathea brought the Holy Grail from Jerusalem to the Isle of Avalon in my country, and there founded an order of monks to watch over it. And there it rested for many years, healing all who came into its presence through its holiness, until by some misfortune it vanished in the reign of King Vortigern, who murdered my grandfather, King Constant, to take the throne of Britain.

"When I became King I swore I would restore the Grail to my people, and so I have searched the world over for it for seven long years. And now I have come to Rome to seek your aid, for surely if there is any news of the Grail's whereabouts on earth, it is here," Arthur finished.

There was a moment of silence when Arthur finished speaking, and beside him Gawain shifted uneasily, unsure of himself in this strange place. Both men were sweating and uncomfortable in their heavy woolen garments.

"But surely, King Arthur," said the Cardinal who had first ushered them into the audience chamber, "if the

Grail really exists—that is, if it can be found—then surely it belongs here? In the Holy City?"

"Yes, of course," said Virgilius quickly. "The Grail must be brought to Rome so that it can be properly taken care of. Don't you agree, King Arthur?"

"They don't know where it is," Gawain whispered to Arthur, with blunt Iceni directness.

"The Grail was entrusted to Britain by Joseph of Arimathea," Arthur said. "And I have vowed to return it there."

"Yes, of course," Virgilius said irritably, "But times change, Your Highness, and men must change with them. We absolve you of the terms of your vow. It is far more suitable that the Grail remain here. I'm sure you see that's for the best."

"I think I have seen a great deal that I never expected to, since I came to Rome," Arthur answered diplomatically. "I am sorry to hear you have no more information of the Grail than I. It seems I must continue my quest."

"You will, of course, keep His Holiness apprised of your success?" one of the cardinals said.

Arthur bowed wordlessly. After several more exchanges of empty pleasantries, the two Britons were allowed to leave the palace.

"What a pack of jackals!" Gawain burst out, as soon as they reached the streets.

"It is very puzzling," Arthur agreed mildly, wiping the sweat from his damp forehead with the back of his hand. "They seemed so . . . venal."

"Perhaps what Merlin has said is true, that goodness resides not in creeds, but in men," Gawain answered after a moment's thought. "Your grandfather, King Constant, did as much ill in the name of the New Religion as Avalon Abbey does good, and both good and ill have been done in the name of the Old Ways."

"True enough," Arthur said, sighing. "But we are no nearer to finding the Grail now than we were when we began, and if even Rome does not know where it lies, I fear our plight is grave indeed."

But when they returned to their lodging, it appeared that their quest was not as hopeless as it seemed, for the others had been putting their time to good use as well.

"There's an old temple up in the hills outside the city," Kay said. "The monks all say it's cursed, but Bradamante spoke to the old laundress, and she says that the common people still go there to pray to the Goddess of the Old Ways. She is said to know the answers to all questions."

Arthur turned to Bradamante. In her tunic and trews the lady-knight looked like a beardless boy—and just now, a hot and irritated one.

"It is true enough," Bradamante answered, shrugging. "I was born in this country, and it is true that many of the countryfolk still follow the Old Ways. But how can the Old Ways help you to find the Grail?"

"I don't know," Arthur answered honestly. "But I will not reject good advice, no matter its source, and if this oracle can answer all questions, perhaps she can answer this one. Can you find someone who will take us there?"

The old woman's name was Graziella, and she plainly thought the British knights were mad. But Bradamante spoke to her in her own language, and at last she agreed to take them to the Spring of Memory, high in the hills above Rome.

The party left that very night, for though Arthur preferred to see only the good in everyone, he was no trusting innocent. Virgilius had been far too interested in the Grail and the power it represented not to keep a close watch on the man who had brought him the news of it. Arthur thought it might be prudent to be gone from Rome before Virgilius thought of more questions he wished to ask.

Once they were outside the city and past the ring of surrounding farms, the hills became a ghostly deserted place in the twilight. The only sound was the jingling of the horses' bits, and the creaking and clicking of the knights' armor as they rode.

Graziella walked ahead of them untiringly until she reached a place where the path divided. She pointed in the direction leading further up into the hills and spoke quickly to Bradamante in her own tongue.

"She says the spring lies at the end of this path. She says she must go home now, for her daughter is waiting for her, but that we will have no trouble in finding the place," Bradamante translated doubtfully.

Bedivere snorted. "That's a tale I've heard before. They say 'you can't miss it,' and next thing you know you're up to your nose in some bog."

"Thank her for her help," Arthur said, ignoring the Welsh knight. Bradamante spoke to the old woman again, and gave her a few coins for her trouble. She returned the way she had come, and in a few moments the knights from Camelot were alone.

"This is a fool's errand," Kay said roundly. "We are all good Christian men. What cause can we have to resort to a Pagan sorceress?"

"It was a wizard who helped me to the throne of Britain," Arthur reminded his foster brother, "and gave both of us our lessons as boys. Merlin taught me not to be too proud to accept help from any source. If this prophetess can help me to find the Grail, then it ill behooves any of us to despise her aid."

After that they proceeded in silence along the path, as the night darkened further and the moon rose, until at last they could hear the sound of running water up ahead. Soon thereafter they reached their goal.

The water issued in a thin stream from the mouth of a grinning gargoyle face carved high above into the rock face, then fell a dozen feet into a basin cut into the rock below. The edge of the basin was strewn with the offerings of the countryfolk: flowers, and honeycakes wrapped in paper, and small dolls twisted out of harvest grasses. These things belonged to the Old Ways, and Arthur automatically crossed himself, lest any of the forces summoned here wish to do him harm.

"You have no reason to fear, Arthur of Britain," a voice said. It was a quiet voice, but it seemed to come from everywhere at once. Arthur grabbed for his sword, then forced himself to relax as a woman in a long hooded cloak stepped out of the rocks. There was a flurry as the knights with him drew their swords, but she did not move.

"Will you drink with me?" she asked. By her voice she could have been almost any age. He could not tell; her face was in shadow.

In her hands she held a silver cup. For a moment Arthur thought it might be the Grail, but it did not shine with the Grail's holy light. She stooped and dipped it into the spring, then held it out to him. Long silver bracelets in the shape of snakes coiled around her forearms, gleaming in the moonlight.

"Who are you?" Arthur asked, taking the cup, gingerly. He had not drawn Excalibur.

"I am the Memory of this place. I see that which has been, and that which is yet to be."

"Show yourself," Arthur demanded.

She threw back the hood of her cloak. To Arthur's surprise, she was quite young. He had expected the Pagan priestess to be as old as the laundress who had directed them here. Upon her forehead was bound a small silver crescent moon, but without it, she could have been any woman. Even her clothes were ordinary.

Once again, she gestured toward the cup he held. Arthur raised it to his lips. The water was sweet and pure, and as cold as the moonlight itself. He drank it all, and handed the cup back to her.

"Why do you come to me, King of Britain? My powers are weak. They wane as the Moon does, not to grow strong again for many generations, while the New Religion shines as bright and steady as the summer sun."

"I come seeking answers," Arthur said. "The people say you know the answers to all questions. For many years I have searched for the Holy Grail. I believed it was my duty to restore it to Britain. But now I wonder: was I wrong? Is that why I cannot find it? Please tell me."

The Priestess of the Spring of Memory smiled, and

her pale face was as lovely as the full moon. "You grow wise with the years, King Arthur. It is a good question, and so I will give you the answer. The Grail was never yours to find. That task is for another to accomplish."

"Then all this has been in vain?" Arthur asked.

The priestess shook her head, smiling gently.

"No honorable action is in vain, King of Britain. Much good will come of what you have done, though you will not live to see it. But go now, for you have been absent from your own place for far too long. It is time for you to return home."

"Wait!" Arthur said. "How can I—?"

But he was speaking only to the moonlight. The woman was gone. She had vanished before his eyes.

"So that's it?" Kay said, in a tone of mingled relief and disappointment.

"I guess we can all turn around and go home now," Bedivere said, to no one in particular.

"Do you believe her?" Gawain asked his friend.

Arthur sighed wearily. "I think she told me no more than what was in my own thoughts, but perhaps it is still true all the same. Perhaps I have been too proud in thinking I was meant to restore the Grail to Britain. If I were meant to find it, surely God would have sent me some sign by now." He paused for a long time, staring down into the spring whose waters sparkled in the moonlight. "I think it is time to go home."

It had been a month since Lancelot had left Camelot. More and more of the running of the kingdom fell to Merlin, Sir Hector, and Sir Bors, for the Queen, inconsolable with grief at the loss of Lancelot, kept to her own rooms. And for the first time in a very long time, Merlin was unsure of what to do. He must remain at Camelot until Arthur returned, for there was no one else who could face the threat that Mordred presented to Arthur's throne, but that was the only certainty. At the moment he was attempting to write a letter to Arthur, and having little success. He could not think of what to say. If only he knew when Arthur was coming home!

With Lancelot gone, perhaps a new champion was needed for Camelot. But who could Merlin choose? Arthur had taken the best of the younger knights with him, and the rest of the able men of Britain were occupied with the running of the kingdom. Even if he had the authority to appoint someone, Merlin could not think which of them could be spared to this task.

Further, though the older generation accepted Merlin and his wizardry, those who followed the New Religion—mostly those born during Uther's reign—wanted nothing to do with the Old Ways. They did not welcome Merlin's interference in the business of government. Though Merlin accepted this philosophically—it was what he had planned toward, hoped for, from the moment he had first had the vision of what Arthur's birth would mean to Britain—there was no denying it was highly inconvenient.

Not for the first time, he wondered if it was time to leave Camelot. Perhaps his fears regarding Mordred were groundless. Merlin had always meant to go home to his beloved forest when Mab's power was destroyed and Arthur no longer needed him, to live there quietly with

Nimue. Perhaps now was the time. If Mordred meant to strike, wouldn't he have done it years ago?

For the first time in many months, Merlin allowed his thoughts to dwell upon the woman he loved. Just as Lancelot and Guinevere had, he and Nimue had been caught between love and duty. Lancelot and Guinevere had chosen love. Merlin had chosen duty.

And Nimue . . . ?

She had always urged him to be the best he could be, to set aside personal desires in the name of his higher calling. She had always been staunch in her belief that Arthur and the good of Britain must take precedence over their own desires. Merlin believed that in her little world of Avalon, Nimue worked as hard for Britain as Merlin did in Camelot, knowing as Merlin did that someday their labors would end and they could be together.

Was now the time?

Merlin hesitated, and sadly shook his head. It was his eager heart that tempted him, as always. Until Arthur returned to Britain, Merlin's task was not complete. The threat that Mordred presented could not be dismissed through wishful thinking.

He heard a faint scrabbling sound and turned toward the door. Opening it, he surprised Llewellyn, a young page sent to Camelot to learn the ways of chivalry here. Llewellyn's people, the Prydain, still followed the Old Ways, and Llewellyn had been fascinated by Merlin, attaching himself to the wizard as his unofficial servant.

"M'lord!" Llewellyn gasped, sprawling backward.

Repressing a smile, Merlin said sternly: "Up to mischief again, young sir?"

"Oh, no, m'lord!" the young page said virtuously. "There's a message—a message has come from the King!"

Guinevere and her senior advisers were gathered in the throne room when Merlin arrived.

Her sorrow had not aged the Queen, for Guinevere still looked as lovely as she had on the day she married Arthur, but it had purified her, the loss of Lancelot hardening her as the sword blade is hardened upon the smith's anvil.

"Merlin," she said in an expressionless voice, "how kind of you to join us. A letter has come from the King."

She held the scroll out to him, though her eyes did not meet his. It was the usual form in which messages that must travel far were sent; a long sheet of paper wrapped tightly around a bronze spindle and inserted in a waxed leather case that could be tightly sealed against water damage. Merlin took the scroll carefully. The vellum crackled in his hands; Guinevere had already unrolled the letter to read it.

"To my Queen and my dear friends—many adventures have befallen me since last I wrote. I have been to Rome, and seen many wonders there, as well as things which cause me great concern, but all of these would take too long to tell, and I must have this missive in the hands of the courier before he departs. Suffice it to say that though my search for the Grail has enjoyed no more success than before, I have been persuaded that I may neglect my kingdom and my people no longer, and—"

"He is coming home," Guinevere said, before Merlin could finish reading.

"He says that Kay and Gawain are well," Sir Hector added. He looked troubled, for he loved both Arthur and Guinevere, and her adultery had divided his loyalties painfully.

"He may arrive as soon as the spring," Sir Bors said. "The winter snows will delay him in crossing the Alps—you may take that from an old campaigner—but he's a resourceful lad."

"A lad no longer," Merlin said. Arthur must be nearly thirty—a far cry from the boy-king Merlin had set on the throne.

"I have called you here to share this news in order to discourage the spread of rumor," Guinevere said, firmly taking control of the meeting. "If rumors of Arthur's return begin to appear, I wish you to be able to confirm them, but until they do, I do not wish the news widely disseminated. As Merlin has often reminded me, Camelot is not without enemies."

And they might well choose a moment such as this, when the people were distracted by the joyful news of Arthur's return, to strike.

There was a murmur of assent from the gathered nobles—the half-dozen men who had seen Uther to his throne and been the first to support his son—and the Queen dismissed them with a gesture. Merlin turned to go as well.

"Stay, Merlin."

He waited until they all had gone, and the attendants had closed the doors of the Great Hall once more. As he waited, he studied the Queen closely. She had changed so much in the past years. He wondered how Arthur had changed as well.

"My lady?" Merlin said courteously.

"What will you do once Arthur returns?" Guinevere asked him.

"I suppose I shall retire from court and tend to business of my own," Merlin said. "He will have no need of me, and neither will you."

"That is a good answer," Guinevere said. Perhaps she thought that sounded a little harsh, for she leaned toward him, and when she spoke again there was real warmth in her voice. "You have spent so much time making Arthur king, following his dreams. Do you not have any dreams of your own, Merlin?"

"My dreams are the same as Arthur's, my lady: of peace and plenty for all. But I have never wished to govern. I will be just as glad to return to my forest, and conclude my days in peace and quiet."

"Peace," Guinevere said sadly. "I do not think that is a thing that any of us can be certain of."

When he left the Queen's presence, Merlin returned to his tower room and his interrupted letter, though this time it was to have a different recipient. For the first time in many years Merlin wrote to Nimue at Avalon, to tell her the glad news that the King was returning, and that soon the king's wizard would be free at last, his duties ended. He wrote the message in tiny even letters on a fine scroll of thin parchment, and when he was done he went to the window and whistled. The pigeons that circled the tower cooed and fluttered, and at last one came spiraling down to land upon the sill.

"There you are, Peregrin," Merlin said. He picked up the small grey bird and tied the message carefully to its leg. "Now go and find Nimue. You can reach Avalon by nightfall if you hurry."

Leaning far out the window, he tossed the pigeon into the air. It spread its wings wide, spiraling down toward the cobblestones for a few seconds, then began to flap wildly until it was soaring westward, toward Avalon.

Merlin watched it go, feeling truly content for the first time in years. Soon Arthur would return, and the years of fear and worry would be at an end.

Soon.

Unblinking black eyes watched the small grey form as it flew toward its destination. Soon it had left the towns and villages surrounding Camelot behind, and once it had, the raven struck, arrowing down through the air to bury its cruel talons deep in the pigeon's feathery back. The two forms fell through the sky like a thunderbolt cast to earth, to strike with a dull thud.

Queen Mab got to her feet, brushing feathers from her hands. The wind whipped her black hair away from her face, causing the crystals braided into it to chime softly.

Sometimes there was a certain satisfaction to doing things yourself. And with Frik spending all of his time mooning over Morgan these days, Mab was thrown more and more on her own resources.

Still, it wouldn't do to upset Morgan just yet. Not while Mab still needed her.

She stooped again and picked up the dead pigeon. Mab plucked the scroll from its leg and tossed the dead bird over her shoulder, wincing slightly as she did so. The shapechanging had taken a great deal out of her; she was less powerful than she once had been. But this time of weakness would end once Mordred came into his power. This time, at last, she had found a champion who would truly be loyal unto death.

Unrolling the scroll, Mab peered at the tiny letters. It was a letter from Merlin to Nimue. Mab found the maudlin human sensibility nauseating, but the news was interesting. Arthur had given up his quest for the Grail and was returning home.

If Arthur was coming home, then Mordred must be here to meet him. At last, it was time. The day for which she had plotted and planned for so many years had come. All she had to do was make sure that all parts of her plan would be ready when the time came.

In her cell, Nimue was at her prayers, telling over the beads of her amber rosary as her lips moved silently. When the Healing Sisters were not practicing their craft, they were at prayer, marking the canonical hours from matins to compline with chanting and hymnations. Her second vows were behind her, and Nimue had immersed herself in study and work. When she took her third and final vows, she would be sealed to Avalon forever.

Was that truly what she wanted? Never to be free again, never to run barefoot along the sand as she had when she was a small child, never to dance and sing for pure joy?

No, she thought in wonder. *That isn't what I want. . . .*

It was as if her spirit were awakening from a long sleep. The thought of spending the rest of her life confined within the walls and the life of Avalon filled Nimue with an echo of the peculiar horror that Merlin must feel to be trapped in an underground cell. This life of prayer and service was not the life of the woman Nimue had been meant to be.

What should she do? How could she take back her word to the Father Abbot after so many years? Her friends, everyone she knew, were here. How could she leave them? And what did she have to leave them for?

Perhaps a walk in the garden will help to order my thoughts, Nimue thought. She set down her rosary on the windowsill and turned toward the door of her little room, but it was already opening.

"Great news—great news, Nimue!" the Father Abbot burst out. "Arthur's coming home!"

Though she was surprised to see him there—for what business did the ruler of the community of Avalon have with a lowly novice?—the news delighted her.

"Thank God!" Nimue said fervently. "Did he find the Holy Grail?"

"Wrong! But what of it?" the Father Abbot said impatiently. "He's coming home. Holy Grail or no Holy Grail—he should never have left."

The Father Abbot did not sound quite like himself, but Nimue was too excited to notice. "Merlin is free!" she said, sinking down onto her narrow cot. "He can start living his own life again!" *With me . . .*

The Father Abbot seated himself beside her and took her hand. "Yes . . . and it *should* be with you, my child," he said, as if he had heard her unspoken thoughts. He gazed deeply into her eyes, until Nimue thought she could almost see green fires dancing in his gaze. "God doesn't want you when you love another." He lowered his voice conspiratorially. "I shouldn't really say this in these hallowed halls: faith is supreme, but love is even better." He patted her hand, rising to his feet. "I'm sure you'll make the right choice when the time comes."

It was all Mab could do to keep from crowing aloud as she scuttled from Nimue's cell in her religious disguise. As soon as she was sure that no one was looking she shook herself violently, and the image of the Father Abbot crackled from her body like an outgrown chrysalis.

She'd been right. Nimue still remembered the bargain Mab had offered her: beauty and youth in exchange for trapping Merlin in a magical place of Mab's creation. While she had thought Merlin necessary to the safety of Britain, the bargain had not tempted Nimue, but with Arthur coming home, the girl would be willing to follow her greedy human heart at last, and take Merlin away somewhere safe.

And then, with Arthur dead and Camelot destroyed, he will see that I was right all along! Mab gloated. She could taste the victory that was nearly hers, and it was sweeter than ambrosia on her tongue. With Merlin out of harm's way, there would be no one left to oppose anything that Mordred chose to do.

But there was much for Mordred to learn before he faced Arthur.

The garden was, as always, a refuge for Nimue. She loved the herbs and flowers that were grown here to form the basis for the stock of medicines belonging to the Healing Sisters. But today it did not work its familiar magic upon her thoughts.

For the first time in many years, Nimue was unsure of her course. In her heart she had always known the truth of the Father Abbot's words—that her true vocation was Merlin. But she had never wanted to stand in the way of Merlin's fight against Queen Mab, for Nimue believed as ardently as Merlin did that the violence and cruelty of the Old Ways no longer had any place in Britain. But now Arthur was coming home to reign over the land that Merlin had protected for so long. . . .

"Sister Nimue."

"Father Giraldus," Nimue said in surprise, dropping a deep curtsy as she turned.

Age had not been kind to the scholarly monk. His hair had thinned until it was only a scant half-circle around the back of his tonsure, and deep lines of dissatisfaction bracketed his mouth. Giraldus was one of those Christians who saw harm in everything outside his own narrow interpretation of the creed, and he had always condemned Nimue's friendship with Merlin.

"I did not see you at prayers," Giraldus went on, studying her closely.

The way he looks at me, you would think I'd been dancing naked in the meadow! Nimue thought rebelliously. But as always, she presented Giraldus with a serene, unruffled face.

"I was praying privately in my cell," she said demurely, keeping her eyes cast down.

The other thing Father Giraldus disapproved of was immodesty in women—by which he meant any degree of self-respect. His sermons were always on the subject of the innate sinfulness of women, of how by Eve's betrayal of Adam, Original Sin had come into the world. He was always trying to get the Healing Sisters disbanded, saying that it was dangerous to make so much use of the old healing knowledge of the Pagans, and that people should look to glory in their next life and not comfort in this one. Sometimes Nimue thought that Giraldus would be happiest in a world that had no women in it at all, if only he could figure out how to manage it.

She would have walked on, but he put out a hand to stop her.

"Then you have not heard the news," he said. "The King is returning home."

Nimue said nothing, but it was hardly necessary to encourage Giraldus.

"He has not found the Grail, but that is hardly surprising. The Grail will only reveal itself to the humble, the chaste, the pure of heart—and the King is a great sinner."

"Arthur?" Nimue asked, startled out of her self-imposed silence. She had only seen the King once, but she'd had many letters about him from Merlin during Arthur's boyhood.

"But he's . . . that is, I have heard that he is very devout," Nimue said piously.

"Hah!" Giraldus barked. "If he were truly devout, he would have found the Grail! No, he's returning empty-handed, which is clear proof of God's displeasure at his liberal ways. Perhaps we can hope that this rebuke will make him properly humble, so that he will take up the true task of the Crown, to purge the land of sinners and heretics."

Nimue flashed him a startled glance. Giraldus made it sound as if he hoped that Arthur would take up the purges and crusades that had marked Vortigern's terrible and bloody reign. "But surely—" she began.

"He has been soft for too long. It is the rot at the root—how can he call himself a good Christian when he has nurtured a Pagan wizard in his bosom since his tenderest years? No, he will see now that it is strength, not mercy, that is needed to sweep away the last of the Old Ways and make the land safe for good Christians once more." He regarded her with a beady gaze that missed nothing. "And you should look to the state of your own soul as well, Nimue. Toleration is very well in its place, but carried to extremes it is nothing but a breeding ground for sin."

That will never be your problem, Giraldus! Nimue thought irreverently. But years spent in Avalon had taught her humility, so she curtsied again, murmuring vague words of agreement.

Satisfied, Giraldus swept on. Nimue looked after him

with troubled eyes. Giraldus traveled far and wide across Britain to preach the New Religion. If he also preached the things he had been saying to her just now, his words of hate and exclusionism would find ready hearers. There would no longer be a peaceful coexistence between the remnants of the Old Ways and the New Religion.

Merlin would no longer be safe. Though the King himself followed the New Religion, he had never persecuted those who followed the Old Ways. But with Giraldus and others like him seeing Arthur's failure to return the Grail to Britain as a sign of Divine displeasure, public opinion would be against the King for the first time in his reign. Arthur was no Vortigern, to rule by terror and force a land and a people who hated and feared him. If he believed it was the true will of his people, Arthur would outlaw the Old Ways.

What would happen to Merlin then? He'd made many enemies through the years among those who were jealous of his influence over the King. They would be happy to take the opportunity to settle old scores with him . . . and Queen Mab, too, would take the opportunity to remove Merlin as an obstacle to her plans.

Merlin would not be safe.

Suddenly the bargain Mab had once offered her became terribly tempting.

"I'll restore your beauty if you take Merlin away to a place I've created for you. You can live with him there to the end of your days."

If Nimue took Merlin away to a place Mab had created, Mab would have no more reason to harm him. And those who followed Giraldus's preachings would have no chance to hurt him, if Merlin were safely hidden away from the world.

She could save Merlin.

But at what cost?

Standing alone in the Abbey garden, Nimue felt her heart beat fast with fear.

Her Nibs was in much too good a mood to bode well for anyone. For as long as Frik could remember, the Queen of the Old Ways had only really been happy when she was hurting somebody, and *entré nous,* Frik just couldn't seem to work up any interest in petty cruelty these days. He couldn't remember when things like that had started to bore him—perhaps it was when Merlin had first become his student—but these days he found Her Majesty very tedious. He'd learned that the mortalfolk feared and loved, hurt and ached just as the Fair Folk did, and Frik had come to share their joys and pain. They had no magic. It wasn't fair to torment them when there was no way for them to defend themselves. It wasn't chivalrous, and Frik had developed an appreciation for chivalry over the years.

Not that it was going to do him any good. Frik stared broodingly out the window in the Great Hall of Tintagel at the waves pounding upon the rocks far below. Though he was here alone—Morgan was in her bower trying on all her dresses, a favorite pastime—he still wore the form of the dashing blond swashbuckler that had so captivated his lady fair. There were times now when Frik forgot it was not his true self—it was true for Morgan, and that was all that mattered.

"Frik!" Mab's harsh voice rang out, and he jumped guiltily.

She'd appeared out of nowhere just the way she always had. She was dressed all in violet and rosy grey—bright colors, for Mab, and another indication of her exalted mood.

"Prepare the horses," Mab said peremptorily. "We're leaving. It is time for me to finish Mordred's training."

"And Morgan?" Frik asked cautiously. The fact that a boy needed his mother had always been Morgan's only protection from Mab's captiousness.

"Forget her!" Mab said contemptuously. "We don't need her anymore."

"Yes, of course," Frik said.

He'd said the same words to Mab a thousand, a million times down through the years of their long association, but this time they meant something different than they had all the other times. This time they meant rebellion.

He would do it. He would break with Mab and stay with Morgan. The two of them could be happy together here. Mab wouldn't care about Morgan anymore now that she had served Mab's purpose, and she hadn't cared about Frik for years. If he were lucky, she'd just go away and leave them alone together at Tintagel. These last few years with Morgan had been a time of true happiness for Frik, and he did not want to go back to bowing and scraping to Mab and her mad plans. Let Mab do as she liked with the rest of Britain so long as she left the two of them to their happiness. Morgan would miss the chance to swagger about as the Queen Mother, but Frik could make that up to her. He knew it.

All he had to do was get Mab out of Tintagel with Mordred before Morgan noticed he was gone. Frik disappeared quickly before Mab could say anything further. What did he care about the rest of the world so long as he was able to stay with the woman he loved?

The woman he loved. Odd words from a gnome, and ones he'd never expected to say or even think, but true. And the most important thing just now was to protect Morgan. All Frik had to do was get Mab and Mordred away from the castle without Morgan noticing.

Quickly he saddled Mab's white palfrey and Mordred's bay gelding, all the while hoping desperately that Morgan would remain distracted by the contents of her closets a while longer. He led the two horses out to the foot of the steps and waited impatiently. How long could it take Mab to tell Mordred the day he'd always dreamed of was here? The boy was quick enough to do things Frik *didn't* like. . . .

If Mab asked why Frik wasn't coming with them, he'd think of something to tell her—that he had to clean up here, perhaps. But Frik didn't really think she'd notice. She hadn't noticed what he did for years—and they'd been good years, too. Frik wanted more of them.

As he fretted, Mab finally appeared, leading Mordred by the hand.

"Careful, my dear. The steps are very slippery." The Queen of the Old Ways looked almost radiant in steel-grey and violet. A dark bride for a black honeymoon, and woe to Britain when it was over!

"Where are we going?" Mordred asked eagerly. In the dim afternoon light there was a gloating sensuality about his sullen beautiful features that made Frik shudder inwardly. Was it possible that he had once been as Mordred was now—heartless, sadistic? He pushed the thought away. It was not wise to be distracted around Mab.

"To my land, the Land of Magic," Mab answered happily.

"Can I create monsters?" Mordred instantly demanded.

"Oh . . . if you wish," Mab said.

"You're so good to me, Auntie."

Come on, come on! Frik thought. Why were they wasting time chattering when he needed them to mount up and ride off before Morgan noticed they were leaving and made one of her scenes?

But Mab could never bear to waste an opportunity to educate her protégé. Even now, she paused on the landing to explain herself to Mordred as she never had to Frik.

"It won't be all fun and games. Arthur's coming back—"

"Ah," Mordred interrupted.

"—and there are things I have to teach you," Mab said proudly.

"Is Mother coming?" Mordred asked.

"No," Mab said. "We don't need her anymore."

They were almost at the horses. Frik trembled inwardly with apprehension, lest Mab should suspect his inner thoughts and punish him for them. And in that moment, his luck ran out.

"Mab!"

Morgan appeared in the doorway at the top of the steps just as Mab and Mordred reached the bottom. She was wearing her green gown with the crushed velvet over-robe—the one Frik liked best—and her beautiful features were contorted with innocent annoyance.

"Where are you taking my son?" she demanded obliviously.

"It's time," Mab said simply.

"Without a word? Without a by-your-leave?" Morgan was very conscious of the royal blood that flowed in her veins—her late father Gorlois, like Lord Lot and his son Gawain, stood almost as near to the throne as the King himself—and liked to receive the deference due to the mother of the future King. Mab was not handling her at all well.

But then, Mab didn't care about handling people.

"I have to make him ready," Mab said, with what passed in her for patience.

"You're not taking him. He's my son!" Morgan snapped.

Blissfully self-obsessed, Morgan had never understood Mab's true nature. If she had—if she had been less self-centered—she would have retreated now. But Morgan was who she was, and it simply did not occur to her after all these years that anyone would treat her with less than the deference to which she had become accustomed.

Frik watched it all, frozen in horror, not knowing what to do. Interfering would only make matters worse.

"He's mine!" Mab flared, turning on Morgan.

"I gave him love! You gave him toys!" Mordred's mother shot back.

From the expression on her face, Morgan was belatedly coming to realize that having Mab for a fairy godmother might have been a bad idea; that perhaps Mordred's childhood should have been arranged differently. But Morgan herself had been little more than a neglected child when Frik came into her life. She had never had the chance to develop the wisdom and maturity that could have saved her and her son.

"I gave him life!" Mab raged, and Frik hesitated, desperately torn between wanting somehow to save Morgan—and to save himself from Mab's wrath. Then Morgan took the decision out of his hands.

"I'm never letting him go!" she said furiously, and took a step forward.

There was a tiny swirl of magic. And Morgan slipped, fell, rolled down the stairs and over the edge of the landing, to drop with crushing force to the flagstones of the courtyard.

"No!" Frik cried in horror.

"That was very clever, Auntie."

Mordred's voice came distantly to Frik's ears as he ran to Morgan and knelt beside her, gazing into her face. Unconcerned, Mordred led Mab past Frik and the dying Morgan, heading toward the horses.

"My love, my love," Frik said helplessly, cradling Morgan in his arms. She was dying, and as life left her battered body, the fairy glamour he had cast over her years before left her as well, leaving her plain and ugly and dressed in rags.

"Frik, my love, am I still beautiful?" Morgan asked painfully.

"Oh yes," Frik said honestly. He did not care what Morgan looked like. He loved her with all his heart. "Beyond words, my love."

He felt a tingle as Mab wrenched away the dashing illusion of handsomeness he had worn for so long, and though he tried, he could not keep himself from asking: "Am I?"

"Oh, yes," Morgan assured him, gazing clear-eyed into her lover's face. "Beyond words. . . ."

Gently Frik bent to kiss her one last time, and as he did, he felt the spirit leave her body, carrying Morgan le Fay where he could never go, to a land where she would always be young and beautiful and loved.

She was dead.

Fury filled him, blotting out fear and self-preservation for the first time in the uncounted centuries of his existence. He got to his feet and turned toward Mab, shaking with rage and grief.

"You killed her!" he shouted.

"Perhaps she just slipped," Mab said archly. Mordred had just assisted her into the saddle and now turned away to mount his own steed. She could not conceal her pleasure that the day she had waited so long for had come, and Morgan's death did nothing to diminish her happiness.

"In any case, what does it matter, Frik? You're holding us up. We have a lot to do," she said impatiently. No vestige of human emotion was present on Mab's porcelain countenance.

"Mab, you evil old crone! May God have mercy on your soul! He obviously didn't have any on the rest of you!" Frik raged.

"Why is everyone suddenly against me?" she said plaintively, and shrugged, coming to a quick decision. "Frik, I'm leaving you with your misery and pain—but with no more magic powers! Now you'll wander through the world ugly and alone, just as if you were human."

She turned her horse toward the gate.

"Good-bye, Frik, I'll miss you," Mordred said good-naturedly. "No I won't," he added with a mocking grin, and urged his horse after Mab's. "Why didn't you kill him, Auntie Mab?" Mordred asked. Frik could hear his voice quite plainly.

"Because that's what he wanted me to do," Mab answered.

Frik stood in the courtyard beside Morgan's body, watching them go. The two riders vanished into the mist, still talking. And then even their voices were gone, and he was alone.

For centuries he had followed Mab's orders and played his own cruel games without thinking—without caring—about the pain they had caused. He had felt a little sorry for Merlin when the boy had been his pupil, it was true, but he had done nothing to help him when he should have. And so, in the end, Frik had been unable to protect Morgan, the woman he loved.

Frik sank down beside her body and wailed his grief.

Enchantment had been all that held Tintagel together for years, and now that the magic was gone it took everything with it. The servants reverted to mice and rabbits and gulls, the fine furniture to driftwood and sea-wrack, and all of Morgan's toys and jewels to bits of colored glass and silver paper. Her fine gowns vanished as though they'd never been, and when everything else had vanished, even the walls and roof began to crumble, rotting away with the neglect that magic had concealed.

And as the castle crumbled away, the sea-mist thickened, and for the first time in many long years, it began to rain.

The rain soaked Frik to the bone, chilling him and making him aware of just how helpless and ridiculous a figure he presented. Even his grief and anger could not distract him from his own discomfort, and at last he got stiffly to his feet, gathered up Morgan's chill body, and made his way slowly up the stairs once more.

At the top he looked down, longingly, at the stones of the courtyard. He was mortal now. How sweet it would be to fling himself down from here and gain sweet and eternal peace.

But no.

There was something he must do first. He did not know how he would manage, when those more powerful and more clever had failed, but Frik vowed that before he died he would see Mab utterly defeated.

He carried Morgan inside, and spent the rest of the day collecting enough wood from the wrecked remains of the furniture to build her a funeral pyre in the center of the Great Hall. There were still scraps of bread and cheese about—for no matter what else had been illusion, the food had been real—and Frik made a meager meal before settling in to keep vigil beside Morgan's body. Most of the roof of the Great Hall had crumbled away, but there was enough left to shelter him.

He wished for so many things that night. He wished he had been a better person when he'd had the chance. He wished he'd helped Merlin more when he'd had the power. He wished he'd been clever enough to know that this day would come, and to somehow spirit Morgan away when there was still time.

He wished he'd never met Queen Mab at all.

The folk of Fairy do not cry as mortalkind understands the word. Their tears are shed for malice, or magic. But Frik wept now, understanding the impossibility of gaining the only thing he had left to desire. How could one de-magic'd gnome destroy the Queen of the Old Ways? Merlin had magic—a considerable amount of it, in fact—and he had never managed to defeat her. Though Frik felt this latest plan of hers would only end in disaster, he was quite certain that Mab would come out of it all right.

And that was something he found unbearable.

When morning came, Frik found flint and steel and kindled Morgan's funeral pyre. Fire was the simplest magic, but even that was beyond him now. When the pyre was burning brightly, he turned and walked out of Tintagel for the last time.

By the time he reached the causeway the fire had begun to spread, for Tintagel, like most castles, contained as much timber as stone. When the fire had consumed all it could, all that would be left was a tumble of old stones, with no one to say what they were or who had once lived here.

Turning his back on the flames, Frik walked on, his mind fixed on Mab's destruction.

There must be a way.

He would find it.

With time.

CHAPTER FOUR

THE BATTLE OF SHADOWS

Mab and Mordred rode away from Tintagel, and as they went, Mordred slowly became aware of things around him that he had never seen before. There were tiny winged women who flitted through the air around him, clad only in a bright rainbow of colored lights, gnarled old dwarves in green coats and red caps who crouched by the roots of trees and watched them ride by. Even the horses were transformed, until Mab rode a shining silver mare and Mordred rode a gleaming black stallion.

At last he was going to the Land of Magic. There Mab would give him the gifts she had always promised him, the gifts that would enable him to destroy his father and all his father's works.

Around the two riders the land slowly changed from the tree-dotted green fields of Cornwall to rolling hills covered with white trefoil blossoms and pale heather. The sky was the silvery grey of mist, and though Mordred looked carefully, he could see no brighter spot where the sun might be shining beyond the mist. The only sparks of color came from the flying sprites. Mordred swatted at one that flew too close, and was pleased to feel his hand connect solidly with the tiny body. He heard its thin wail as it sailed through the air to land heavily against the ground.

"Now Mordred," Mab said, "you mustn't be rude. These will be your subjects someday."

"If they're to be my subjects, then that means I may do just as I like with them," Mordred said logically. But the sprites steered clear of him for the rest of the ride.

Soon they reached a place where an immense stone henge had been erected, gigantic pillars of pale granite set in a ring, with stone lintels laid across them so that the structure resembled nothing so much as an enormous ring of cyclopean doorways leading to unknown destinations.

"This is the way into the Land of Magic," Mab said proudly.

She gestured, and the doorways filled with rainbow fire. Through them, Mordred could see visions—of marching armies, of strange weapons, of machines that flew through the sky spewing fire.

War.

He liked it.

Mordred smiled. "Which door shall we choose, Auntie?" he asked eagerly.

Mab did not answer, but rode forward, through a door that showed Romans fending off blue-painted savages who fought with clubs and spears. Mordred eagerly spurred his own horse after her, but once he had ridden through the gate, the warriors vanished.

Mordred stood beside Mab in the center of a silver path that arced through a vast cavern. He could hear the sound of water lapping somewhere far below, but the cave was so dark that he could not see it. All around him, the walls glittered with a dull crystalline shine, and in the distance he could hear a faint chiming.

This is rather disappointing, Mordred thought privately. Frankly, he'd been expecting something more impressive than a cave.

"I have brought you Mordred!" Mab cried, throwing her arms wide. Her shout echoed through the vast cavern. "Come, Mordred. We have much to do."

She took his hand, and suddenly the two of them were in a completely different place. *This is more like it,* Mordred thought. The room had a fireplace, a table, and chairs, but what it had most of was books, large dusty impressive-looking tomes that probably contained all manner of vile spells. Mab ripped through them with her customary destructiveness, flinging them from the shelves and tossing them aside as she searched for a particular object.

"Ah," Mab said at last, turning toward Mordred with a small black glass bottle in her hand. "Here it is."

Mordred regarded the bottle with interest. Whatever was inside seemed to be glowing.

She pulled out the stopper before seizing a battered and tarnished silver goblet from the top of a shelf. She poured it full from the bottle—the liquid *did* glow, then began to bubble and smoke. She handed the goblet to Mordred.

"Drink this," Mab said. "With its power you will be able to persuade anyone mortal of anything."

Mordred stared down into the goblet. "And why would I want to do that, Auntie?" Persuasion hadn't actually been in any of his future plans.

"You will turn Arthur's knights against him, and use them to destroy Camelot and all that it stands for!" Mab cawed in her raven's voice. "And then Merlin will see that it was wrong to oppose me!"

"But aren't we going to destroy Merlin too, Auntie?" Mordred asked. He sat down in a large ornate chair, brushing away a few cobwebs first. The goblet he held still bubbled and foamed.

"Leave Merlin to me," Mab said. "I've made plans that will remove him from the World of Men completely. He will be powerless to help Arthur."

"That's all very well," Mordred said, getting up again and walking over to where Mab stood, "but don't you want him dead? Auntie? Tell your favorite nephew."

"Merlin is a wizard," Mab said. "He has the Old Blood running through his veins. The potion's powers won't affect him. I don't want you to fail, Mordred," she said, turning to him and stroking his cheek. "You mean so much to me."

But not as much as Merlin does, Mordred thought with an unwelcome pang of realization. He'd always known that Mab had created Merlin. But Merlin had betrayed her, and Mordred had been sure that Mab had written Merlin off years ago.

Suddenly he wasn't so sure anymore.

"Drink," Mab urged him.

Mordred did, cautiously. Despite the fact that the goblet in his hands was hot, the liquid it contained was cold—bitingly cold. It burned freezingly all the way down his throat, numbing his mouth and tongue. He coughed and sputtered, dropping the cup.

"I don't feel any different," he said when he could speak.

Mab patted his shoulder. "It won't begin to work until you return to the mortal world—but beware. Its power will wane with the waning of the year. At Samhain it will end."

"That should be plenty of time," Mordred said complacently. "Now. What other presents do you have for me, Auntie?"

Once he left Tintagel Keep, the now-mortal Frik wandered helplessly—aimlessly—through a world grown dark and cruel. He had thought that there could be nothing worse than to be Mab's eternal victim, but he had been wrong. Stripped of the magic that had been his since the beginning of Time, he was forced to fight for his survival in a world where his gnomish appearance made him every man and woman's enemy. There were times when Frik, tired, hungry, and cold, yearned simply to lie down in a ditch and let Lord Idath take him away to the Land of Winter.

But he wouldn't. Not while Mab was larking around, gloating over her hopeful victories. There must be some way to stop the old besom!

There was no one he could turn to for help, no one left alive who would look kindly upon him, save for one man.

Merlin the wizard.

Down deep inside himself, Frik cringed at the thought. He could not bear to accept Merlin's forgiveness when he could not forgive himself. But Merlin would understand his grief. Merlin would help him. The boy had a kind and generous heart, and was dedicated to Mab's destruction. Merlin would forgive Frik his part in all the abuse and maltreatment he had suffered in the service of Mab's ambition.

And it was time to face facts. Frik had nowhere to go and no one to turn to but Merlin. Perhaps between the two of them, they could think of something that could destroy the powerful Queen of the Old Ways. Almost despite himself, Frik's faltering steps turned north, toward the forest where Merlin had been born.

We had some happy times here, Frik thought to himself as he surveyed the little forest hut. It wasn't kept quite as it had been in Ambrosia's time—when Frik had been a frequent, though invisible, visitor—but it was tidy enough. All right and tight, waiting for the day that Merlin would come back to it.

Frik sat down on a stool and stared morosely into the cold hearth. The harsh wind of autumn blew through the chinks in the thatching, and Frik shivered in his threadbare mountebank's costume. He was cold—and try as he might, no amount of will could light a fire in the fireplace, or even generate a little heat. Life wasn't much fun without magic . . . and yet Merlin had struggled so hard against it, both against learning it and against using it.

It was very puzzling.

Frik's shoulders slumped. There was no point in putting off the horrid realization any longer. Merlin wasn't here. Part of Frik had known all along that he wouldn't be. Merlin would be at Camelot—and soon, so would Mordred, armed with all of Mab's venomous ingenuity. Frik had come on a fool's errand—but down deep inside, a small voice insisted that there was something he needed to do here in Barnstable Forest. Something important. Something vital.

Frik gazed bleakly about the hut. Little curls of autumn leaf had blown in under the tattered door curtain, and spiders had strung veils of lace between the shelves and along the walls. The little cottage had the look of a place that had been abandoned forever, but surely that could not be true. This was Merlin's home. He loved the forest and the wild lands. He must be planning to return here.

When?

When Arthur was dead and Mordred ruled in Camelot? When Mab had won? Even if Merlin were willing to abandon his vendetta against her, Mab wouldn't just let Merlin walk away. She was too vengeful for that. She would want her renegade wizard to bow down, to acknowledge her supremacy—and, try as he might, Frik could not imagine Master Merlin doing that.

Unfortunately, Frik couldn't imagine Merlin winning a battle against Mab either. Mab was an elemental force of nature, the Queen of the Old Ways. No mere human—

or half-fay wizard—could destroy her, not when she drew her power from human belief. Only when every last one of them had forgotten her would she lose her malign potency.

Frik put his head in his hands and thought longingly once more of Lord Idath and his soft dark all-comforting cloak. In the Summerland there was no cold, no hunger, and no pain. Frik was sure that he would not mind being dead very much. And surely Lord Idath would have to take him in. He was mortal now, after all. And all that was mortal were Lord Idath's subjects.

Frik gazed woefully around himself, self-pitying thoughts of Mab's invincibility and Lord Idath's kingdom swirling together in his mind. And suddenly he realized why he'd come here, why he'd never quite despaired in all the long days since Morgan's murder. There was something here that could help him destroy Mab.

Slowly Frik got to his feet, pacing around the interior of the hut, casting his mind back through the years. As if it were yesterday, he remembered the day Merlin had escaped from the Land Under Hill back into the mortal world and Mab had gone in search of him. She had returned in a terrible temper—alone—vowing vengeance against Merlin for betraying her, and Frik had not dared to ask her what had happened that day in the World of Men. But later, when her anger had cooled, Mab had boasted of the things she had done that day in the forest to hurt Merlin. She had boasted of her part in Ambrosia's death.

And of what she had done to Herne.

Once, like Ambrosia, Herne had been a cleric of the

Old Ways, serving Lord Idath in his aspect as Lord of the Wild Things. But as Vortigern's oppression had grown, Herne had set aside his priestly horned crown to become the champion of the people, feeding the hungry and protecting the weak from his home here in the greenwood. Herne had watched over young Merlin as he grew up here within the forest, and when Ambrosia had been killed, Herne had tried to save Merlin from Mab's vengeance, only to be destroyed for his efforts. But even though he had renounced his ancient power and priesthood, Herne had given Mab quite a fright, Frik knew, for Herne had still held the Horn of Idath, one of the thirteen sacred treasures of Britain, and even Mab could not stand against its effects.

So long as all thirteen of the treasures existed, the realm of Britain would endure no matter what evils beset it. Aeons ago most of the treasures had been lost to their ancient guardians. The Horn of Idath was one of those few treasures that remained visible in the mortal world. Only a Lord of Fairy, such as Herne had been—or a great wizard—could sound this horn, but once it was blown, it had the power to strike terror into those who heard it, to suspend time . . . or to call its maker, the Lord of Winter, to aid the wielder.

Herne was dead. But Merlin still remained.

A giddy wave of hope washed over Frik, forcing him to sit down for a moment. Mab had taken the Horn from Herne, but she had not dared to bring it back with her to the Land of Magic, for then Idath, its master, would have known where it was—and asked Mab some very awkward questions, Frik was sure.

And so Mab had hidden it here, somewhere in the forest. If Frik could only find it, and bring it to Merlin, the wizard would at last possess a weapon that even Queen Mab feared.

All Frik had to do was find it.

In the days that followed, Mab showed Mordred all the secrets of her underground dominion. Mordred feigned appreciation, and never let Mab suspect the fury that was slowly growing deep inside him.

She was going to spare Merlin. Her firstborn—the wizard whose malfeasance had caused Mab to create Mordred.

Mordred could not remember how long he'd known he was competing with Merlin for Mab's affection. She'd always called Merlin her enemy, but Mordred, even as a child, had known better. Mab wasn't finished with Merlin. She'd forgive him in an instant if he came back to her, and then where would Mordred be? He wasn't a wizard. He didn't have any of the Old Blood. While Merlin was alive, he was *second best*.

It was intolerable.

In a just world, matters would have righted themselves naturally. Mordred would have killed Merlin, and eliminated his rival for Auntie Mab's affections. She'd always promised him that he'd get to do that just as soon as he grew up.

But now she'd changed her mind. Now she was planning to hide Merlin somewhere else while Mordred got rid of dear Father and that trollop he'd married. Once he'd seen the full extent of her power, of course Merlin would want to return to Mab, and then Mab would love him best . . . and where would that leave Mordred?

Obviously, this could not be allowed to happen. And so Mordred would learn all Mab could teach him, take all the weapons she was willing to give him, and use the power he gained in ways she had never imagined. Arthur would die—and so would Merlin, no matter where Mab hid him.

It would all be for the best.

She'd see.

He searched in the high branches of trees, under thorn-bushes, beneath the surface of ice-crusted woodland pools, in an ever-widening spiral that had Ambrosia's cottage as its center. The search was tedious, and Frik was never afterward quite certain of how long it took him, only that the forest turned from autumn brown to winter grey while he searched. The Horn of Idath was here. He knew it. And he would find it, even if he had to sift through every scrap of the detritus of thirty winters.

If Frik had still been able to call upon even a scrap of magic, the search would have been quick and simple, but Frik was as helpless now as any human, and far less used to managing things without the power of magic. Frik was—had been—a creature of magic. Without it Frik was not a normal mortal, but a crippled gnome. He felt the loss of his powers keenly.

But even though Frik was now mortal and magicless, he still had the ageless patience of fairykind. And at last he found what he sought.

The Horn of Idath was wedged high in the branches

of an oak tree. The tree's wood had grown tight around it, and in any other season it would have been invisible. But in winter the gleam of gold and gems stood out brightly against the grey bark. He had not quite believed it was here, but he had also not dared to doubt.

Carefully Frik climbed the tree, and worked patiently with a small knife he had found in the forest cottage until he had freed the Horn from the wood. It had snowed last night, and it had begun to snow again as he worked, but Frik noticed neither the cold nor the fat wet flakes that mantled his shoulders and crusted his eyelashes. All he could see or think about was the Horn. Now at last it was in his possession. Its magic made his fingers tingle.

He climbed stiffly down from his precarious perch and stood at the base of the tree, holding the recovered Horn in his two hands. It was a huntsman's horn, with a long strap of gilded leather attached so it could be slung over the shoulder. Frik had seen Herne carry it that way so many times as he watched Merlin grow up here. Its mouthpiece was gold, and the white curve of the Horn was banded in gold, the bands studded with emeralds, sapphires, and opals.

Its fatal beauty tempted him to sound it, but Frik was neither a wizard nor a Lord of Fairy. The Horn would not work for him.

But it would work for Merlin.

He must go to Camelot. If Merlin was not there, surely someone would know where he was. Merlin was the king's wizard, after all.

Carefully Frik wrapped the Horn up in a bit of cloth and tucked it away safely in his backpack. He had a long journey ahead of him, but for the first time since Morgan's death, he had hope.

If only he could reach Merlin before Mordred did.

"I cannot teach you magic," Mab said regretfully to Mordred. "But I can *give* you magic."

The two of them—mistress and protégé—were seated in the Great Hall, the largest chamber in Mab's cthonian palace. Its silvery walls soared hundreds of feet into the air, toward a vaulted ceiling lost in shadows. High narrow windows of stained glass glittered darkly, like sheets of black ice, and the walls were hung with banners that had once been gay and flaunting, though they were all dark and tattered now, and festooned with cobwebs. The long table at which the two of them were seated was the only thing that did not show the effects of age and neglect. A single sheet of black glass a dozen yards long, it hung in midair without any visible means of support.

"I like presents," Mordred said. He sat at Mab's left hand, wearing the elaborate black velvet costume she'd given him, a vision in black and silver. He wore rings and brooches of onyx, jet, and black diamonds, and a black 'crown set with rubies.

"You have learned all that I have to teach you," Mab said reluctantly. "Even now, Arthur is crossing the Channel on his way back to Camelot. It is time for you to take your armor and your sword and go to meet him. The Armor of Night is made from the skin and scales of the last dragon. Wearing it will make you invulnerable to every weapon except one: Caliban. Caliban cannot be given—it must be taken. You will need the Armor of Night to claim the Black Sword."

"Caliban?" Mordred asked with interest.

His days in the Land of Magic had been filled with many new experiences. Armored wraiths had taught him to become a deadly fighter with any weapon. The ghosts of long-dead generals had taught him strategy and tactics. All so that he could take the throne of Britain for his own. But despite the wonders he'd been shown, Mordred had not been taught any magic. Now, it seemed, he was about to get some.

"Arthur has Excalibur, but all of the great magics create their own opposite. No weapon can stand against Excalibur, except one. Caliban, the shadow of Excalibur. Now it will be yours."

"I want it now, Auntie," Mordred said. "I'm quite a big boy, you know. You don't have to keep me away from sharp objects."

There is something you're not telling me, Mordred thought privately. For the first time, he missed Frik. The gnome was a coward and had always been his mother's groveling sycophant, but Frik could usually be tormented into revealing all the secrets he knew.

"I know," Mab said, reaching out to pat his hand. "But I don't want anything to happen to you."

Mordred smiled and raised his cup in a silent toast. *I don't believe you,* he told her silently. *But it* will *be true. Trust me on that.*

The following day—so far as day and night could be measured here in the Land of Magic—Mab took Mordred

to a chamber he had never seen before. There were racks
of weapons along the walls, and in the center an arming
bench. Mab gestured, and armor appeared on the arming
bench.

It was a dark pewter color except where the light fell
directly upon it, when it shone with a deep iridescence.
Flinging off his cloak and tunic and kicking off his boots,
Mordred eagerly donned the scaled trousers and tunic.
The boots and gauntlets were smooth, but of the same
heavy grey leather as that which backed the scales. He
transferred a few daggers from his old clothes to the new
and then, fully garbed, he turned expectantly to Mab. She
did not disappoint him.

"Here is your device—the sign of the eclipse," Mab
said, handing Mordred a surcoat. "As the moon eclipses
the sun, so the Old Ways will eclipse the New Religion—
and your reign that of King Arthur's."

The surcoat was of black velvet edged in silver lamé,
and on the breast, in blackened silver, was a dark sun, the
sign of the eclipse. Mab helped him slip the surcoat over
his head, and then belted it about Mordred's waist. At last
she held out his helmet.

"Wearing this, you are invincible."

The helm was a dull and forbidding grey, and concealed most of his face. Great steel bat-wings swept out
from each side of it, giving it the look of some demon's
skull.

Mordred liked it at once. He swirled his black cloak
around his shoulders and took the helm from Mab, tuck-
ing it under one arm. Almost ready.

But instead of handing him a sword as Mordred expected, Mab held out a key. It was impossible to tell what color it had originally been. Now it was a dull greenish black with age and neglect.

"What's this?" Mordred asked blankly.

"It is the key to your destiny," Mab told him. "I have given you three gifts—your strength, your power of persuasion, and your armor. You must take Caliban for yourself. Make me proud, Mordred!"

"I shall exceed your wildest expectations," Mordred assured her, smiling his twisted smile. Let her think he meant whatever she wished. Mordred had his own plans for the future, and they did not include the survival of any rivals.

From earliest childhood Mordred had known he was very special to his Auntie Mab. She lavished attention on him and brought him gifts, and never, ever, told him he was wrong.

Then he had found out that he was only second best in her eyes. Merlin came first. If not for Merlin, Mab would never have created Mordred, never sent Frik to charm his mother into falling in with Mab's schemes. All along, in Mab's every thought, Mordred came second.

It was intolerable.

Even when she spoke of what he would do in Camelot, Mab never spoke of the harm he was to do Merlin. It was only Arthur, Guinevere, Camelot, that he was to destroy.

Never Merlin. Never Mab's perfect special half-breed pet, the wizard to whom she had given far more of the Old Ways than she had ever given to Mordred.

But Mordred had a special surprise in store for his

Auntie Mab. He'd do all that she asked. He'd make Britain a howling wilderness, devoid of life.

But he'd kill Merlin, too.

Then she would love him best.

She'd have to.

A moment later he was alone in the room, staring down at the tarnished key. He looked around, but there didn't seem to be any lock here that would fit it. Shrugging, Mordred stepped out into the hallway. It was a different hallway than it had been a few minutes before, but Mordred wasn't surprised. He'd grown up with the Old Ways, and was used to the strange ways that magic worked.

He looked up and down the hall, searching for the lock that matched the key. He already knew that Mab would make this as easy for him as possible. She'd always indulged him.

But Mordred was beginning to feel that indulgence wasn't quite enough, somehow. There had to be more to life than this. He'd always had a bright future ahead of him, and somehow it had disappeared when he wasn't looking. He felt cheated.

"Perhaps I can help you."

Mordred whirled toward the sound of that unfamiliar voice, and found himself staring at a man he had never seen before. His hand groped for the dagger at his belt, but somehow he suspected that this stranger wouldn't be an easy victim.

The stranger was dressed in grey leather that was studded all across the shoulders and front with tiny silver skulls. He had flowing red hair and a full red beard, and his eyes glowed a fiery Otherworldly scarlet. Ivory antlers branched from his forehead, and the black cloak that flowed from his shoulders was darker than a starless night.

"Who the devil are you?" Mordred demanded rudely.

"I am Idath, the Lord of Death," the stranger answered austerely. He stepped aside, and behind him Mordred saw a door that had not been there a moment before.

"And?" Mordred clenched his fist over the key in his hand.

"You have one last chance to turn away from the path you follow now, Prince Mordred. By the Ancient Law I must warn you that he who takes up the Black Sword Caliban may not lay it down until its task is accomplished. Theseus bore this sword, and Herod. Consider carefully what you do here."

Mordred regarded him insolently. "King Herod has always been one of my boyhood heroes. Now do run along. I'm afraid I have a very busy afternoon planned."

The horned man drew himself up to his full height, though he did not seem affronted by Mordred's impertinent words. "Mock if you will—choose how you will. But know that for you as for all mortalkind there is no escape. We *will* meet again."

Mordred laughed, a little startled. "I suppose we will," he said. He'd helped enough creatures out of this life to know that Death came for all, but to meet him now was an unexpected bonus to visiting Mab's domain.

"I don't suppose you'd like to tell me something I *don't* know?"

Idath smiled, and for just an instant the Lord of

Death didn't look grim and old. "You know that Excalibur grants victory in battle to its wielder, and Caliban is its counterpart. But Caliban grants its wielder nothing but endings. When Caliban is drawn, it brings about the end of an age. All are swept away by its magic."

I'd like that, Mordred thought. All his life—his short unnatural life—he'd been restless and unsatisfied. He'd thought it was because he had a great task ahead of him, but the more he learned about his destiny, the less that thought comforted him. Mab had taught him to be clever and clear-sighted. He had grown to adulthood with supernatural speed—and he had no reason to think he would age any more slowly now. Where normal men could expect threescore and ten years of life, Mordred could hope for, at best, a dozen years. All the magic of Fairy could not grant immortality.

In a way, it was just as well. At some point Mordred would have destroyed everything that there was to destroy. Here in the Land of Magic he had discovered that he could not imagine anything beyond that moment. Perhaps this way he would die before everything was gone.

But the thought that someone, somewhere, might escape his attentions was a troubling one. At least with Caliban at his side Mordred could do his best to destroy everything before his time came.

Mordred smiled his sweetest smile at the Lord of Death. "We'll meet again," Mordred said.

He stepped forward and fitted his key into the lock. As he'd expected, the key fit perfectly. He turned it and pushed open the door.

He staggered back, stunned by the brightness and

heat. He looked around quickly to see if Idath were still there, but the Lord of Death had vanished.

Good. Mordred hated it when people saw him caught off guard.

Standing in the doorway was like standing in the open mouth of a furnace. From experience—and experiments—Mordred knew how unhealthy the inside of a furnace could be. Surely Mab didn't mean him to go in there?

Maybe he'd gotten the wrong door.

But no. Auntie Mab had said that the key would open the door to the Black Sword . . . and that the armor would protect him so that he could reach it.

Blinking furiously against the flames, Mordred slid the bat-winged helm over his head. The heat and the brightness receded, and he could see.

The lake of fire stretched before him, and now in the distance he could see a glittering tower wreathed in clouds of steam, or fog. Mordred took a cautious step forward. There did not seem to be any other landmark in the inferno ahead, so he would make the crystal tower his destination. The fire was no real barrier. The Armor of Night would protect him, Mordred realized, and he was utterly without fear. Moving cautiously, he stepped out into the flames.

He quickly realized that he could not walk across their surface, but the lake was only a few feet deep. Cinders crunched beneath his boots as he stepped forward. He could wade across.

The constant roar of the flames was annoying, but the greatest hindrance Mordred actually faced was the constant hot wind that blew toward him with enough force to stagger him. But even there, his dragon-scale armor bore the brunt of the gale, and his inhuman strength took care of the rest.

I'm sure this would test the ingenuity and valor of one of Arthur's muscle-bound paladins, but I'm hardly in that class. No, upon careful consideration I'd have to say I'm something else entirely. . . .

In fact, there was a distinct sense of anticlimax as Mordred reached the pillar. It was not glass, as he'd first thought, but an enchanted ice that the flames could not melt, and the cold that it radiated was nearly as painful as the heat of the flames had been. Embedded in its depths he could see the Black Sword, but there did not seem to be any opening in the ice through which he could get to it.

Mordred rested the palms of his gauntlets against the surface of the ice, ignoring the bite of the cold. At the touch of his blisteringly hot dragonskin glove, water welled up beneath his fingers, trickling down the shaft of the pillar, but melting his way through—even if it was possible—would take too long. Patience was not on the short list of Mordred's virtues.

Drawing back his fist, Mordred struck the pillar. The ice cracked beneath the impact of his supernatural strength but did not shatter, and in his impatience he struck it again and again. The transparency of the ice went dull and white as its interior fractured under the impact of the blows. Mordred dug his fingers into its surface, flinging handfuls of the ice into the flames.

"Interesting," he said aloud.

Everywhere the ice struck, the flames died out, exposing the bed of coals beneath. They were white with ash, glowing red in their depths.

"But not really helpful," he decided.

Mordred turned back to the pillar, and was relieved to see that the ice had not magically repaired itself. He scooped out as much of the cracked ice as he could, but digging his way in to the sword would take almost as long as trying to melt his way in.

"Mother always said I was too impatient," he said.

There was a deep hole near the base of the ice pillar. Mordred leaned against the column, shoving against it as hard as he could.

At first nothing happened, but then there was a low groaning, and a series of sharp cracks like breaking bones. He felt a sort of grating vibration beneath his hands, and the top half of the pillar began to shift away from him. Slowly, with a sound almost like tearing, it tilted, then toppled, just as if it were a tree whose root had been chopped through. A hundred feet of ice struck the fire lake, throwing up a huge wave of fire that rippled outward in all directions, exposing the glowing coals of the lake bed. Instead of splashing back to fill the gap, the fire continued to recede, and the circle of embers grew. Mordred watched, fascinated, as the great column of ice melted away, dousing the fire lake as it dwindled. Soon the fire was only a thin line of red on the distant horizon, and Mordred was standing on a bed of coals, seeing by their dim red light.

He glanced back at the ice. Caliban was thrusting up out of the melting stump. Mordred reached out and drew it free.

In every way Caliban was Excalibur's opposite. Its blade was dull and pitted, and the quillons and pommel were shabby and unadorned. The only decoration anywhere upon it was the image of a comet cut crudely into the haft itself.

Mordred frowned, gazing at it. A black sword for an ill-made knight, but Mordred was no knight, and didn't want to be one. He rejected all of that chivalric futility. If he carried a weapon onto a battlefield, it would be something more efficient and less romantic than a sword.

As if it knew and could understand his thoughts, Caliban rippled in his grasp. Surprised, Mordred nearly dropped it as the shape of the metal flowed and changed, but he held fast, and when it had stilled again, he found himself holding an ax.

Like the sword it had been, the ax was dull black from its narrow curved blade to its long utilitarian haft. Except for the image of the comet cut into the shaft of the ax just below the head, the new weapon had nothing in common with the sword it had been a moment before—nothing except for the force of magic and the aura of deadly purpose that infused it.

Mordred tossed the ax up into the air and caught it again, laughing. Now he was ready to go . . . home.

Wouldn't his father and his dear stepmama be surprised to see him?

The heliograph had sent word that Arthur and his knights were in Calais. It was a matter of a few days—perhaps less—before the King returned to Camelot after a seven-year absence.

And what would greet him there? A Queen who did not love him—whose behavior was a scandal in open court—the threat of a son begotten in sorcery.

And worse to come.

Merlin watched the stars, as his first teacher Blaise had taught him, searching for messages in the endless dance of stars and planets. But lately there had been a new wonder in the sky: a celestial wanderer like none he had ever seen before, moving swiftly through the houses of the Zodiac, trailing glory behind it.

The ancient Greeks had written of these "hairy stars," or *comets,* and Merlin knew there was nothing of sorcery about its appearance. But the manifestations of the natural world often served as warnings, and Merlin wondered if this comet might be one such. Even if it was not, it would soon be visible to even a casual observer, and the superstitious might read all manner of dire portents into it, to the returning king's misfortune.

Merlin knew he must do all that he could to protect Arthur. He had considered what he should do ever since word had come that the King was returning, and now there was no more time to ponder. Reluctantly, Merlin had reached a conclusion. For the safety of Camelot, he knew what he must do.

Telling no one where he was going—or even that he was leaving—Merlin summoned Sir Rupert and rode toward Sarum.

Am I so unwilling to give up my hatred? Merlin wondered as he rode toward the ring of stones. They were visible in the distance, silhouetted against the white sky of a spring evening: great stark menhirs that had once marked a temple of the Old Ways.

He pondered the question carefully. Since his sixteenth year he had hated Queen Mab. She had killed his birth-mother Elissa and his foster-mother Ambrosia. She had maimed Nimue. But time could soften the edge of both love and hate. Merlin was willing to set aside his anger in the name of a greater good. Let Arthur return home to a kingdom that was as much at peace as Merlin could make it.

Are you sure this is a good idea, Merlin? Sir Rupert asked as he walked up the hill toward the stones.

"At my age, I'm sure of nothing, old friend," Merlin told the enchanted steed, "but I do know there's no harm in trying."

If you say so, Sir Rupert answered dubiously. He shook his head vehemently, so that the buckles on his harness jingled. He stopped, switching his tail back and forth. *I have my doubts.*

Merlin laughed at the animal's skeptical tone as he dismounted. Slapping Sir Rupert companionably upon the shoulder, he walked the last of the way to the stones. A twitch of his fingers summoned his wizard's staff, and he was glad of its support as he walked into the fairy ring. He had no guarantee that this would work.

He stopped in the center of the stones. It was evening, and the mist was rising on the Downs, giving his purely mundane surroundings a magical insubstantiality.

"Mab!" Merlin shouted. "Queen Mab!"

"I am here, Merlin."

The Queen of the Old Ways walked out of the nearest slab of stone as if it had been an open doorway.

Merlin had not seen her since the night Arthur drew Excalibur from the stone, but she had not changed. She was still the exquisite creature who had dazzled his boyhood dreams and captivated kings.

"It has been a long time since you called upon me, Merlin."

Her dark-rimmed pale eyes watched him expressionlessly as she waited, and suddenly Merlin found it hard to begin.

"I've come to make peace," Merlin finally blurted.

Mab watched him, and Merlin had the feeling that if there were still any honest laughter in her soul, Mab would have laughed at him then.

"You vowed to destroy me," she pointed out.

"Things change," Merlin said. "They've changed for you. Can't you see it? All my life you have fought to destroy the New Religion and return Britain to the worship of the Old Ways. But don't you see? The time of the Old Ways is past. All things change. Let them change, Mab."

"And be forgotten!" Mab hissed. "I won't surrender! I'm too close to winning!"

"If Mordred kills Arthur, nothing will change, Mab. The people will fight, but none of them will fight for the Old Ways. It is too late for that."

He took a step toward her, studying her face. Queen Mab had given him life. Her blood ran in his veins. Her actions had shaped his life.

"Please, Mab." He stretched out a hand to her.

"These were once your people. Don't hurt them now. Let Mordred come to Camelot as a friend, not an enemy—"

With a gesture almost too quick to see, Mab struck out at Merlin and sent him sprawling.

"Never!" she cried. "Mordred will not betray me! He is loyal! He will destroy Arthur and Camelot, and the people will return to me!"

"Never!" Merlin shouted from the ground. "Mab— think!" he pleaded, struggling upright. "They are human beings, with human hearts. They must be ruled through love, not fear. Those who fear you will leave you—as I did."

Mab had raised her hand to lash out at him once more. She stopped, and Merlin saw her struggle to understand what he had said . . . and fail. She was what she was: the Queen of the Old Ways, of Air and Darkness, as unchanging as the seas and the stars.

"You were right to fear me," Mab hissed at last. "I could destroy you here, dear Merlin—but I won't. I have other plans for you and for your precious Arthur. You left me—but Mordred did not. Soon he will reach Camelot. And when the people see his power, they will return to me. I will not be forgotten!"

"No, Mab!"

He had not tested his powers against her for years, but Merlin knew that his only hope of keeping Mordred from Camelot lay in stopping her now. He flung out his hands, drawing magic out of the living earth.

The winds began to rise, and the sky took on a glowing greenish hue. An oak tree sprouted beneath Mab's feet, growing with supernatural speed, surrounding her and trapping her within its heart. It continued to grow, putting out branches and leaves, towering toward heaven as the storm whipped around it.

There was a flare of light and the sun and moon wheeled through the sky, rising and setting with unnatural speed. Mab burst out of the trunk in a lethal shower of splinters. The great tree split in half and fell away. In moments it had withered and decayed away to nothing.

"You cannot defeat me!" Mab hissed. "Magic cannot destroy me—*it just makes me stronger!*"

She gestured, and Merlin flew backward. He struck one of the standing stones with a cry of pain, and slumped to the ground.

"Poor Merlin!" Mab said with false sweetness. The winds that whipped her robes and her hair into a Medusa-like tangle died down. "Always too little and too late!"

She vanished, but her words echoed through the air around him: *too late—too late—too late* . . .

But too late for what?

At last there was stillness. Merlin groaned, painfully pulling himself to his feet. He could see a thin line of pink along the eastern hills: sunrise, not sunset. Though it had seemed that only minutes had passed, his confrontation with Queen Mab had taken the entire night.

He'd tried. But Mab had not listened—*could* not listen. All her dreams were of the past, projected into a future that could never be. Though she drowned Britain in blood and fire once more, she could never regain the love she had once received from her followers. She had forfeited it through fear and anger, and anger and fear were all she had left.

No, Merlin thought, he no longer hated Queen Mab. But he pitied her.

And he feared for Britain.

On a horse the color of cinders, Prince Mordred rode toward Camelot to claim his birthright. He was conceived in treachery and nurtured in ambition, and his only skills were cruelty and destruction.

Arthur was not yet here, but Arthur's Queen was. Between them, they could arrange a splendid homecoming for his dear father. . . .

CHAPTER FIVE

THE BATTLE OF MIRRORS

 uinevere was on her knees before the Virgin, clutching a pearl rosary in her hands as she told her beads. She seemed to spend more and more time these days storming Heaven on her knees, as if the sheer number of her petitions could compel Heaven to answer.

But God and His Holy Mother remained silent upon the subject of what Guinevere was to say to Arthur. Her husband would be here tomorrow, and she did not know what she would say to him when he arrived.

She did not love him. She knew now that she never had. She had wanted to please—please her older brother Gawain, please their father, please the glamorous boy-king who had been so dazzled by the very sight of her. It was all very flattering, but Guinevere realized now that in all of that consideration she had given no thought to what she herself wanted—if she had even known.

But years passed and times changed. She knew now. She wanted Lancelot, and she did not care what she had to do to get him. Overthrow Camelot—always Arthur's dream, never hers—renounce the New Religion and return to the Old Ways; it didn't matter. She had always wanted to be loved and needed, to know there was a place where she belonged, and she had found that place in Lancelot's arms. And now that she had found her happiness, she would not give it up without a fight. She would do whatever it took to get Lancelot back.

A thousand times since Lancelot had left Camelot she had thought of swallowing her pride and going to Merlin to beg the wizard to help her find where her lover had gone. But Guinevere had been born a princess of the Iceni, of blood as royal as Arthur's, and she knew that she had a duty to keep Britain safe until Arthur returned.

But when he did, her duty would be over.

Despite her resolve, she dreaded telling him—about Lancelot, about her feelings—though that would not stop her from doing it. She knew that what she had done was a sin in the eyes of the New Religion.

But Arthur gave me no choice! From the beginning he shut me out—how could I have done other than what I did? Oh, Holy Virgin, you who know the griefs of women, open Arthur's heart and make him understand that I—

There was a sound from behind her.

Still on her knees, Guinevere turned, the rosary swinging from her fingers. There was a man standing in the doorway of the chapel, watching her at her prayers.

"Hello, Mother," he said.

He was tall and slender, and his skin was as pale as

lilies. His cherry-black hair hung loose about his shoulders, and he was dressed all in severe and funereal black, from his silver-buttoned tunic to the plaid that was draped across his body and brooched at his left shoulder with an ornate clasp.

"Who are you?" Guinevere asked warily, getting to her feet and looping the rosary through her belt. "I gave orders I was not to be disturbed."

"Oh, forgive me," the young man said, sweeping her a low mocking bow. "We haven't been properly introduced, I know. My name is Mordred. And you're the Queen. But you know that already."

"I don't know you," Guinevere said. "And why do you call me Mother?"

Mordred feigned a stricken expression—badly, as if he wanted his audience to know he was only pretending. "Oh, well, you'll have to admit it's a natural slip of the tongue. My father's wife, my stepmama . . . you don't mind if I call you Mother, do you? I think family ties are *so* important in these uncertain times."

"You're Arthur's son?" Guinevere asked numbly. How could he be? He looked nearly as old as Arthur.

And where were her guards? If this intruder was mad—or worse, somehow telling the truth—she wanted aid to be within easy reach.

"He hasn't told you?" Mordred asked with false concern, walking into the room.

He moved with catlike elegance, the picture of knightly grace, save for the fact that he wore upon his belt not a sword but a war-ax. No true knight would carry such a weapon.

"Well, I'm not really surprised, I suppose. My mother, his sister—"

Mordred broke off again in theatrical surprise, gazing at Guinevere from wide grey eyes.

"Oh, I suppose he didn't tell you *that,* either. No, Arthur isn't quite the plaster saint he's made himself out to be. Isn't it wonderful?"

"What do you want?" Guinevere demanded in a low voice. Mordred stopped directly in front of her, smiling a guileless smile that Guinevere found unaccountably chilling.

"I want what everyone wants. My rights. I'm Arthur's heir—and at the rate he's going, I'll have precious little competition in that line. In fact, I'd go so far as to say I'm your only hope for a Crown Prince for this dreary little backwater. So why don't we just . . ."

He put a conspiratorial hand on her arm. Furious, Guinevere shook him off and stepped back.

"Monster! I'll see you burn first," Guinevere flared. "Guards!" she shouted.

"I wouldn't say that if I were you," Mordred said. "These things have a terrible way of recoiling against the speaker, Your Highness."

The guards finally appeared, four men wearing the white-and-gold livery of Camelot. They stared from the Queen to the well-dressed young man in bafflement, unable to understand why they had been called.

"Put him in the dungeon," Guinevere said, pointing at Mordred.

"Oh, I don't think they'll do anything like that," Mordred said lightly. "After all, I'm an honored guest here at Camelot. Prince Mordred, son of Marie of the Border Celts and Good King Arthur. And you were about to tell them to escort me to your finest accommodation and treat me with all honor. Weren't you, Your Highness?"

He smiled at her with heartless brilliance. The Old Magic vibrated on the air. All at once Guinevere felt confused, feverish. She looked at Mordred, then at the guards, and smiled uncertainly. Was that what she'd been about to say? She couldn't remember. She looked back at Mordred, who smiled encouragingly at her.

"Yes, that's right," Guinevere said slowly. "Escort him to our finest accommodations. Treat him with all honor."

She watched, numbly, as the guards led Prince Mordred from the chapel, feeling so ill and dizzy that she knelt on the cold stone floor again, leaning forward to press her face against the cold slate flags.

After several minutes, her thoughts cleared, and she remembered the truth. Mordred had bewitched her!

She got to her feet, her heart hammering with alarm. Where had he gone, and what was he doing?

And why had he come? Guinevere ran from the chapel, fearful of what she might find, but everything seemed normal at first. The castle's inhabitants were going about their daily business, the servants and the young pages walking briskly toward their destinations in a purposeful fashion. Her guards were back at their posts, just as they ought to be.

There was no sign of Mordred.

Perhaps it is I who have gone mad. Perhaps there was no Mordred. Perhaps he was only a fantasy her mind had produced, a sin of Arthur's to equal and even surpass her own. Incest was a far darker sin than adultery, and if there had truly been a child . . .

But if Mordred is real, why is he sneaking around Camelot like this? And where is he?

Then she heard a burst of laughter from the door to the chamber that held the Round Table. No one had been in there except to clean it since Arthur had taken most of the Knights of the Round Table away with him on his quest.

She peered through the half-open doors. Though it had been deserted the past several years, the room was full now. Torches lined the walls, and servants moved to and fro with tankards of ale. Though the table had no head or foot, each knight's name marked his place, and Mordred sat now in Arthur's seat, the Siege Perilous, surrounded by a group of the younger knights.

He was speaking earnestly to them, too low for Guinevere to hear him, using the same hellish power of suggestion that had beguiled her in the chapel. When Mordred spoke, Guinevere knew, his hearers would believe anything he told them, no matter how outlandish . . . including that a man only a few years younger than the King himself could be Arthur's trueborn son.

Madness that it was, Guinevere no longer doubted that it was the truth. All she knew of Morgan le Fay was that she was the daughter of the Duke of Cornwall and the Duchess who had been Arthur's ill-starred mother, but her name suggested that she was in league with dark forces. Morgan's son was undoubtedly the product of the same Pagan magic Morgan worshiped, here to destroy the peace and prosperity Britain had found under Arthur's reign.

Suddenly Mordred broke off what he was saying and got to his feet.

"Is someone there?" he called, staring toward the doorway.

Guinevere shuddered at the sound of his voice, and shrank back. When he resumed speaking, she hurried away before he caught her there listening to him. She did not know what it was that he meant to do here in Camelot, but she knew he must be stopped. Somehow.

Merlin had gone off on one of his mysterious errands, so even if she could bring herself to call upon him, he was not here. But Sir Hector and the rest of the royal council were. She must summon them at once and tell them all that she knew and suspected about Mordred. Perhaps they could think of some way to imprison him until Arthur returned, though how one could imprison a man who could convince anyone of anything Guinevere did not know. There must be some way to stop him.

Frightened and confused, Guinevere prayed for a miracle.

They had landed at Dover the day before, but Arthur had not sent word ahead to Camelot of his arrival. If the people knew they were coming, there would be holidays and celebrations, and in his heart, Arthur did not feel he deserved them. He had failed on his quest, after all. The Grail was still lost.

But Britain was just as he had remembered it, lush and verdant, heartbreakingly lovely, and he knew, seeing it, that he had made the right choice in coming home. He could not understand, seeing it with the fresh eyes of long exile, how he had ever been able to bring himself to leave it, and vowed he would never leave it again.

Only now that they were home could he bring himself to admit how battered and weary his surviving companions were. Seven long years of adventures had taken their toll. Even the horses they rode were thin and jaded, their coats dull and their gaits shambling. The once-bright banners that they had carried through the gates of Camelot with such high hopes were faded and tattered, as were the ideals of the men who bore them. The bright dreams Arthur had cherished as a young man were gone, lost somewhere in all the long years of wandering.

But now, at last, he was home.

"Camelot . . ." he whispered, gazing down at the city on the shore of the lake. It was evening, and the setting sun touched the walls and the rooftops with gold. "It's built. Lancelot kept his word."

A stubborn spark of pride swelled within his heart. No matter what else he had failed at, Camelot was real. His golden city of peace and charity had been built. Tears of thanksgiving rose in Arthur's eyes.

"We have to ride in with banners held high, Sire," Gawain said, beside him. Loyal Gawain! The first to follow him, always there, faithful and uncomplaining.

"You're right, Gawain," Arthur said. "Lift up your banners and your hearts, men!" he shouted. "We're home!"

Joy and thanksgiving kindled a last spark of energy among the weary company, and the knights rallied, sitting straighter in their saddles and raising their pennons to jaunty angles. Even the horses caught some of their masters' eagerness, and pranced like young colts as the small band rode forward, down through the gates of Camelot.

Guinevere had summoned the Royal Council to the throne room to tell them about Mordred, but at once things had begun to go wrong. Merlin would have understood better than any of them, but he was nowhere to be found, and before she could explain to the others about Mordred, a party of the younger knights forced their way in to the Great Hall, demanding an audience with the Queen. Members of the Queen's Bodyguard followed them.

"What is it that you want?" Guinevere demanded coldly. She recognized only a few of them—Sir Hoel, Lord Caradoc, Lord Melegraunce—but those she recognized had been troublemakers even before Arthur left, and in his absence had constantly challenged her authority. She thought they were some of the men who had been gathered with Mordred around the Round Table.

"We want you to step down, Your Highness. You're unfit to rule," Sir Hoel said.

Guinevere stared at him coldly and did not reply.

"Gentlemen," Sir Hector said, "Let's be reasonable."

"When did *she* ever listen to reason?" Lord Melegraunce demanded, gesturing at Guinevere as she sat upon the canopied throne. "We're tired of a frivolous Queen and an absentee King. You say Arthur is coming back, but when? Where is he? We want someone fit to rule us seated on the throne of Britain—"

"In that case, I'll crown my donkey," Guinevere said tartly, "because you're a jackass, Lord Melegraunce, and you always have been!"

"Better a jackass than a trollop," someone called from the back of the angry crowd.

There was a sound of clashing steel, as several of the knights of the Queen's Bodyguard drew their swords.

"Gentlemen, gentlemen," Sir Hector said desperately. "Please! We must not be so hasty. The King will return to Camelot within the week. Surely we can reason together about this matter. Lord Melegraunce, Sir Hoel, your concerns do you credit. Put up your swords. I'm sure we can settle these matters to our mutual satisfaction."

More knights and nobles had pushed into the throne room while Sir Hector had been speaking, until the room was dangerously crowded with armed men jostling one another.

"Down with the Queen!" someone cried.

"Prince Mordred and Britain!" someone else shouted.

"Where is everyone?" Arthur asked wonderingly.

The courtyard they had ridden into was deserted. Though it was nearly the dinner hour, when the life of the castle drew inward for the night, there were no servants going about their business, no horses waiting for stabling. The courtyard—the entire town that they'd ridden through, in fact—was as silent and still as if it had been enchanted.

"Something's wrong," Gawain said, worry in his voice.

Arthur flung back his faded black cape and swung down from his horse. He gazed around the deserted stableyard, his eyes wary, then gestured curtly for his men to follow him. Something was wrong in Camelot, and he meant to discover what it was. Though the castle had not been finished when he left, he had designed it. He knew his way.

But when he reached it, the great doors stood unguarded, and the corridors of Camelot were deserted as well. There were no servants to be seen, no guards to challenge the men they could only perceive as intruders. All was as silent as if the castle's inhabitants had been put to sleep.

"I didn't expect this kind of homecoming," Arthur muttered to Gawain as he reached the doors of the throne room. He flung them open and stopped in shock. Though there had been no one elsewhere, the throne room was jammed with people, and all of them seemed to be arguing at once.

"What's wrong here?" Arthur shouted.

Silence spread in the wake of his outcry, and the crowd parted to let him and his companions pass, though few of them recognized the tall blond bearded man as their King.

But Guinevere recognized him. His Queen was more lovely than ever before. As he came toward her, she stepped down from the throne and watched him advance, expressions of fear and longing mingled on her face.

"Guinevere . . ." Arthur whispered.

He clasped her shoulders, but instead of greeting him with joy, the Queen hung her head in shame. He put a hand beneath her chin and raised it to look into her eyes. They were filled with anger and grief.

All around him, the room was filled with the silence of guilty, frightened men. Arthur looked up, gazing at each member of the Royal Council in turn. Sir Bors would not even meet his eyes. He turned to Sir Hector and Lord Lot.

"Where's Merlin?" Arthur demanded. "Where's Lancelot?"

They shuffled uneasily, unwilling to speak, and Arthur's trepidation grew. What terrible thing had occurred in his absence? He knew that a letter could have missed him as he traveled, but surely . . . ?

"I'll tell you," a new voice said.

Arthur turned toward the doorway. A young man dressed all in black stood leaning negligently against the doorframe. Arthur had never seen him before.

"Who the devil are you?" the King asked. The day had been a long one and his temper was close to fraying.

"Elegantly put," the young man said, straightening up. His voice held a faint mocking smile that filled Arthur with alarm. " 'Who the devil?' " he repeated musingly. "Yes, indeed."

Something in Arthur's words seemed to amuse him a great deal; he smiled as he swaggered toward the King. " 'Who the devil?' " he repeated once more. "Well, don't you recognize me?" he asked as he advanced.

"No," Arthur said bluntly. "Should I?"

"I'm hurt," the young stranger said. "Here . . . in my

heart." He touched his breast, and his smile grew more cynical. "Not usually my most vulnerable spot," he added confidingly.

An expression of malicious triumph seemed to kindle like flame in his pale grey eyes as he stopped before Arthur. He reached out and clasped Arthur's shoulders overfamiliarly.

"I recognize *you,* Father. I'm your long-lost son, Mordred!" he cried in mock delight.

Whispers of consternation and disbelief filled the room like the sound of a rising wind. "How is that possible?" someone gasped. Arthur stared into Mordred's eyes and knew.

"There will be a child. Mab will see to that. He'll be the future, and he'll destroy us." The terrible words Merlin had spoken on that long-ago day echoed in Arthur's ears now. The fruit of that single careless heedless act stood before him, as dangerous as Merlin had prophesied.

"He'll be the future, and he'll destroy us."

Merlin had told him that Mordred would be his enemy, but Arthur was a straightforward and honest man, unused to subtlety. An enemy was someone who met you on a battlefield with an army, not someone who came to your home while you were away.

"Morgan le Fay is your mother?" Arthur asked, hoping against hope that he was wrong. Deep in his heart, Arthur still hoped that he and Mordred could be friends.

"Not *is,* Father, *was.*" Mordred strolled past him, past the Queen, toward the throne, talking all the while.

"She passed over into a better world. She sleeps alone at last. A great loss. One day she was laughing, smiling—the next, gone like a summer breeze. In the midst of life, etcetera, etcetera, and so on and so forth." His tone made a mockery of the conventional obsequies, as did the briskness with which he changed the subject.

"It's why I'm here," he said, turning back to face Arthur and gesturing to include not only the throne room, but the entire castle. Morgan le Fay might have been his mother, but it was clear that Mordred had not loved her. The force of his smiling hatred was a palpable presence here in the throne room.

"I don't understand," Arthur said.

Mordred regarded Arthur with a false expression of surprise. "Why, to protect your interests . . . *Father*. You see, your interests are my interests. Whilst you were away on this great spiritual quest to cleanse your soul . . . how should I put it? You were being betrayed."

Another ripple of dismay coursed through the room.

"Mordred! That's enough!" Merlin snapped from the doorway.

As the people in the room turned to look, Merlin hurried toward the two men standing before the throne. He had ridden back to Camelot from Sarum as fast as he could, and at that, he had nearly been too late. Mordred was already here, and from the look of things, so was trouble.

"It isn't!" Mordred protested. "Come, Merlin, let's speak truth at last! Father—"

"This isn't the time," Merlin interrupted sharply, but Mordred would not be silenced.

"It is—it is! Father, Lancelot betrayed you with the Queen."

"What?" Arthur gasped, stunned. But Mordred wasn't through.

"Or should it be, 'The Queen betrayed you with Lancelot'?" Mordred wondered archly, mocking them all. "No matter. There's no point in being pedantic. You were betrayed."

Behind him, Arthur heard Gawain—Guinevere's brother—groan in anguish. Both factions that filled the room were arguing and jostling each other now, as revelation piled upon revelation rocked the foundations of their world.

"Guinevere?" Arthur whispered, turning to look at her.

"This isn't the place to discuss this matter," Merlin said. With a decisive gesture he swept Arthur and Guinevere out of the center of the crowd and off behind the safety of a pillar.

"Oh, I think it's the perfect place," Mordred called from behind them.

"Is it true?" Arthur demanded, glaring down at his Queen. His beard made him look older, as did the lines of exhaustion that marked his face.

"Arthur," Merlin said quickly, trying to stop the terrible disclosures. "You've only just returned. Arthur, we must talk—"

"Guinevere. Is it true?" Arthur asked remorselessly.

"Yes. It's true," Guinevere answered defiantly, glaring up into his eyes.

Arthur's face contorted in sudden fury. In that moment, Merlin feared he might have struck her, only Mordred pushed himself forward into their midst once more.

The engaging redheaded toddler had grown into a dark and dangerous young man, Merlin saw. He was as heartless as any of the fairy race, yet more vicious than Queen Mab at her worst—as if Mordred, monster that he was, dimly suspected the wrong that had been done to him by what Mab and Morgan had made of him. But this was not the time or place for pity. Mab's creature must be stopped.

"Mordred, you've no right to be here," Merlin said.

"I've every right here," Mordred said. "We all have. This isn't a private matter. It concerns all of us."

He gestured toward the men with him, who nodded and mumbled in agreement. Merlin realized that somehow, though he could not have been here in Camelot for very long, Mordred had amassed a dangerous majority of the knights to his cause.

"Didn't you think of me at all?" Arthur demanded of Guinevere, oblivious to the events around him. The haven he had dreamed of for all those long years of absence was gone, swept away as though it had never been. That was what hurt the worst.

"You left me alone for years—didn't you think of *me?*" the Queen shot back. "What about *my* honor, finding out that my husband had a child by a woman called 'Morgan le Fay'?"

"Good one," Mordred murmured appreciatively in the background. "Come, Father," he said bracingly, trying to elbow his way past Merlin, "this is becoming distressingly personal. You're forgetting it's a matter of state."

"A matter of state?" Merlin echoed, baffled. Mordred

was dangerously clever, and Merlin could not be certain of what he was driving at.

"Well, we *are* talking treason here, aren't we, my lords?" Mordred said with feigned innocence.

The men behind him—even Sir Hector and Sir Bors—nodded agreement, and there were some shouts of "Treason!" from the rowdier knights. Only then did Merlin see what Mordred's plan was.

Under the old law codes bequeathed them from the Romans, the man was the unquestioned master of his household—he *was* his household—just as the King was Britain itself. Adultery was betrayal of the marriage vows. When a woman betrayed her husband, she betrayed her family.

But when a Queen betrayed her husband, she betrayed her country.

Treason.

Mordred meant for Arthur to execute his Queen. And no matter how deserved the punishment, such an act would divide the country terribly. For the last seven years, Guinevere had been the Crown, the only ruler the people knew. For the King to return and abruptly execute her would give rise to all manner of destructive speculation.

"We must consider this calmly," Merlin pleaded, desperation filling his voice. The Queen stared at Arthur, her eyes filled with contempt, but Arthur stared at Mordred as though Mordred were something the like of which he had never seen.

"Yes," Arthur said finally. "We must. Guards! Take the Queen to her bedchamber and keep her there. At least this way I can be sure you'll be there alone," he said to her in a low voice.

Guinevere stared at him with scorn, saying nothing. When the guards came to her, she led them out as though they were a guard of honor, not of shame.

"Oh, Jenny—why?" Gawain said, as she passed him.

"You of all men have no right to ask me that," Guinevere said to her brother, stopping before him. "You followed your heart to go with Arthur when I begged you to stay with me. Well, I followed mine as well." She turned and walked out.

"Well," Mordred said brightly in the silence that followed. "What shall we do with the rest of the afternoon? A little tennis?"

"We must decide what to do about this," Arthur said. "Merlin—Knights of the Round Table—come with me."

When Arthur had left on his quest, this room had barely been finished. Like the table it contained, the chamber was round. Its walls were a deep celestial blue, and upon them were painted the images of the great kings who had been Arthur's ancestors, stretching back to that noble warrior, Brutus, who had fought at the siege of Troy. The walls also held images of the saints who concerned themselves most with Britain—Columba, Patric, George— and the timbers of the roof were carved with angels. All the figures, painted and carved, seemed to gaze down on the round table below.

Lord Lot had given this table to Arthur as a wedding gift. From the white rose of chivalry painted in the center, spokes of green and white radiated outward across its thirty-foot diameter, symbolizing the beauty and the holiness of Britain, until the whole surface of the table looked like a starburst. Around its rim were painted the names of the noblest members of the order of knighthood it symbolized. Bors—Bedivere—Gawain—Perceval—their names were there along with those of so many others. The table was without a head or a foot, a perfect circle that symbolized the perfect unity of Arthur's kingdom, but today the men gathered about it were divided as never before.

"It *is* treason," Sir Hoel—Mordred's partisan—said stubbornly. "When Guinevere betrayed you, she betrayed the Crown and the Country."

There was a murmur of approval when Sir Hoel finished speaking, but Arthur stood firm. The years had left their mark upon him, Merlin saw, darkening the gold of youth to the bronze of maturity. In his dark tunic and cloak, covered with the dust of the road, Arthur looked nothing like the splendid youth who had set off upon his doomed quest so long ago—but in spite of his failure to achieve the Grail, he looked more kingly now than ever before.

"I don't see it as treason," Arthur said. "She betrayed me and only me." Though worn and tired, he spoke patiently.

"It's the law of the land," Mordred called. He was standing in the doorway, underscoring the fact that there was no place for him within the room.

"That's enough!" Arthur snapped.

"No, Sire. Mordred is right," Sir Boris said slowly. He was a knight of the old school, scarred by the events of Uther's reign, and Guinevere's adultery had been something he could not forgive. "You're the King. And that makes her adultery treason."

"But then we must condemn her to death!" Gawain said, outraged.

"Do you really think we should do that?" Merlin asked conciliatingly. He stood in the corner of the room, not a member of the knightly company, but there as Arthur's adviser. If only they would stop and think about the enormity of what they were doing, surely they would choose mercy, just as Arthur wished to.

He desperately wished he'd had a chance to speak with Guinevere before Arthur—and Mordred—had arrived. Mordred must have gotten here first, and Merlin would have given a great deal to know more about the enemy facing them now.

That Mordred was the pawn of Mab, Merlin already knew, but this was the first chance he'd really had to take Mordred's measure. He did not sense that Mab had taught her protégé any of the Old Ways, since for all his eldritch upbringing, Mordred was the child of two mortal parents, and thus his ability to learn magic was limited. But if Mab had not taught Mordred sorcery, it was clear that she had bestowed upon him many of the old fairy gifts. Mordred was beautiful and charismatic, and men would believe in his words and follow him without thinking of what they did. Mordred was using that unnatural ability now, to make them listen to him, to keep them from questioning how it was that Arthur could have a full-grown son when he was not yet thirty.

But what could Mordred hope to gain from forcing

Arthur to execute the Queen? The Iceni, Guinevere's people, were still half-Pagan. And because of that, when Arthur executed their Princess for something many of them did not consider a crime, they would rise up against him. There would be war. That was what Mordred—what Mab—wanted. A war. A war that Mab thought she could win. And though Merlin knew that she must inevitably lose, the loss would come at an enormous cost in human lives.

Lord Lot was speaking now.

"It's the law," he said. He was Guinevere's father, and this public shame seemed to have aged him ten years in a matter of hours. The lines of care were etched deeply into his face, and his beard was almost white.

"It's harsh," Merlin said, hoping once more to sway them to compassion.

"It's meant to be," Sir Boris said.

Merlin's hands sketched soothing gestures in the air. "This is a time when we should temper justice with mercy," he said coaxingly. If only they would stop and think, it might curb their rashness before someone was hurt. "After all, your religion proclaims it. 'Let he who is not guilty of sin cast the first stone. . . .' Now, I know I've been guilty in my time, and I suspect you have been, too." He smiled at the men around him, and the tension in the room eased, just as Merlin had meant it to.

"I have to confess I've sinned a little," Lord Lot said, looking more reminiscent than guilty. The others laughed. Only Gawain and Arthur still looked grim.

"So," Mordred said, stalking into the room and

standing directly across the table from Arthur. "We make excuses for her because she's a Queen."

"No," Merlin said, feeling his spell of goodwill dissolve like morning mist. "Because she is *human*."

"No, because she's *Arthur's wife!*" Mordred shot back remorselessly, keeping the argument focussed on the invented crime of privilege. "Are we going back to one law for the rulers and one for the ruled?" He leaned forward, placing both hands on the table, his rain-colored eyes flicking restlessly from side to side.

"Is that the way it is?" he demanded, and with each word he spoke, the malign magic of his voice sowed dissent and wooed his listeners away from their better selves.

"Arthur?" Mordred demanded, gazing directly into the King's eyes. "I thought Camelot was to be different," he sneered.

All eyes looked toward the King. Arthur had to answer, and he said the only thing that he could. "It is!"

"Then show the world you mean it!" Mordred answered immediately.

The two men locked eyes. Arthur desperately looked for a way out of the trap Mordred had set. The laws of Britain were sacred to him. Not for anything would Arthur wish to return to the anarchy and unbridled tyranny that had been the essence of both Uther's and Vortigern's reigns. Arthur knew that upholding the law was the right thing to do—but now, somehow, Mordred had made it wrong, turned the law into a tool for hurting people and doing great injustice. And in the face of that hideous cleverness, Arthur was lost.

"Merlin," Arthur said at last. "What should I do?" His voice was desperately tired.

Merlin looked at Mordred—waiting, gloating. Mab's monster child had left none of them any choice. Mab had finally learned how to use the good in men to destroy them.

"In the end, you must uphold the law," he said evenly.

All around the room, the stricken consciousness of what they had allowed to happen showed at last on every face. Sir Boris sat with both hands clasped over his mouth, as if he wished to call back the words that had helped to condemn the Queen to death.

Arthur did not bow his head. He was too kingly for that. He got slowly to his feet and stared steadily into Mordred's eyes as he spoke. "Guinevere will be tried for treason," he said in a low voice.

A murmuring filled the room as every man there spoke at once—approving, denying, who could say? Rising above the voices was the sound of Mordred's slow mocking applause, as though Arthur's agony had been a performance staged for him alone.

"A splendid decision, both fair and just, eh, Father?" Mordred said delightedly. He seated himself contentedly at the Round Table, as though he had a right to be there. "Now, let's drink and enjoy ourselves." Behind him, his cronies laughed and agreed, pleasure on their vulpine faces.

"I want you out of Camelot!" Arthur shouted, loathing filling his voice. He began to walk around the perimeter of the Round Table, toward Mordred and the door.

"But Father, I only just arrived," Mordred said innocently. "I thought we'd reminisce about old times and play happy families."

"Stop him talking!" Arthur pleaded, goaded halfway to madness by Mordred's spiteful self-absorption. The boy prattled on as if he did not know what harm he had caused—or worse, knew and did not care.

"You can't mean that, Father," Mordred said as Arthur approached him. "I'm your devoted son, the crown prince, your one and only heir." His face still wore that maddening half-smile.

The greatest horror of it all was that everything that Mordred said was true, Merlin realized. He *was* Arthur's heir, the crown prince. But if all he had wanted was recognition, he would never have staged his entry into Camelot in this fashion, forcing a public trial of the Queen that would leave a war in its wake. Mordred's every action was a lie. He hadn't come to gain his rightful place but to destroy the kingdom—and Arthur—completely.

"Get out of my sight," Arthur spat, leaning over Mordred.

"Embrace me, Father," Mordred said, rising to his feet. There was a curious note of warning in his voice as he confronted his father, their faces only inches apart.

"Never!"

"Or I'll take what is rightfully mine."

"Guards! Seize him!" Arthur shouted, turning away as if even the sight of Mordred was intolerable.

The black-mailed guards moved forward to carry out Arthur's command, but Mordred shoved them back with enough unnatural strength to send the men flying across the room.

"Please don't get up. I know my way out," he said blandly.

Holding his hands fastidiously away from himself—as though he had just performed some distasteful task—Mordred walked toward the doorway and ascended the three steps. Then he stopped, turning to face Arthur one last time.

"I'm sorry, Father, but I'm going to destroy you," he said, and his voice was still bloodlessly polite. It gathered venom with his next words. "And this time your pet wizard won't save you."

Mordred turned away again and walked out. And as he went, two-thirds of the knights who had filled the room followed him.

The Queen was sitting at her window, a length of embroidery in her lap. The last light of day framed the window in silver. Someone should have come to light the candles, but none of the servants had dared to enter with the guards on the door, and so Guinevere sat alone in the dark.

She must be told, and Arthur could not bear to face her. Rather than leave the task of bearing these ill tidings to someone else, Merlin had come himself.

Guinevere looked up as he came in. In the evening light, her face was expressionless.

"You are to be tried for treason," Merlin said, his voice gentle.

"Mordred," Guinevere said, as if that name explained everything. Sorrow had touched both her and Arthur with royalty, and she had never looked more queenly than in this moment. She turned away from the window and stood. "Arthur's son. Was that your doing, Merlin?"

"Not mine," Merlin said, "but that of my great enemy, Queen Mab of the Old Ways. Mordred is the tool with which she means to destroy us."

"Arthur, and Camelot, and me—and you," the Queen said dispassionately. "But I will go first, I think, burned at the stake as if I were a heretic, when my only sin was to love a worthy man. When is the trial?"

"Tomorrow," Merlin said reluctantly. "I'm afraid it won't take very long."

Guinevere said nothing.

"If there's anything I can do—" Merlin began.

"You!" the Queen said in sudden fury. "When did you ever do anything for any of us that didn't end in disaster, Merlin? It was you who made an enemy of Queen Mab—you who let Mordred live to grow up—you who encouraged Arthur to go on this senseless quest—you who brought Lancelot to Camelot. . . ."

For a moment her grief almost overcame her, and she swayed and nearly fell, but then she regained her formidable self-control and glared at him icily. "If you want to do something for me, Wizard, then free me from this prison so I can go in search of Lancelot! I won't die for your and Arthur's sins."

Merlin hung his head. "I cannot do that, my lady."

"Then leave me." Guinevere's voice was hard. "And when I die, my blood will be on your hands—and Arthur's."

Merlin walked slowly away from the Queen's chambers. There was just enough truth to Guinevere's accusations, though hurled in the heat of thoughtless anger, to make Merlin writhe inwardly. His war had been with Mab, and he had drawn Arthur into it thoughtlessly.

But to make him a tool of the Light! Merlin argued. *I wanted Arthur to be a force for good!*

But it was the goodness in Arthur that was destroying him now.

And what of Mordred? How could everything have gone so wrong so dreadfully fast? It was as if Mordred were a lighted match that had found ready tinder. Merlin should have done something the moment he knew the child had been born—but what? Mordred had only been an innocent baby then. Wouldn't destroying him have made Merlin as evil as Mab? And what else could Merlin have done?

He pressed his hands to the sides of his head as though he could silence the accusing voices that way. What could he have done differently? What could he have changed? All the choices he had made had led him to this end. It was Mab's greatest trap, and Merlin could see no way out.

He wandered through the secret passages of Camelot for hours, wrestling with his thoughts, and at last he reached a decision.

I am not guiltless in all of this. Guinevere was right: if I had not brought Lancelot here, none of this would have happened. The fault is mine, and so if I meddle now, I can hardly complain of a little more guilt . . .

Slowly he ascended the twelve-dozen steps to the top of his tower and went inside. He closed and barred the door behind him, and with a gesture set the candles and braziers alight.

Fire, you once told me, is the simplest magic. Where are you now, I wonder, Master Frik? Though Frik had been Mab's creature, Merlin did not think that even he would have countenanced what Mordred had become.

With a savage gesture, Merlin swept a pile of books and papers from the surface of his worktable. They were plans for some additions to Camelot, but they didn't matter now. There was no future left for Arthur's dream unless Mordred could be stopped.

Working quickly, Merlin set a mirror, a candle, and a bowl of water upon the table. He wrote quickly on a small scroll of parchment, and tied the scroll to an eagle feather he found in a box. He hefted the bundle in his hand. Too light. After a short search, he added a large gold ring. It had the king's symbol, the Red Dragon, inlaid upon it in scarlet enamel. Arthur had given the ring to him a long time ago as a mark of royal favor. Now it would serve another man equally well.

Merlin tied the ring to the feather and the scroll and set them beside the bowl of water. Then he turned to the mirror.

Merlin did not really like magic, but over the years he'd become very good at it. This mirror was formed of a solid piece of glass that had come from a place where a star had fallen to earth. The glass was a dark opaque green, smooth as water, and had been shaped into a slightly concave bowl about eight inches across. When it had come into Merlin's possession, he had set it into a frame of blackthorn wood inlaid with silver knotwork around the edge. Just as the knot formed a tangled line impossible to unravel, so did human lives twine and coil together, until it was impossible to disentangle one person's destiny from the next's.

He picked up the mirror. The candle flame was reflected in it, distorted into streaky shapes by the curve of the glass.

Lancelot, Merlin commanded silently. *Appear to me, in the name of the Powers which spin out the destinies of Men. Be you in the Land of Men, the Land of Death, or the Land of Magic, appear to me now!*

Slowly, faint colored shadows gathered in the bottom of the glass. As they collected, they formed vague shapes, and suddenly Merlin saw Lancelot. The best knight in the world was camped by the side of the road, staring into the flames of a small fire. Black Bayard cropped grass placidly nearby, and Lancelot was roasting a rabbit on the point of his sword. Everything about Lancelot's actions spoke of a time of long and pointless wandering, without purpose or goal.

Mab's magic must have touched him as well, for I think he would have gone home to Joyous Gard to be with Galahad if he had found it possible. And now I shall meddle in his life once more, but with Elaine dead, there is no one left to hurt. . . .

Summoning up his magic, Merlin picked up the small bundle he had made and dropped it into the bowl of water. It did not strike the bottom, but vanished out of sight as if Merlin had dropped it into a deep hole. A moment later, he saw Lancelot start, as though someone had thrown something at him, and then the vision in the magic mirror vanished.

Merlin sighed, straightening up, and blew out the candle. He had done as much as he could to repair some of his errors—it was little enough, and it might come to nothing at all, but a man must try.

Perhaps it is the fact that we try that is the important thing, and not whether we succeed or fail. I wish I knew for certain, but in the matter of the meaning of life I am as blind as any mortal.

He was weary—Magic always took a great deal out of him—and it was time to seek his bed. Today should have been a day of rejoicing at Arthur's safe return. Instead it had been a day of tragedy and sorrow, and tomorrow would bring fresh troubles of its own. Mordred had prudently disappeared after Arthur had tried to have him arrested, but Merlin was certain the boy was still around, waiting for the appropriate moment to continue his destructive agenda.

But as Merlin walked in the direction of his little hut at the edge of the village, he passed by the room that held the Round Table, and saw pale light streaming out through the open doors. As Merlin looked in, he saw Arthur sitting alone beneath the light of the burning candles. The remains of a hasty supper of bread and cheese lay untouched at his elbow, and Arthur was still in the worn and threadbare riding clothes he had returned to Camelot wearing. His hair was still dusty from the road.

He looked up as Merlin's shadow fell across the Round Table.

"Did you tell her?" he asked.

Merlin nodded.

"And?"

"She wasn't pleased," Merlin said mildly. "But she blames Mordred, not you." *And she blames me, but there's no need to burden you with that as well.*

Arthur fell silent for a long moment, staring down at the honored names painted around the rim of the Round Table.

"I can't let this happen," Arthur said, as if his words continued some other conversation that the two of them had been having. "They'll burn her at the stake."

Merlin came around the table and put a comforting hand on Arthur's shoulder. Beneath the scale armor that he wore, Arthur was so thin, worn down with cares and privation. He had wanted the Holy Grail so much. . . .

And sometimes we do not get what we want most, Merlin thought, thinking of Nimue. *Sometimes, desire must be enough.*

"It's the only way to save the kingdom," Merlin said.

But before the Queen was executed, there would have to be a trial, and perhaps there Arthur could find some way to sway his nobles—appeal to their sense of mercy, and make them agree to spare the Queen's life. He did not tell Arthur that he had sent for Lancelot. Lancelot might not arrive in time. Merlin did not wish to add the heavy burden of hope to Arthur's shoulders.

Arthur sighed heavily. "How many of my knights will side with Mordred?"

"About half, I think," Merlin answered.

"That many? Why?" Arthur asked, honestly surprised.

Because you left them, Merlin thought simply. But even if it was the truth—or *a* truth—he couldn't bring himself to be so cruel. Still, Arthur deserved an answer.

"When they found out you had a child by Morgan le Fay, some of them felt they'd been betrayed. Others have gone over because they want to be on the winning side." *And because Mordred can make them believe anything he says, at least for a while. And that's long enough.*

Arthur sighed. "You taught me everything about how to be fair, and good, and just. But you could not teach me to be King. I did not realize how hard it would be, Merlin. A King must be so much more than a man."

"I know, Sire," Merlin said gently. "Go to bed, Arthur. Tomorrow will be a wicked day."

And in the morning the comet rose in the western sky as the sun rose in the east, brighter and more baleful than ever before.

CHAP+ER SIX

The Battle of Cruelty

The Queen's trial was brief. There was only one question to be answered: had Lancelot and Guinevere been lovers?

Guinevere took the stand in all her finery, the crown glittering upon her head and her fingers covered with rings. She wore a long golden brocade supertunica over a dress of scarlet samite, and her hair was coiled and braided with pearls. She looked every inch a Queen.

The King sat in his high seat with Excalibur laid unsheathed across his knees, in token of the fact that the offense before the court was a capital crime. He wore a simple tunic in golden velvet embroidered with the Red Dragon, and a gold coronet upon his head. He had not shaved off his beard, but it had been trimmed and combed.

The room was filled with nobles, many of them now

wearing armbands carrying Mordred's device: the eclipse. Mordred had chosen not to appear himself in the courtroom, but his influence was palpable. As Merlin took his place behind the King, he could feel the waves of hostility radiating from the watching spectators. They had come for blood, not justice.

"My lords—" Merlin began. He intended to remind them once more that mercy was a great virtue, and that Arthur had shown himself willing to abide by the law by agreeing to the trial.

The crowd did not let him.

"Kill the wizard, too!"

"This is his fault!"

"Down with the Old Ways!"

"Burn the wizard!"

"Be silent!" Arthur shouted, half rising from his throne.

The crowd's shouting dimmed to ominous murmurs.

"The wizard—Merlin—has no place here," Sir Boris said with painful honesty. He had been chosen to prosecute the case because there could be no question of his favoring Mordred. "This is a court of law, not a place for trickery."

Merlin bowed his head, acknowledging his defeat. He had worked for so long to make Britain a Christian kingdom in which magic and the Old Ways would have no place, and all he had wished for had come to pass. But somehow, it did not feel like a victory now.

"Merlin is free to be here, just as any of you are," Arthur said, but he had lost the hope of Merlin influencing the jury, and he knew it. Merlin retreated to the edge of the room, his words unspoken.

"Let the trial begin," Arthur said.

"The Queen stands accused," Sir Boris began, reading from a scroll of charges, "of . . ." For a moment it seemed as if he could not continue, then the old knight took a deep breath and went on. "Of treason, viz. of betraying the King with the knight known as Sir Lancelot of the Lake. How say you to this charge, Your Majesty? Yes or no?"

He gazed up at Guinevere. She met his eyes unflinchingly.

"I say yes, Sir Boris. I have loved Lancelot of the Lake."

The room broke into pandemonium, a sound of whooping and wild yells more appropriate to a battlefield than a courtroom. But in a sense, a battlefield was what this was.

Sir Boris looked toward Arthur, misery in his gaze. "The Queen stands accused by her own words. The charge is treason. And the sentence, Sire?"

Arthur looked desperate to escape, but there was no escape to be found. The Queen was guilty by her own admission, and there was only one penalty for treason.

"Death," the King said, bowing his head.

The little convent garden at Avalon was still and serene, though spring had come late this year and was filled with peculiar portents. There were unseasonable fogs and apparitions, strange lights in the sky. Migrating birds had not returned, and hibernating animals were slow to waken from their winter sleep. The brothers who kept the Abbey's bees said that their charges were troubled as well, refusing to leave their hives to go in search of nectar. It was as if the orderly progression of seasons had been suspended, pending some unimaginable revelation of Nature or Magic.

Nimue's life, too, had been jolted from its accustomed path, and things that were once certainties were now indefinite. All the rules had changed, now that Arthur had returned, because Arthur's return meant that Merlin was free.

And in great danger.

Nimue glanced around the cloister garden, holding her cowl protectively close about her face to hide her scars. The courtyard was completely deserted at this hour—everyone was in the chapel saying the noonday prayers, even Father Giraldus. Nimue should have been there as well, but she was not. The unvarying walls of Avalon that had been her home for half her life now oppressed her, and in her heart Nimue felt it was time to leave.

To be with Merlin.

But there was one last thing she must do before she could be with him. Merlin's war against Mab had begun because of the death of his foster-mother Ambrosia at Mab's hands, but her attempt to kill Nimue had given it the fuel that had kept the fires of enmity burning in Merlin's heart all these long years. If she went to him as she was, the scars on Nimue's face would always remind Merlin of his vow to war against the Old Ways, and keep the two of them from finding peace.

And Mab had promised Nimue that Merlin would find peace and happiness in a land far from the everyday strife of Britain.

Nimue believed her. Mab had no reason to lie. With Arthur coming home, all the struggle, all the politics of a royal court would begin once more, and as more and more of the land turned to the New Religion, there was no place at that court for Merlin. Father Giraldus was only the first of those who would see Arthur's return without the Grail as a signal to plunge Britain into an orgy of repentance. Merlin and all the gentle survivals of the Old Ways that still lingered in Britain would be their target. After all his years of service to Britain, of selfless sacrifice, to be hated for something he had never been would break Merlin's heart.

And to keep it from happening, Nimue would at last accept the devil's bargain Mab had offered her so many years ago. She had pledged her life to God, but she had not yet taken her final vows. And God had given her, as He had given all His creation, free will, and a heart and a mind to use with it. So she would do this for her own happiness—but more than that, she would do it for Merlin's happiness . . . and safety.

She hesitated, knowing the step she was about to take was irrevocable.

"Mab," Nimue said aloud.

There was a flicker of magic, and Mab appeared behind Nimue, in the shadow of an archway. The Queen of the Old Ways looked dark, almost funereal, in her somber spider-silk robes. There was little of glitter or glamour about her now, only a dark purpose implacable as the night.

"I'm here, Nimue," Mab said.

There was still the ghost of royalty in her graveyard voice. Mab had once been Queen within these walls, had reigned from this holy place over all of Britain and the Western Isles. Here, if nowhere else, Mab still wore the aura of her queenliness, as if to say that though Time could diminish her, the years could never truly destroy what she had once been.

"You made me a promise, years ago," Nimue said, turning to face her. "Will you keep it?"

"Yes," Mab said simply. "But what made you change your mind?"

As she spoke, she stalked past Nimue into the center of the courtyard, glancing about herself at Avalon Abbey as if to measure the strength of her eternal enemy, the New Religion.

"The King is coming home, and Merlin is free to be with me. I've discovered that all I want is Merlin," Nimue said. Her voice trembled as she turned to face Mab. It wasn't the truth—or not all of it—but let the Queen of the Old Ways see into her heart and read the truth there if she could! One thing that Nimue's life had taught her was that Truth was a complex thing that could not be caught in a simple net of words.

"Will you agree to live with him in a place I choose?" Mab asked, her back still to Nimue.

"If you make me whole again," Nimue answered steadily. *Whole!* This was the crux of the bargain. Nothing else really mattered. If she were whole, Merlin would no longer fight against Mab in her name.

Mab turned to face her, and for the first time Nimue realized how tiny the Queen of the Old Ways was. She looked like a carved saint's statue from the cathedral at Winchester, like something strange and powerful and alien.

"I have to warn you, Nimue. If you go to this place, you can never leave it," Mab said.

It was almost as if some human softness was struggling to be born in Mab's heart. She watched Nimue with anxious eyes, as if every care must be taken with the terms of this bargain.

"Will Merlin come to me there?" Nimue asked. None of this mattered for herself, she insisted silently. It was all for Merlin.

"Yes. He will," Mab answered, almost reluctantly. Nimue didn't understand her remorse. Surely this was a triumph for Mab, and not a failure?

But it was not necessary for Nimue to understand, only to make this pact that would take Merlin out of the World of Men before it could deliver its final blow to his warrior spirit. In that moment Nimue was more than a woman, more than the inculpable bride of the White Christ. She was the Goddess Herself, ageless and abiding, harsh with necessity, who bore the warrior-prince she would someday lay to eternal rest in his narrow bed of earth. Merlin was her son, her lover, her victim, and she must play unflinchingly her part in the glorious pageant of his life.

Nimue pulled back her cowl, exposing her burned and branded face.

"Then do it, Mab."

There was a flash of lightning that turned Nimue's bones to silver and crystal, a moment when the warm spring sunlight was replaced with the unflinching light from the heart of a star. Nimue felt as if she had been turned inside out—as if she had been remade. And then she was whole.

She put her hands to her face, and could not keep from crying out with joy as she felt smooth unblemished skin beneath both her palms. Gone was the roughness, the stiffness, the scars that had made a warped mask of a young woman's face all those years ago. Nimue was whole again, untouched by the cruelty of the world.

"Now come with me," Mab said, and she held out her hand.

Trembling inwardly, Nimue laid her own hand against Mab's. Mab's skin was cold, her flesh as hard as if it were carved of wood. And when Nimue's warm mortal flesh touched Mab's immortal form, both of them vanished, leaving Avalon as if neither of them had ever been there.

Darkness, and light. Nimue opened her eyes to see pillars of stone replaced by pillars of wood. She stood in the middle of a vast enchanted forest.

The trees were bathed in a strange red-gold light, making them look as if they were made of metal. Somehow Nimue knew that this was not a forest in the real world, no matter how much it resembled one, but was in-

stead a part of the Land of Magic where Mab ruled as
Queen. There was a crystalline chiming borne upon the
air, as though the harps of a thousand bards were playing
at once, and the air was scented with a delicious perfume
more wonderful than anything Nimue had ever smelled
before.

Mab stood beside her. The Queen of the Old Ways
looked at home here, as if she belonged in this enchanted
forest. She gestured, indicating something that lay ahead
of them.

"All this I have created for Merlin—and you. Keep
him here, Nimue, and all will be well for both of you. If
he leaves, the two of you will be parted forever. It is in
your hands."

"I understand," Nimue said.

"Then go! Wait for him here. He will not be long,"
Mab said imperiously. In the blink of an eye she vanished, and Nimue was alone.

She had been born a princess, and had lived many
years among the holy women of Avalon. Her life had always been filled with the presence of other women, but
now, for the first time, Princess Nimue was alone. She
threw back the cowl of her robe, relishing the feel of the
fairy breeze upon her unblemished skin, and set out to
explore the home that Mab had made for Merlin and
Nimue.

The strange golden light that came from neither sun
nor moon illuminated everything she saw, making ordinary objects seem to glow with a sourceless light. Nimue
soon found that the path through the forest led to a large
clearing, and in the center of the clearing was a large

round hut, its thatched roof extending nearly to the ground on every side, so that it most resembled a large haystack.

Nimue had never seen the forest where Merlin had grown to manhood, but he had told her of it many times, and her surroundings seemed to match his description down to the smallest details.

Why, this is Merlin's home! Mab has re-created it here.

Or had she? Perhaps this was Barnstable Forest itself, taken outside of time by some spell of Mab's, and turned into a sanctuary for Merlin. It was possible. Anything was possible with the Old Magic.

Nimue walked into the hut, knowing what she would find. On her right were shelves filled with cups and dishes and with pots and jars of good things to eat. There were bunches of herbs hanging from the ceiling along with golden strings of onions and garlic. On her left was a long table flanked by two benches, with a mortar and pestle sitting on it. On the back wall of the room—the center of the hut—was the hearth. The hearth was swept and scrubbed, the broom and a bucket standing ready beside it. Iron pots hung inside the fireplace, and a three-legged stool stood nearby.

Nimue pushed aside the blanket that served as a door and stepped into the inner room. There was a small window in the back wall, closed off with wicker shutters. There was a wardrobe for clothing and a rustic bed heaped with fur coverlets and homemade quilts. The room smelled of lavender, and a small harp hung upon the wall.

I can be happy here, Nimue realized gratefully. Deep in her heart she had feared that a place created for Merlin would seem strange to her, but the little hut was as homely and familiar as bread.

She went back into the outer room and began to build a fire. She would make tea while she waited for Merlin to come. She had no doubt he would come soon, just as Mab had said.

Each day that passed in Camelot made things worse. At first the people had been stunned by the news of the Queen's death sentence. Only Mordred's followers seemed pleased at the thought of it. But as the days passed and Mordred's influence grew, more and more of the people of Camelot began to demand that the sentence be carried out immediately. It was as if some terrible spiritual rot had set in, turning the hearts of the people against the thought of mercy and simple kindness.

The comet was visible now in the morning sky—a disastrous omen. The people called it the Red Dragon, and talked of it coming to punish Arthur for his sins. They would have burned the Queen themselves if they could have gotten their hands on her, but Arthur had stood firm.

Merlin had used every trick he knew to find Mordred in order to stop him spreading his poison, but Mab had prepared her catspaw well for the task of destroying Arthur. Mordred refused to come out and fight. Instead, he hid himself in the twisting alleyways of the town, always eluding Merlin's searching as he spun the twisted lies that so many were so ready to believe.

Without a single shred of proof, the people believed

that Mordred was Arthur's son, despite the fact that common sense would say that Arthur was not himself old enough to have fathered a son Mordred's age. They believed that Arthur meant to set himself above the law, to persecute and oppress them with unjust laws that he and his friends would never feel the bite of, when all of Arthur's life had been spent erasing the distinction between rich and poor, knight and peasant.

They believed that Mordred was their salvation. And that was the greatest lie of all, for Mordred had come to Camelot to destroy it.

Merlin had tried to explain this to Arthur, but the grief-stricken King would not listen to his wizard's strategies for opposing Mordred. With every hour since his return, Merlin had felt Arthur withdrawing from his responsibilities, as if the exercise of kingship had simply become intolerable.

Merlin knew that in his heart Arthur believed that his beloved subjects would still see reason. That if he showed himself obedient to the law and burned the Queen, the people's anger and discontent would cease and they would acclaim him once more, as they had on the day he drew Excalibur from the stone.

But that was many years ago, Arthur, Merlin thought sadly. *Everything changes. Spring to autumn, morning to night, glorious young King to guilty politician, bargaining to buy back what he thoughtlessly gave away in the morning of his youth.*

The direction of his thoughts made Merlin sad. Arthur had nothing to be guilty for. He was doing his best, doing just what he had always done. He was upholding truth and asking no one to do anything that he would not do himself.

And because Arthur was who he was, Guinevere must die. Arthur had delayed setting the date for Guinevere's execution as long as he could, but in the end he had no choice but to carry out the sentence.

Tomorrow, at noon, the Queen would be burned at the stake.

"I just don't understand it," the burly man in the leather hood said plaintively.

He stood almost seven feet tall. In addition to the hood that covered the upper half of his face and his thick neck, he wore leather trousers, boots, and laced bracers on his massive forearms. Iron-Head Gort was a formidable man.

Merlin glanced around the dungeon. He supposed it was rather homey, if you liked that sort of thing. There was a rack over in one corner, an Iron Maiden on the wall, and several stands of pokers and branding irons, along with an empty brazier. None of them had seen any use since Uther had died, of course, but Arthur had kept the Royal Executioner on. After all, the man had done nothing wrong. There was no reason to turn him out of his job.

"I've been the Royal Executioner all my working life," Gort said. "Vortigern . . . Uther . . . I've always given satisfaction. But I must protest, Master Merlin. Have I failed in some way? Is the King unhappy with my work?"

He gazed anxiously at Merlin. Even seated on a low

stool in the corner of the royal dungeon, Gort loomed over Merlin the way a granite cliff would loom over a willow tree.

"No. Of course not," Merlin said soothingly. "I've certainly heard no complaints. Why, everyone says Iron-Head Gort is the best there is."

He'd come to bring the details of the Queen's execution to Gort himself, as Arthur was simply unable to do it. Coming down here to discuss the details of her execution would have been impossible for the King, racked with guilt at his failure to protect the greatest of his subjects.

"Then why is the Queen being executed at noon?" Gort demanded.

He was a big childlike man, who would never dream of hurting anyone except as a part of his job. But this was the first time Arthur had ever called upon his services, and he was anxious to give satisfaction.

"All executions—whether by fire, ax, or rope—take place at dawn. The sun rises up, the condemned goes down. It's all very symbolic and beautiful, you know. But now the King has said she's to die at noon." Gort shook his head. "I don't know, Master Merlin. I just don't know."

Merlin knew. Though he had given Arthur no reason to hope for such a thing, the King was not a fool. Arthur was hoping that Lancelot would come to rescue Guinevere.

Merlin hoped so, too, but he dared not use his magic to see if Lancelot had understood his message. If Mab or Mordred suspected that Lancelot was coming to save Guinevere, they would surely stop him.

"And another thing," Gort added. "This is the Queen of Britain's execution! Shouldn't we make it a special occasion? Not just a simple burning at the stake—anyone can have that—but a real exhibition? She could be torn in pieces by wild horses, or there's always beheading—the crowd loves a good beheading—or hanging with a silken rope, or—"

Merlin raised his hand to stem the flow of professionalism from the Royal Executioner. "The King was very specific, Master Gort," Merlin said. "The Queen is to be burned at noon tomorrow. I can't tell you any more at the moment, as this touches on highly secret matters, but we all trust you'll put on a good show." He smiled coaxingly.

"Well, I'll try," the executioner grumbled, unmollified. "But sometimes I don't know what this younger generation is coming to. No pride in craft, that's their problem. None."

Merlin spent the night before the Queen's execution in his tower workroom. He did not know what it was that he waited for, but if Lancelot were to come in the night, he could be more use inside Camelot's walls then he would be elsewhere.

But the hours passed without disturbance, and slowly Merlin's hopes failed. Lancelot would not come in time. The Queen—Arthur's proud, loving, reckless lady—would die, and a part of Arthur would die with her.

Soon the eastern sky began to lighten with the promise of a new day. Merlin glanced out his window toward the west, where the shadows lay blue upon the ground, still hoping that he would see Lancelot riding to his lover's rescue.

He did not see Lancelot. But in the sky above the western hills, a baleful red star with a tail of bloody fire glowed against the dawn sky.

"It is only a comet?" Arthur asked Merlin.

The two men stood alone in the throne room, looking out over the courtyard where the Queen was to burn. The day had turned cloudy, finally hiding the red star in the west, but terrible things could still be seen. The cobblestones around the platform that held the stake were already piled high with logs and branches awaiting their victim.

"What?" Merlin asked lightly, trying to cheer him. "Did I teach you astronomy on all those cold winter nights for nothing? It is a comet, Arthur, no more supernatural than the fixed stars of the sky."

"But why must it appear *now?*" Arthur said, and to that question, Merlin had no answer.

It was going to be a wonderful day, Mordred thought to himself gleefully. Today, no matter what Arthur did, Mordred could claim the first in a chain of victories that would end with Arthur's death.

If the King burned the Queen, Arthur would have been dealt a mortal blow to his human heart—and such blows, Mordred had been given to understand, were fatal. Why, just look at how Frik had carried on just because Morgan had died, completely missing the point that nobody needed her anymore. A human heart made its owner soft, vulnerable.

Mordred had no intention of being either soft or vulnerable.

He'd put the days he'd spent in hiding since the Queen's arrest to good use, convincing those bored gullible buffoons, the boys of the chivalry—who had sat around Camelot growing fat and lazy while Arthur wandered Europe on his fool's errand—that he, Mordred, was their only hope for a life of danger, excitement, and privilege.

Of course, he hadn't put it to them quite that way. *Honor,* he'd said, and *fairness,* and *equality,* and *simple common decency.* And they'd rallied behind him—meeting in cellars, drawing up manifestos, wearing his device, pledging to overthrow the weak tyrant who currently occupied the throne of Britain.

It was enough to make a cat laugh, really, and Mordred relished every moment of the joke. Not as much as he'd enjoy watching his father's wife go up in flames, of course, but Auntie Mab had encouraged him to savor the small joys of existence as well as the great.

By eleven o'clock people were moving into the courtyard to await the show, and Mordred moved with them. He felt safe: even if Arthur still meant to arrest him, he could hardly do it right at the moment he was burning the Queen. Besides, with one thing and another, Arthur had never actually gotten around to formally banishing Mordred from Camelot. Mordred had just as much right to be here as anyone else—and he did so want a front-row seat.

But it was always wise to be prudent, so he kept a fold of his cloak pulled up over his face, and kept out of sight of the windows that overlooked the courtyard. Soon enough, he wouldn't have to skulk in corners.

His time would come.

Very soon now, his time would come. . . .

Could pride shield her from the flames? Guinevere wondered. She did not think so, any more than prayer could strike down evil.

She sat at her dressing table, gazing into the mirror as she removed her jewels for the last time. She had dressed in her finest and queenliest robes to hear Mass and receive the last rites of the Church this morning, but she would not need jewels and robes of state where she was going now.

She stripped off her rings and her bracelets and set them aside. She unpinned the heavy pearl and gold brooches at her shoulders and let the stolla fall from her shoulders, then reached up to unclasp her necklace and set it upon the table before her. She removed the pearls in her ears, and last of all she lifted the heavy golden crown from her head.

How she had loved it the day she had first seen it, lifting it from its satin-covered box to admire it. She had been a child then, to think that crowns made queens. She knew far better now.

She unpinned her braids and began to run a comb through her long chestnut hair. The day was overcast, the sun pale, but she would not live to see if tomorrow's weather might be better. At noon Arthur would give her to the flames.

He has always loved anything better than me! she raged unfairly. She had given him no reason to love her, and despite that he had done all he could to save her. But in the end, when he had been forced to choose between her life and his kingdom, he had chosen Britain.

It was the action of a King.

If only—Guinevere clasped her hands together and tried to still their shaking. She had broken so many of God's laws—what awaited her after death? Heaven? The pains of Hell? Epona's green meadows where the favored of the White Horse Goddess gathered? She did not know. It did not matter. She would not have traded one hour she had spent in Lancelot's arms—one kiss—for the promise of life eternal. If death was her fate, she would go to meet it like a Queen.

There was a tapping on the door, and Guinevere rose to her feet, shrugging off her rich brocade robe so that she stood clad only in her shift of scarlet linen, a plain belt of golden disks about her waist.

Has noon come so soon?

Bishop Wace entered the room. For this sad occasion he was dressed in a simple white monk's robe. Guinevere could see a company of guardsmen behind him.

"My lady," the Bishop said reluctantly. "It is time."

The crowds howled like a mob in the Roman arena as she appeared. If not for the protection of the guards, they would have torn the Queen limb from limb long before she reached the stake. They jeered at her helplessness, shouted threats and accusations at her as the guards pushed their way through them.

Gort was standing beside the stake. He reached down to help the Queen ascend the platform, then tied her hands around the stake with a length of stout rope. Chain would have been better—rope would burn through—but rope would do well enough. Before the rope burned through, the Queen would be dead.

Guinevere looked toward the windows where Arthur stood watching, and her eyes held unwavering accusation.

Once she was securely bound to the stake, Gort stepped down from the platform and took up an unlit torch. He touched it to the coals of a waiting brazier, then swirled it alight, brandishing the torch so that all could see. He looked toward the throne room windows. Arthur was supposed to be standing in full view, watching the execution. He was supposed to give Gort the order to light the fire.

But the King did not come forward, and after a moment Gort turned away and thrust the torch into the kindling piled around the edges of the platform.

The flame caught at once, making an uprush of golden fire. The wall of heat drove the crowds back. Their excited roar took on a higher pitch. In the throne room above, Arthur moaned and took a step backward, shutting out the sight.

"I can't bear to watch," he whispered. "The sin was mine, not hers."

He looked helplessly, pleadingly, at Merlin, but Arthur's former mentor was powerless to help him. This trap was composed not of magic but of morality, and against that force the greatest wizard in the world was helpless.

The flames spread greedily. There was fear on the Queen's face now as she felt their bite. Almost against her will she struggled against the executioner's ropes, trying to evade a fate she knew now was inevitable. The last possible moment for rescue—or pardon—had passed.

"Merlin," Arthur groaned. "It's too late."

Her fear, her struggles, were like a knife twisted in Arthur's heart. Guinevere kept looking toward him, willing him to share in her fate. The flames were higher now, and hotter, and billows of smoke from the pyre rolled up, filling the courtyard and obscuring Guinevere's struggling body. In a few moments more the pain would be too great for her to remain silent. She would scream, and then her body would begin to burn.

"Merlin—!" Arthur begged, not even sure what he cried out for.

In his voice Merlin heard the cries of the child he had loved and raised: *"Master Merlin, make it stop, make it go away!"*

I cannot stand by and allow this to happen, no matter the cost. Merlin stepped forward into the window, saw gratefully that clouds still filled the sky, and *reached* for them with his magic.

What is there shall be here—even heaven sheds a tear!

There was a rumble of thunder, and the rain began.

The first droplets of rain struck the flames like thrown stones, dissolving in tiny puffs of steam. Mordred turned away from the pyre. It no longer interested him. He had seen people burn to death before. What interested him now was his father—he wanted to watch Arthur's face as his beloved Queen turned to ashes. The rain cascaded down torrentially as if the sky itself wept in anger at the Queen's plight. The sudden storm was so loud that until the doors into the courtyard at last gave way, no one inside quite realized that Lancelot had been battering at them.

In the window above Mordred could see Merlin. For a moment their eyes met. Merlin thought they were simply enemies, but Mordred knew better. They were rivals—rivals for Mab's love.

Her love was the only thing Mordred had ever really wanted.

Behind Mordred, Black Bayard surged through the guards as Lancelot hewed about himself with his shining sword. Its name was Joyeuse, but there was little cause for joy in Camelot today. Before the sun set, wives and mothers would mourn the unjust deaths of men slain to prevent an unjust death.

All around the courtyard people shouted and ran, both toward the battle and away from it. The scene was pure chaos, and the fierce downpour only made things worse. Only one dark-clad figure stood immobile, staring up toward the throne-room windows as the people around him shouted—half in praise of Guinevere's rescue, half demanding that Lancelot be burned as well.

Mordred.

He watched the window where Arthur—weak, broad-minded, accommodating Arthur—came hesitantly

forward to peer down at the Queen's magic-born salvation. Mordred stared fixedly toward the King. He did not
turn to see the source of the sounds of battle, murder, and
sudden death that came from behind him.

Lancelot was the best knight in all the world, and he
was fighting for his heart. He flung back a dozen men as
he fought his way to the pyre and severed the Queen's
bonds with one stroke of his gleaming blade.

None of that mattered to Mordred. All that mattered
was Arthur, and Merlin, and the fact that Arthur had
cheated.

Mordred always enjoyed watching someone abandon
all his principles.

She stood on a bed of half-burned wood, her bare feet
blistered, as pillars of steam rose about her. Her scarlet
linen tunic was sodden with rain, her hair seal-slick
against her skull. But Guinevere laughed, pulling herself
free, and looked no longer to the window where the King
watched.

"Come on!" Lancelot shouted. He held out his hand
and pulled her up before him. Bayard danced and fretted,
alarmed by the soldiers all about him. Then Lancelot
turned, and, spurring his stallion, galloped away from
Camelot with the Queen in his arms.

Merlin stepped away from the window and sat down on
the nearby bench. He was weary to the bone. He had
passed a long and sleepless night, and if Lancelot had not
arrived, they would be watching the Queen burn even
now, despite his spell. *Lancelot has all of knighthood's*

virtues, and every one of its failings, but there are two things about Lancelot that will never be a part of any bard's tale: he always leaves everything till the last minute, and he always makes the wrong choice.

But what was the wrong choice, under these circumstances? The one Arthur had made—or Lancelot's?

"Thank God," Arthur whispered fervently, staring after the lovers as if he wished he could join them.

"And you, of course, Merlin," he said, recollecting himself. Arthur turned away from the window and looked down at Merlin, concerned.

"It had to be done," Merlin said simply.

"It's strange," Arthur said, almost to himself. "When I married Guinevere, I didn't love her. It was truly a marriage of state. But when I returned from my quest—when I realized I had already lost her—my feelings changed. I found that I really did love her then. If I had loved her at the beginning, would I have needed to go on my quest?"

"Some say that the Grail is love, Arthur," Merlin said gently. "If you have found love, perhaps you have truly found your Grail at last."

"But it's too late," Arthur said sadly. "Too late for all of us."

He walked to the doors and flung them open to address the waiting guards. "Summon my council, and the Knights of the Round Table. It is time to decide what to do about Mordred."

"Thank you for Jenny's life," Gawain said.

Arthur's companions—Gawain, Sir Bors, and the others—had gathered around the throne, waiting for

Arthur to say the words that would make the world seem sensible once more. But before they could begin to think about the problems that faced them, Gawain had stepped forward to offer his simple thanks.

Arthur's first follower, his lifelong companion, was haggard with sleeplessness and worry. But his eyes shone with loving trust as he clasped Arthur's arm and murmured his words of gratitude.

Perhaps we can make it work after all, Merlin thought, watching the two of them embrace. Arthur's dream had been a worthy one, and he had managed to pass his vision on to others. Perhaps men of good will, all working together, could manage to prevail, just this once.

"Thank you, Gawain," Arthur answered, sitting down on his throne. "I—"

But Arthur would never complete his sentence.

The doors of the throne room flew open again. A band of nobles pushed in to the chamber, and Mordred was at their head.

"What is the meaning of this?" Arthur demanded, coming down from his throne. Beside him, Gawain drew his sword, his face clouded with anger.

"You *tricked* us, Father!" Mordred cried. They were words of moral indignation, but the tone was the cheated surprise of the spoiled child. "You pretended to condemn the Queen to the stake, then you had her rescued by your damned wizard!"

There was a murmur of angry surprise and agreement from Mordred's band—joined, unfortunately, by some of the Knights of the Round Table.

"You hadn't even the courage to set her free yourself!" Mordred stood his ground as Arthur advanced upon him, until the two men were standing only inches apart: Arthur, tall and strong and fair, his full beard making him look older, and Mordred, small and feline and dark, with the mark of Fairy on his every feature.

"That's true," Arthur answered steadily. "I should have done."

But Mordred did not give the King's bold honesty a chance to win supporters for his side.

"One law for you and another for the rest of us?" he accused, throwing his arms wide as if to invite all his on-lookers to judge the fairness of that.

"We can't live like that!" cried one of Mordred's men, as if on cue.

"Do you hear?" Mordred demanded, a faint cool smile on his face. "They can't live like that." The words were heartfelt, but Mordred's voice was lightly ironic, as if he did not believe in the very things he urged his fol-lowers to accept so passionately.

"I call upon all trueborn Britons to rally to freedom's flag!" Mordred raised his voice and swept the room with a rallying glance, his fist upraised. The room rang with shouting and cheers. "Depose this—"

But Arthur could be mocked no longer. His face twisted with contempt, the King struck Mordred a power-ful backhand blow, stopping his lying silver tongue at last.

There was a hiss of steel as knights—on both sides—drew their swords and the room fell silent. Only Mor-dred's supernatural strength kept him from falling to the ground. As it was, he staggered back, and there was a thin thread of blood at the side of his mouth.

"You caught me by surprise, Father," he said, moving back to stand before Arthur again. For once there was honesty in Mordred's voice, and a kind of twisted joy, as though Arthur's virtues made him even more worthy of destruction.

"I know how that is," Arthur answered. He smiled without humor.

There was a long moment of silence in the throne room, then Mordred spoke in a low, even, and horribly compelling voice, his eyes never leaving Arthur's face.

"Nobles, the time for talking is over. Those who value right and justice, follow me."

Mordred turned away and left without another word. And, terribly, many of Arthur's own sworn knights followed him, until less than half the men Arthur had originally gathered in the throne room remained. Slowly Gawain sheathed his sword, the last of the knights to do so.

Arthur walked through his men to the doors Mordred had left hanging open, and violently slammed them closed. The crash echoed through a room gone unnaturally still.

"So it is war," Arthur said into the silence.

"Can't we just . . . give him what he wants?" Sir Bors asked. The old knight glanced at Merlin as he spoke, but he could not meet Arthur's eyes.

"You mean the kingdom?" Gawain demanded. "He already nearly got Guinevere's life."

"But he didn't!" Sir Bors shot back. "She didn't burn. Arthur's . . . wizard . . . saved her."

Sir Bors looked pleadingly at Arthur, his eyes begging the King to understand. Sir Bors was a knight of the old school, a believer in royal privilege. He would not have cared if Arthur had pardoned Guinevere a thousand times. Arthur was King. It was his right to do as he chose . . . but for Arthur to cheat his way out of a promise using the power of the Old Ways was something Sir Bors's honest Christian soul found hard to forgive.

"That is true," Arthur said. "Merlin is my oldest friend, Sir Bors. He saved me from myself when I had lost my way. But I won't need anyone to save me from myself any longer. Mordred has come to Camelot as a usurper, but I will not surrender my throne to him. When the time comes I will face him on the battlefield, and as God is my witness, I will do what is right. Are you with me, men?"

"Yes!"

"For Arthur!"

"For Camelot!"

But to Merlin's ear the shouts of victory were hollow. War had come to Arthur's golden city, and Merlin was not wanted here. He slipped from the tumult of shouting, cheering men and disappeared.

The rain had ended. The smell of smoke, though lingering, was faint, and Gort's men had already cleared away most of the pyre. Only a smear of wet ashes on the cobblestones remained to remind onlookers that here a Queen had nearly died by fire. The clouds, robbed of their moisture, had vanished, and the sky above was the robin's-egg blue of spring. A year ago, on a day very much like today, Merlin had looked out over the country surrounding Camelot and wondered what he should do about Lancelot and the Queen. Now, at last, that matter was settled, though he would never know what happened to the two of them. *They will become legends, just as I dreamed, but I will never know the end of their tale.*

Merlin walked through the city, toward his little hut on the outskirts of the town. There were few people on the street for the time of day, and those that Merlin saw looked furtive and ashamed. A great sense of guilt hung over Camelot, as though everyone in it was conscious of having helped to commit a great wrong and now was filled with shame.

Mordred's doing, just as the coming war was. But this war would not be fought for lands or crowns. This war would be fought for the hearts and minds of Arthur's people.

And all I can do is hope—from afar—that Arthur wins it, Merlin thought bleakly. *Especially as my help seems to do more harm than good.*

In his heart, Merlin knew that his time—the time of all creatures of the Old Ways—was passing, as swiftly and inexorably as the sands that fell through an hourglass. Soon all of them would be gone, their brief season over.

Assuming, of course, that Arthur wins.

Merlin's ruminations were cut short when he rounded a corner and came within sight of his little house.

It had been burned to the ground.

CHAPTER SEVEN

THE BATTLE OF DECEPTION

Sifting through the wreckage and cleaning up what he could took Merlin most of the rest of the afternoon, and it seemed to him that every time he looked up into the sky, the baleful red eye in the western sky glowed brighter, as if it were gloating over the tragedy to come.

The burning of his home was only a harbinger of what would happen if he stayed at the King's side. He was no longer welcome here. Whether for good or ill, the day Merlin had worked toward from the moment of his foster mother's death had come: Britain belonged to the New Religion now, not the Old Ways.

But what of Mab, and her creature, Mordred?

Merlin sighed, shaking his head as he brushed his hands clean and turned back toward the castle. Mab's cruelties had grown more extreme as the years had passed, and Mordred was a monster. But if Merlin had learned one lesson from Arthur in all the years of loving him and raising him and—at the last—letting him go, it was that you could not fight another's battles.

Defeating Mab was not something Merlin could do for the people of Britain. He could oppose her influence over his own life and try to protect those whom he loved. He could arm the King and his people with the spiritual and moral tools to take up the fight themselves. But he could not do it for them.

If Love is one great secret, then surely this is its match: to be truly wise, one must be able both to love and to let go. I have done the one. Now the time has come for me to do the other.

He walked slowly back to the castle to make his farewells.

The tower room where Merlin had spent so much of his time these last few years already had a deserted look to it, as if somehow these inanimate objects knew that Merlin had no more use for them. He lit the lamps and braziers against night's shadows and spent several hours tidying the room for its next occupant, destroying herbs and potions that would only cause trouble, burning his notes and personal papers lest others find them and make them into something they were not meant to be. At last the room was impersonally tidy, with little trace of its former occupant.

By now it was late, though Merlin doubted that Arthur had yet sought his bed. After the trauma and emotional excesses of the day the halls of Camelot were quiet and still. He would speak to Arthur, and do what he could to ease the King's mind. Arthur was as loyal as he was kind, and having his friends at odds with one another could only hurt his generous heart further.

Merlin paused in his search for the King at a doorway that led out into what had been the Queen's garden. Guinevere had loved her garden, and people had brought her rare plants from every corner of Britain and beyond to fill it. The air here was lush with the rich spring scent of new life.

He wondered again where Guinevere was now—if she was safe, if she was happy. But these were riddles to which Merlin knew he would never learn the answers, for Guinevere and Lancelot had ridden out of Arthur's story and into their own.

He was about to go on, when there was a movement in the garden. "Who's there?" Merlin called warily. A figure dressed all in white hurried toward him. "Father Abbot," Merlin said in surprise.

"I rode all night to get here," the old man said. "Nimue's gone."

"She's gone?" Merlin echoed in dismay.

"She left you a message," Avalon's Father Abbot continued briskly. "She'll be waiting for you at the door of magic."

That isn't the Father Abbot!

Merlin came down the three shallow steps that separated him from the white-robed figure. Did the old man's eyes gleam red in the faint light? "You're a liar," he whispered softly.

The figure before him reeled back in shock. "Merlin! How can you say that?"

"You're a liar!" Merlin shouted.

The figure of the Father Abbot turned away, beginning to laugh. His laughter rose to a mad cackle as he took a few steps into the darkness then turned back to Merlin, shaking off the form of the Father Abbot as a dog shakes off a coating of mud, revealing Queen Mab beneath the disguise.

"I'm glad to see you haven't lost all the skills I taught you," she said in her hollow voice.

"I've lost none of them," Merlin answered. "And it was Frik who taught me." *Not you, never you—you could not even give that much of yourself, Queen of Air and Darkness!*

Amazingly, Merlin's words had struck a nerve. "Don't mention that ingrate. He's left my employment— without a reference!" She glared at Merlin.

Morgan le Fay dead, Frik gone—Mab is chancing all she has on Mordred's success.

But Mab wasn't finished speaking. "Anyway, Nimue *has* gone, and she *does* want you to join her . . . when you're ready." Before Merlin could frame another question there was a flicker of lightning, and between one flash and the next, Mab was gone.

Curiously, Merlin did not doubt that Mab was telling the truth. It had been true from the very beginning that Mab could not use the power of the Old Ways to kill, but it was equally true that she had never been as interested in killing her enemies as turning them to her cause. Now she wanted him gone to smooth the way for Mordred's victory. But the Queen of the Old Ways had never really understood mortals. This fight had never been Merlin's, but

Arthur's and Mordred's. If Merlin left, it would not make much difference to the outcome of the battle.

He turned and walked back into the castle, in search of the King.

Merlin found Arthur where he had expected to find him: in the chamber that held the Round Table. The King was asleep where he sat, his elbow upon the table and his head resting on his hand, as though he'd fallen asleep brooding. Excalibur lay unsheathed upon the table beside him, its silver blade gleaming in the dim light.

Not wishing Arthur to know that he had caught him napping, Merlin retreated to the doorway and cleared his throat. When he saw Arthur startled into wakefulness, he entered again as though for the first time.

"Merlin," Arthur said as he entered.

The King's face was haggard with the terrible griefs he had endured in the seven short days since his return to Camelot. He rose to his feet and cleared his throat nervously.

"My noblemen don't want you with us against Mordred. They say that if you come, they won't follow me."

Arthur's face was filled with shame. He had not wanted to say these things to Merlin, but royal necessity compelled it.

"Ah," Merlin said, bowing his head in understanding. It seemed his decision to leave wasn't wholly his to make after all.

"What will you do now?" Arthur asked.

Merlin forced himself to smile for the King's sake. It would be cruel to add to Arthur's pain, and in truth, he'd already known it was time to go. But there was a vast difference between leaving willingly and being booted out.

He smiled ruefully, walking around the edge of the vast table to where Arthur stood.

"I'll close my books, break my wand, and retire," he answered lightly. "I have a life, and a chance to live it."

Some of the guilt in Arthur's expression vanished. "Nimue?" he asked hopefully.

"I'm going to meet her now," Merlin answered, making up his mind in that moment. "Will you be able to deal with Mordred?"

Arthur smiled, and for a moment the joyful fearless boy he had been gazed out again from his eyes. "It's just one more battle. And right is on our side."

Merlin embraced him then, and Arthur hugged his old tutor fiercely. Tonight Arthur might believe that the Fellowship of the Round Table had been destroyed, but Merlin knew that the Round Table had been nothing more than a glorious experiment, and if it had failed, the failure was not forever. There would always be those who strove for freedom and equality, and the magnificent legend of the Fellowship of the Round Table would be a beacon to them in their strivings.

"I'm proud of you, Arthur," Merlin said, gazing deeply into the king's eyes.

Then there were no more words to be said. Merlin had never liked partings—none of the ones he had known in life had been happy. He turned and strode from the room, putting a brave face upon things for Arthur's sake. But he could not keep himself from pausing in the doorway for one last look back.

Will I ever see you again, my boy? And if I do, will it be in victory—or defeat?

But it seemed to be Arthur's turn to console his old friend.

"Don't worry about me," Arthur said. "I have Excalibur."

He smiled at Merlin, touching the enchanted sword that lay on the Round Table beside him.

Carrying the Horn of Idath with him, Frik journeyed south from Nottinghamshire in search of Merlin. Before he had gone very far, garbled rumors of the troubles at Camelot began to reach him.

Arthur had returned. Guinevere had committed treason. She'd been executed—no, she'd escaped with her lover, Sir Lancelot of the Lake. Arthur had a son named Mordred. Merlin had been banished. Mordred had taken the throne. No, Arthur was going to war against Mordred, to keep him from ever gaining the throne.

That last bit at least was true, Frik reflected, looking at the preparations all around him. Arthur was certainly going to war—and who else could he be fighting but Mordred?

Well, I hope Arthur trounces the little beast! Frik thought viciously. Each time the gnome thought of Mordred, he remembered his mother, Frik's beloved Morgan. Mordred could have prevented her death—Mab would have given him anything he asked for—but he hadn't. He'd been too selfish to think of anyone but himself.

"You! Fellow!"

The call roused Frik to attention. He'd stopped in the

little village for a drink of water and some fresh news—and, frankly, to see what he could steal, for without his magic, Frik was reduced to theft and scavenging to feed himself. But he hadn't had a chance to do either yet, so at the moment his conscience was clear.

"Me?" Frik asked nervously. He'd wrapped a scarf about his head to conceal the most obvious of his gnomish features, but with his pale skin and goggling eyes—and no hope of using magic to change his appearance—Frik could pass for human only among the very nearsighted these days.

"You," his interrogator said. He was a large, loud, middle-aged man in a leather apron—probably the village blacksmith. "I haven't seen you around here before."

"No. Er, ah, well—that is to say—"

"Do you want to fight for the King?"

The unexpectedness of the question took Frik by surprise. He'd expected to be accused or attacked, not offered a job.

"For the King?" Frik asked. *Against Mordred,* his heart said.

"And who else?" the man said belligerently, striding over to where Frik stood beside the horse trough. "You aren't one of the Black Prince's—that Mordred's—sympathizers, are you?"

"No," said Frik passionately. "I want him dead."

"Good man," the blacksmith said approvingly, clapping Frik upon the shoulder and nearly sending him sprawling. "Come along to the tavern then, and we'll get you kitted out. We're mustering at Colchester—Sir Bors is to lead us. How are you with a bow?" his new friend asked, walking toward the tavern with his arm around Frik's shoulders.

"Well, actually," the gnome confessed modestly, "I'm rather good with a whip. . . ."

If he could find Merlin, Frik would deliver the Horn of Idath to him. If he could not, at least this way he could do *something* to strike back at Mordred.

And at Mab.

Though Lancelot would not let Black Bayard slow for several miles, it soon became clear that Arthur had sent no one in pursuit of them. He'd wrapped his cloak tightly around her, but Guinevere still shivered from her wet hair and her damp linen shift. The blisters on her calves and feet stung, a grim reminder of how close she had come to perishing in the fire.

"How did you know to come?" she asked, when Lancelot was finally willing to stop for a rest.

He pulled off his glove and showed her the ring that he wore. It was red-gold, with the red dragon of Britain inlaid in its wide band in enamel. It was Arthur's ring, the one he had given to Merlin before he had left. She had often seen him wear it.

Merlin.

Tears prickled at the corners of her eyes, and she angrily brushed them away. Merlin had been a true friend to her at the last. He had sent for Lancelot.

"When I left Camelot, I tried to go home, but I could not find my way. One night as I sat beside my fire, close to the sin of despair, this ring appeared out of nowhere, with a message that you were in danger. I came as quickly as I could, but I was almost too late!"

If Arthur had not delayed as long as he could, you would *have been too late,* Guinevere thought. She had been wrong to condemn her husband so harshly. Arthur had loved her after all.

If only he had stayed. If only we had come to know each other. How different everything would have been then!

But though her heart ached for what might have been, Guinevere could not regret her choice. She loved Lancelot as she could never have loved Arthur.

"Where shall we go?" she asked.

"To Joyous Gard," Lancelot answered. "It is my home, and I have been too long away from it. I hope you will be happy there. I can only hope that Galahad will grow to love you as much as I do."

It took them many weeks to find their way back to Lancelot's castle, for this time Merlin and his magic were not there to smooth the way. But at last they found a cave near the forest of Broceliande where the Old Ways were still powerful, and when they passed through it, Guinevere could smell the sea and hear the cry of the seabirds.

"We are home," Lancelot said simply.

In the distance, Joyous Gard gleamed on the cliff above the sea, a castle forged from the fabric of dreams. Its steep conical roofs were plated in pure gold, and black pennons flew from every spire. Seeing the mourning banners, Lancelot sighed heavily.

"Poor Elaine," he said. "She did not deserve her fate."

Nor did I, if you'll remember. "God forgives all, Lancelot," said Guinevere, rather tartly. "None of us was free to act as we chose. Mab controlled all of us as if we were her puppets."

"Cold comfort," Lancelot said, smiling at her wanly. "But come, my lady. Joyous Gard will make you welcome."

They rode down the hill and across the sand in the direction of the castle. As they came within sight of its gates, the gates opened, and a knight rode out.

His armor glistened like polished silver in the sun, and his helm was crested with angel's wings. The horse he rode upon was whiter than sea-foam, and upon its blue saddlecloth was embroidered the image of a glowing golden cup.

The Grail.

The knight stopped when he saw them, reining in his horse. He pulled off his winged helm, and the sun shone down brightly on his pale hair.

"Galahad!" Lancelot said.

"Father," Galahad replied coolly. "So you've come home at last."

He had grown into a tall young man of sixteen. His hair was still the same white-blond it had been when he was a young boy, and his eyes were the color of the winter sky. He was as bright as Mordred was dark.

"I tried to get here sooner," Lancelot said. "This is Guinevere. I'm giving her sanctuary here at Joyous Gard."

"Sanctuary can only be given by the Church, just as forgiveness is. Once it would have mattered to me, but no longer. Joyous Gard is no longer my home."

"You can't leave!" Lancelot said, agitated. "Where will you go?"

"I will go in search of the Grail," Galahad responded serenely. "If I cannot live without love, I will love only God, for God is always worthy of love and never betrays it."

Lancelot looked away, unable to meet Galahad's eyes.

Guinevere laughed angrily. "Have a care what you promise, Grail Knight, for there is always someone listening. And there is no love without betrayal."

"Then I will never love," the young knight said simply, "for love is the beginning of death." He slid his helm back down and picked up his reins. Without another word, he rode on.

Lancelot gazed after him without speaking. The only one who he believed could have absolved him of his guilt for Elaine's death, Guinevere knew, was Galahad, and now that would never be.

"I wanted to love him," Lancelot said simply.

"Let God do that," Guinevere answered. "We have each other."

After a long moment, Lancelot and his lady rode on, through the gates of Joyous Gard.

Merlin left Camelot and walked until dawn. His destination was the Enchanted Lake, for nowhere else could a Door Into Magic be found in the world of modern Britain, and Mab had told him that Nimue waited at the Door Into Magic. But Mab and her sister, the Lady of the Lake, were not on the friendly terms they had been in Merlin's childhood, and the Door Into Magic was probably not in the center of the Lady of the Lake's watery domain as the entrance Merlin had used in childhood had been.

You weren't planning to walk all the way there, were you, Master Merlin? a familiar voice asked from behind him. Merlin staggered forward at a sudden shove between his shoulderblades, and turned to see Sir Rupert gazing at him out of wise brown eyes.

"Sir Rupert, old friend!" Merlin said in delight. "But I turned you out to grass years ago!"

I'd be a poor friend if I didn't come when I was needed, wouldn't I, Master Merlin? the enchanted animal replied. *Where are we going?*

"To the Door Into Magic—wherever it is," Merlin answered. He swung himself into the saddle and settled his weight on Sir Rupert's back. "I may be in for a long search."

No. I know where it is. Sir Rupert answered. The horse snorted and shook his head, then trotted off.

Sir Rupert moved at his own pace, and Merlin did nothing to hurry him. A great sense of peace had enfolded him. He had brought a long life of service to an honorable end, and now he went to enjoy the fruit of his labors. In his heart, Merlin did not doubt that Arthur would prevail. After all, he had Excalibur. And Excalibur would always bring victory to a just man who wielded it in a just cause.

By midday they had reached the edge of the Enchanted Lake. The boundaries of the lake and the magical domain it encompassed were always fluid, and today the lake verged upon a vast wild forest whose trees had never felt the blade of Man's ax. Merlin could feel its magic tugging at him, calling him home.

He rode along the edge of the lake until he reached a sheer stone cliff that was so tall he could barely see its top. Its stone face was striped and stippled with the marks that ancient rivers had worn in the stone. In the center of the cliff a deep fissure led into the rock.

We're here, Sir Rupert said.

"Nimue!" Merlin shouted. "Nimue!"

His voice echoed back from the rocks on every side, but then, as though it were the spring breeze itself, he heard Nimue's voice.

"Merlin. I am here," she said.

Merlin rode into the shadow of the opening, then dismounted from Sir Rupert and peered into the darkness, testing the wind that blew from the cave. It was ripe with magic, and the sound of Nimue's voice seemed still to echo in it, like the faint aftersong of churchbells.

All magic goes in threes, Merlin thought suddenly.

Frik had told him that once, long ago. The great tides of a man's life were threefold: as child, as lover, as victim. Twice before Merlin had gone into darkness, and each time had changed him.

The first time he had been a child, traveling with Frik into the Land of Magic to meet Mab. What dreams he had dreamed of his future in those days! That journey had begun with a voyage through a long dark tunnel, and even then he had felt the terror of the living rock pressing down upon him. When he had left the Land Under Hill, he had left the innocence of childhood behind him.

The second time he had been a young man, carried into the dark dungeons beneath Vortigern's castle to die. For weeks he had lain on cold stone, feeling the whole weight of the castle pressing down upon his chest, locked away from light and air and freedom. That was the moment that had led to Nimue's maiming, to the beginning of his helpless, futile war with Mab. When he had entered Vortigern's dungeons, he had left peace behind.

This was the third. Once more Merlin must make the trip into the unknown. What would he leave here, and what would he gain?

Slowly Merlin walked into the darkness, leading Sir Rupert behind him. The stone passage was narrow and dark, and soon Merlin had left the pale clear daylight behind, to walk blindly through blackness. A ghost of his old fear of entombment rose up to taunt him, but this time the magic in the air soothed his old fears. No matter where this passage led him, Merlin was going home.

Soon the corridor ahead began to fill with light—a ruddy, sourceless illumination that cast no shadows. Merlin walked toward its source, and soon he had passed out of the cave, and into the Land of Magic that Mab had promised him.

It was a different environment than Mab's own darkly-brilliant realm, though Merlin did not doubt that it was somehow connected to that place. But there were many kingdoms within the Land of Magic, and this one was a dominion that had been created to Merlin's own measure. It fit him as closely and as well as his own boots did.

He was in a forest. Though the trees were in full summer leaf, their foliage was the brilliant red and gold of autumn, as if here it was every season at once. Merlin could see each twig and leaf as clearly as if it were noonday, though the sky far above his head was a velvet starless black, for the light here owed nothing to either sun or moon. The sound of Sir Rupert's hooves was muffled in the thick soft drifts of fallen leaves that covered the ground, so that the loudest sound Merlin heard was the creak of Sir Rupert's saddle and the soft rush of the wind through the trees. Animals that had never known what it was to fear man scurried on their way as he passed. Merlin saw rabbits and squirrels, larks and doves, even a young doe with her fawn beside her.

Every creature that he saw was the ghostly silver color of Otherworld animals, more proof—if he had needed it—that the cave had led him into the Land of Magic. The very air was filled with the scent of it, a perfume that assuaged a longing deep in Merlin's soul that he had never realized was there. He was Mab's child as well as Elissa's, and all his life, a part of him had longed to return to the magical land that had given him being.

Now he was home.

And more than that—both halves of his soul were at last at rest. For this forest was more than beautiful, it was familiar as are the places of earliest childhood. This was Barnstable Forest, where Merlin had been born—but a Barnstable Forest made perfect beyond all mortal possibility.

"Welcome home!" Bran the raven called from a branch above his head. Merlin smiled and waved to his old childhood companion. He knew where he was going now, and his steps quickened as he followed the path that led to Ambrosia's forest cottage. Even after so many years, he thought of it as hers; the place where he had first seen the light of day, taken his first steps, discovered the magic of love.

The cottage was just as he remembered it, for memory always idealizes reality. The curtain was drawn back from the doorway, and he could see the fire burning in the fireplace inside the cottage. There was a sweet tang of woodsmoke in the air, carrying with it the promise of a thousand summer afternoons to come.

Hearing his arrival, Nimue stepped out of the cottage, stooping as she came through the low door. She wore the simple white tunic she had worn at Avalon, but now there was no cowl pinned closely about her face. Once more Nimue greeted the world boldly and unafraid.

"Look," she said, and her hand went to her face, caressing the unblemished smoothness of her cheek. "Look where we are!"

Home. Merlin was home, with the woman he loved. Everything he had ever wanted was here.

Nimue lifted up her skirts and ran to him, flinging her arms about his neck and kissing him unreservedly upon the mouth. Merlin put his arms around her, trembling and weak with a hope too long denied. *This is what I've always dreamed of,* he thought. Home . . . and Nimue . . . and freedom.

A quiver seemed to pass through the forest when their lips met. Merlin tried to lose himself in the moment, but to his wizardly senses, this place rang with the sound of magic, closing around the two of them, locking them tightly together. He felt Nimue shudder against him as though she felt it too, and clutch him as securely as if she would protect him from dangers as yet unseen.

A moment later she drew back, holding his hands and gazing at him with the open peaceful love he had longed to see on her face all these years. Nimue had weathered the storms of her life and come at last to this safe harbor. She was at peace with herself at last, and that made her more beautiful than the removal of any scar possibly could.

"Come," Nimue said, laughing as she tugged at his hand, urging him toward the cottage.

"Wait," Merlin said reluctantly. He gazed around himself, feeling the frisson of magic. "This is all Mab," he said, reminding them both. No matter how innocent a paradise this appeared, it had all been created by Mab.

"Oh, forget her!" Nimue said in loving exasperation. "We've wasted so much of our lives together already. Now it's our turn," she whispered, coming into his arms once more. "Isn't it what you always wanted?"

Nimue's honesty and openness convinced Merlin that there could be nothing to fear. Sincerity was the one weapon Mab could not wield. For whatever reason, Mab meant them to be happy.

Merlin followed Nimue into the cottage, and here, too, everything was perfect, just as he'd always dreamed it would be.

Afterward, they lay together on the wide bed and talked of their lives. Merlin spoke of Arthur, of Mordred, and the pain that he had expected to feel was curiously muted.

It was as if he spoke of events long in the past, events that no longer had the power to hurt. Arthur, Guinevere, Lancelot, even Mordred, all were figures in a tapestry of myth, a tapestry woven long ago.

From that moment began a golden time in Merlin's life. His days held the carefree recklessness of childhood, but with the wisdom of age Merlin was able to savor their rarity, their perfection, even as he lived them. There had been so little of joy in Merlin's life, so little peace for a man torn always between his fairy and mortal natures, that he never tired of this tranquillity.

Perhaps this was what the Christians sought from their Paradise; days of unending bliss without the possibility of sorrow. And Nimue was there with him, a part of that joy. Together he and Nimue ate and slept, laughed and made love, wandered through the forest and bathed in its crystalline pools in the eternal day that had no twilight.

But nothing is eternal.

The forest provided everything they needed, but water must still be drawn and firewood gathered. One day—he did not know how long after he had passed through the Door Into Magic—Merlin was walking alone in the forest. Each stone and tree around him was familiar to him from childhood.

Save one.

It was an old oak, its trunk bent and gnarled with the storms it had weathered. It stood apart from its fellows, alone in its solitary majesty, and Merlin had never seen it before.

Where had it come from? Everything here beyond the Door Into Magic was an exact counterpart to something in the Barnstable Forest of his childhood, and so this must be as well. But a tree this magnificent took centuries to grow. It didn't just appear overnight. If it had been in the forest in which Merlin had spent the first years of his life, he could not have failed to see it.

Cautiously, he approached the tree. Was its manifestation an omen—and of what? He reached out—

It was summer, but the air was cold and the vegetation sparse, and somehow he knew that little the farmers had planted this spring had grown. The air was filled with a thin dry fog that veiled the sun and left a film of black grit on everything, even the food and the surface of the water. In the west, the tail of the wandering star stretched across half the sky, turning the heavens to blood and night to day. The ground beneath his feet vibrated with the tramp of marching men, and in the distance he could hear outcries, and the clashing of swords.

Merlin drew back with a gasp. The spell of contentment that had enfolded him since the first moment he had kissed Nimue was gone, shattered by the feel of the tree bark beneath his hand. Once more he remembered the outside world, where Arthur faced Mordred and war reclaimed a land which had not known it for a generation.

It is nothing to do with me, Merlin told himself. *Once, perhaps, but no more. Those days are through. I am through. This is where I belong now.*

But he was troubled, and took care not to go to that part of the forest again.

In the days following Mordred's declaration of war, Arthur rallied his men to oppose the usurper. Barons who barely knew that the King had returned to Britain received curt summonses to come with their men-at-arms to Camelot.

Some, loyal supporters of the Crown, did as they were bid. But more stayed away, flocking to Mordred's standard, the banner of the eclipse.

They do not even know why they fight for him, but they do, Arthur thought bleakly, gazing out the windows of his throne room. All around him, the castle rang with the preparations for war—in the distance, regular as the beat of a ticking clock, he could hear the ringing of the blacksmith's hammer upon the anvil.

Before Arthur had taken the throne, the people had automatically believed that the King was above the law. Many of them still believed it. It had been Arthur who had been the one to say that the King must be subject to the same laws as his people, that justice and fairness, not might and force, should rule Britain. But now that Mordred was saying that Arthur placed himself above the law, the very people who had upheld the King's new idea were now willing to fight to the death to destroy it.

Merlin had warned Arthur before he left that Mordred had the ability to cloud men's minds. Now Arthur was seeing what that ability could do.

I should have killed you the first moment I saw you, Arthur thought grimly. But in those days—only a few short weeks ago, but it seemed like another life—he'd still had some ideals left. He'd believed that love could make a difference.

There was a footstep behind him in the throne room.

"How goes the muster, Gawain?" he asked without turning around.

"Well enough," Gawain answered. "Fewer than we'd hoped, of course. Mordred holds the north and west. He's struck again at Winchester, but the garrison there managed to beat him back. The fighting was savage. Mordred's men fight like animals; the men are more terrified of him than of the Devil Himself, they say."

Gawain sighed. "He's only toying with them, of course. Trying to draw us into a chain of skirmishes that will sap our strength."

"Of course," Arthur echoed, turning to face Gawain. Gawain had been a grown man when Arthur had still been a boy. There were threads of grey in the Iceni prince's hair now. *We grow old. We all grow old, leaving our life's work undone.*

"It's me he wants, not those men. If it were my kingdom, my crown, my throne—power—I could understand, even forgive him, God help me. But that isn't what Mordred wants. It's me. He's out to destroy everything I have given my life to build."

"You will not lose, Sire," Gawain said, clasping Arthur's arm in support. "Mordred is but a beardless whelp—he'll run from the first real show of steel, and the rebels with him. And you have Excalibur."

"I know." Arthur's hand touched the hilt of the wondrous sword belted at his hip. For a moment his eyes were far away as he relived the moment he had drawn Excalibur from the stone.

Mab had been there that night. She had cursed him. The words came back to him as sharply as if she were here with him now. *"His reign begins in blood,"* she had said to Merlin, *"and it will end the same way."*

"But it doesn't have to be mine," Arthur said aloud.

"Sire?" Gawain answered, perplexed.

"That was the other thing I wanted to see you about," Arthur said. "As you know, Mordred is my son. But I've disinherited him. Whoever rules after me, I don't want it to be him."

"Sire!" Gawain protested automatically.

Arthur smiled. "I may be King, but I'm still mortal. If—when I finally face Mordred—I die, who will rule Britain after me?"

"I— Well— There are—" Gawain's words stumbled to a stop. "Aside from Mordred, you have no heir, Arthur," he admitted reluctantly.

"I want *you* to be my heir, Gawain," Arthur said. "It was what Lord Lot wanted for you once, you know."

"I don't want it," Gawain said hoarsely.

Arthur laughed. "And I don't want you to have it! But if I'm dead, I don't want *him* to have it either, or have a bunch of princes squabbling over my crown the way they did at my father's funeral. Humor me, Gawain. You're still my brother-in-law. Do this for me."

"Kay will think he should have been the one," Gawain warned, surrendering to Arthur's wishes.

"I love Kay, Gawain, but I know him too well. If a problem can't be solved with a sword, Kay goes and gets a bigger sword. He's not the man to rule a kingdom."

"Very well, Sire," Gawain said. He knelt before Arthur, more stiffly than he had once but still as readily. "Before God and beyond death, Sire, I am your man."

*　　*　　*

The tent was black. The furnishings were black, the tapestries were black, the pillows were black, even the torches were black. Mordred liked black.

And he saw no reason why he shouldn't have everything decorated just the way he liked it, no matter what anyone else thought, because when you came right down to it . . .

I'm going to be the next King of what's left of Britain, and they're not.

Mordred smiled his sweetly chilling smile. He sat alone in his tent, Caliban across his knees. The weapon was still as he had made it when he drew it from the ice, a slender-headed ax with a long hooked blade. Its shaft was the same black metal as its head, and strong enough to shatter any blade . . . except one.

Excalibur.

For symmetry's sake—and in his own way, Mordred was an artist—Caliban should be a sword, so that the black blade and the bright could clash upon the field of battle. He'd thought about changing it back off and on over the past weeks, but when you came right down to it, Mordred wasn't much of a man for swords. Swords meant knighthood, and ceremony, and honor, and Mordred didn't care for any of those things. Mordred liked to kill, and he liked to win. And after he'd won, he liked to smash what was left.

An ax was a better tool for smashing things than a sword.

He leaned his head against the back of his chair and half closed his eyes. The red light of the Dragon Star seeped through a crack in the walls of the tent, working its malign magic. A strange dry fog filled the air, causing men to sicken and die, and spring this year had never warmed into summer. The crops—those Mordred hadn't burned—had failed in the fields. There'd be famine this winter, whoever won the battle to come.

Then I'm really doing those sniveling peasants a favor by cutting them down now. But do I get any thanks for it? Of course not!

Twelve weeks before, Mordred had ridden out of Camelot to York, the northernmost of the great Roman walled cities. But he hadn't attacked the city of York, though he'd come at the head of a sizable army. No, he'd pretended to be one of his own men's servants, slipped into the city, and vanished amid its teeming populace.

A fortnight later, the fruits of his labors had begun to ripen. Just as at Camelot, there were meetings in cellars, circulated petitions, an anonymous execution or two. And then the people had risen up, thrown out the garrison, and installed Mordred—*Prince* Mordred, future King of England—as the ruler of York and the North.

Mab had warned him these tricks wouldn't work on everyone. But as far as Mordred could see, they worked on enough people—and once you had a mob of well-armed, weak-minded followers, you didn't need either logic or persuasion: everyone else pretty much did what you wanted them to.

And when the time was ripe, Mordred would meet Arthur and his army on the field and crush them utterly, then lay waste to the kingdom in a way that would have turned Old King Vortigern positively *green* with envy.

"You're wasting time!" a familiar voice hissed. "The

power that I gave you to cloud men's minds will not last into the dark half of the year!"

"Hello, Auntie Mab," Mordred said without moving.

A moment later he got gracefully to his feet and stepped down from the black-draped dais his chair rested on. He held out his hand to Mab. "I've missed you so," he said, leaning over to kiss the air beside her cheek.

"Don't change the subject!" Mab hissed. "Arthur should be dead by now. Why isn't he?"

"I don't like to rush things," Mordred said sulkily. "And if we're going to play Twenty Questions, where's Merlin? With all I've done to Arthur in the past three months, you'd think that damned wizard would be around to pull his prize pupil's chestnuts out of the fire, but no one's so much as seen him."

"Don't worry about Merlin. I've taken care of him," Mab said.

"Is it too much to hope you've killed him slowly and horribly?" Mordred asked, turning away from her.

Mab didn't answer.

"I see," Mordred said, and this time his voice shook with the effort it took to keep his tone light. "Can I offer you a drink? No? I think I'll have one. It's been a long day."

Mab still said nothing. Mordred crossed to the table, where a decanter of black glass stood surrounded by golden goblets inset with cameos of carved jet depicting the Seven Deadly Sins. He picked up the nearest one, poured it full, and drank without concern. No one in his camp would dare to try to poison Prince Mordred . . . and if they did, well, it simply wouldn't work. He did, after all, have the strength of ten because his heart was black.

"What are you waiting for?" Mab demanded abruptly. "You must take the throne before Samhain, or all is lost."

Mordred drank again, leisuredly. So Mab had protected Merlin, hiding him somewhere out of Mordred's reach, had she? It was no more than he should have expected. She still loved Merlin best, still wanted to keep him safe. But Mordred had no intention of leaving any rivals on the field by the time he was through.

None.

The goblet crumpled in his hand, and he set it down carefully.

He turned to face Mab, leaning back against the table.

"I'm waiting, dear Aunt, for the right time. The time when Arthur has gathered together positively every last bit of support he can possibly muster and gotten it all together in one place so that once I've killed the King and every man in his army there won't be anybody left to oppose me," he said as if explaining the matter to a child.

And Merlin will come to save Arthur. He must! And I will kill him, too, and then there won't be anyone else left, will there, Auntie? You will have to love me best of all. . . .

"You're a good boy, Mordred," Mab purred, oblivious to the tenor of Mordred's inner thoughts. She walked over to him and stood on tiptoe to kiss his cheek. "You'll make me proud of you, won't you, Mordred?"

"Oh yes, Auntie," Prince Mordred said. "I quite guarantee it."

CHAPTER EIGHT

The Battle of the Forest

imue could hear Merlin singing as he chopped wood for their fire. Though there was neither night nor day here in the Enchanted Forest that Mab had made for them, they had fallen into a regular pattern of waking and sleeping and performing simple homely tasks. Neither of them realized that each time they slept it was for a longer period, until one day soon they would sleep without wakening.

Nimue stirred the porridge for their morning meal and stared into the flames, alone with her thoughts.

They did not make for pleasant company.

With each passing day, Nimue's secret guilt grew harder to bear. Certainly Merlin had come to the Enchanted Forest of his own free will, but he had also come because she was here. Though he said that Arthur had no further need of him, Nimue knew that did not mean that

Merlin's work in the world was done. His purpose was as it had always been: to defeat Mab. And if Mab still feared Merlin so much that she would construct such an elaborate trap for him, then he must be very near to succeeding. If he went back into the world, perhaps Merlin could still defeat Mab.

But that was where Nimue's part came in. She was the one trapped by the Enchanted Forest, not Merlin. She could never leave—but if Merlin left, he could never return. Nimue would be trapped here forever. Alone.

If Merlin thought about leaving, Mab counted on Nimue telling him that. Begging him to stay. Keeping him here because he loved her, and turning their love into a weapon for Mab to use against them.

That is not right! Nimue thought sadly.

But what *was* right? To drive Merlin back out into the world, where men like Mordred and Giraldus waited to destroy him? She had only agreed to Mab's bargain to save Merlin because she thought that his work in the world was at an end, and because she believed that if that were so, then Merlin's happiness and safety were the most important things in the world.

But Nimue was beginning to suspect that she was wrong.

All through the weeks that followed, the two commanders—Arthur and Mordred—moved their playing pieces across the chessboard of Britain, never actually coming to grips. Every day the comet grew larger in the sky, and it seemed as if the land were under a curse of famine and darkness.

Many said that the King was to blame. Arthur had sinned, and the land was blighted because of it. The dragon star was a sign of his wickedness.

Sometimes Arthur wondered if it was true. A King should rule his land, and he had abandoned it to search for the Grail, just as Guinevere had abandoned him for love. A King should rule his people, and instead his people flocked to Mordred's standard in greater and greater numbers with each passing day.

But Mordred's army pillaged and raided as Vortigern's had once done, laying waste to the countryside and terrorizing good people who wanted nothing more than to be left alone peacefully in their homes. Even though they had abandoned him, Arthur had sworn to protect them, and he would do his best to do that for as long as he lived.

And so as the red star grew ever brighter in the sky, Arthur gathered together all those who were still loyal to him and prepared to do battle against his son for the people of Britain.

"Do you think he'll come?" Gawain asked.

"He'll come," Arthur said grimly.

The plains of Sarum were shrouded in a thick grey fog that made it almost impossible for a man to see someone standing six feet away, but Arthur knew that Mordred's army was out there somewhere. Perhaps at the edge of the forest. Though he knew his own army was behind him, he could not see them either. Each day the cursed mist grew thicker. Perhaps soon they would all be fighting in the dark.

Mordred had asked for a parley, to discuss the terms of surrender. Even though he knew it was a trap, Arthur could not refuse to meet Mordred. He would lose what little support he still had among the nobles if he rejected this seeming chance for peace.

And there was always the chance that Mordred really meant it.

If all he wants is a kingdom to rule, I will give him the north. I would give him the whole kingdom, except that I know what he will do to my followers. I owe them my protection, and so I cannot abdicate, but I can divide my kingdom: give him the north, and leave the south to Gawain. I thought things would never come to this—I thought there could be nothing worse than Mordred's rule—but I was wrong. If we do not make peace, we will destroy the whole land between us.

The sun was already high in the sky. Normally battles—or parleys that might end in battles—started at dawn so that the combatants could have as much daylight as possible in which to fight, but since the red star had appeared in the west, darkness continued long past sunrise. Mordred had not yet appeared, and it was nearly noon.

In the distance, a horn sounded.

"That's the signal," Arthur said. He started to ride forward.

Gawain stopped him with a hand on his horse's bridle.

"At least wait until we see them, Sire. Mordred doesn't want peace. He wants you dead."

"And I want him dead, may God forgive me," Arthur said.

A few moments later, the white flag appeared through the mist. Arthur and Gawain rode toward it. In his hand, Gawain held a hunting horn with which he could signal the start of battle if the parley turned out to be an ambush.

Mordred rode a black horse, and his armor was a dull iron grey. He wore a helm with fantastic bat-wings sweeping out from the sides, and a black surcoat and cloak. Upon his chest his symbol, the eclipse, shone in dull silver. Beside him rode the knight who was carrying the flag of truce. As far as Arthur and Gawain could see, the two men were alone.

"Mordred," Arthur said.

"Father," Mordred said mockingly.

There was a moment of silence.

"Well?" Gawain said. "This *is* a parley. What are your terms?"

"Oh, I never had any terms," Mordred said lightly. "I just wanted to see if you'd come. You see, I'm ready to kill you now, and I thought this would be the most convenient place. Shall we fight?"

They were really going to do it. Frik gripped his spear nervously. There were rumors that Mordred wanted to surrender, but Frik knew the little reptile better than Arthur did. Surrender was the last thing on Mordred's mind. And when Mordred didn't surrender, they would fight. And Frik would be there in the thick of it.

He couldn't believe he was betraying his principles this way. Frik was a devout coward. But his principles could do nothing to assuage his anger at Mab. Oh yes, he had helped her do her worst. But now he wanted to make amends, and fighting for Arthur would be a good start.

Suddenly he heard a horn sound three long blasts—the signal to charge. *Just as I thought.* All around him men began to cheer. The man ahead of Frik began to trot forward. Frik took a tighter grip on his spear and followed.

All around him, unseen in the mist, the two armies rolled toward each other like tides. Then they met, and the ring of steel began to echo across the plains of Sarum.

Merlin lay drowsily beside Nimue in a drift of fallen leaves, looking up at the starless sky. The leaves formed a canopy of gold, their brilliant sparkle making up for the lack of sun and moon. A gentle breeze played over his face, ruffling the feathers on his cloak. Though he knew he had come here through a cave, Merlin had no sense of being enclosed in any way. Perhaps this really was Barnstable Forest, somehow magically perfected by Mab.

As always, thinking of Mab disturbed him, as though there were something he had forgotten.

"This is so beautiful, isn't it?" Nimue said.

"Yes," Merlin answered, his train of thought vanishing at the sound of her voice. He wondered what he had been thinking in the moment before she spoke.

Whatever it was, it couldn't have been very important.

The fighting had been going on for hours. Most of the horses had been killed by archers, and Gawain and Arthur were both fighting on foot. They had become separated in the fog.

An armored man wearing Mordred's colors rushed at Gawain. The Iceni prince slashed at him, and he fell, only to be replaced by another. No matter how many of Mordred's men Gawain killed, there were always more to replace them. This one Gawain stabbed through the belly, then braced his boot against the dying man to yank the sword free. All around him, Gawain could hear the roar of battle and the shouts of the dying. He hoped none of them was Mordred.

He wanted to kill Mordred himself, for Jenny's sake.

Gawain had seen Mordred a few minutes earlier, before the last wave of attack. In his bat-winged helmet the usurper was easy to spot, but Mordred could have been easily identified even if he wore the same armor as his men. Mab's brat fought with unnatural strength and demonic ferocity. One blow from his ax was enough to cut a man in half. Gawain could not imagine the number of men Mordred must have slain today.

But numbers did not matter. Despite Mordred's ferocity, Gawain knew that Arthur's forces were winning. Whatever spell Mordred had cast over his troops to get them to fight, it seemed to be failing. They were fleeing the battlefield, and Arthur's troops were not. Today, victory would belong to Arthur.

Gawain cut down another man, felt someone behind him, and turned quickly, but there was no attack. Mordred stood a few feet away, maddeningly calm and composed. There was not a scratch on him, or even a drop of the blood of the men he had slain.

"Gawain. What a pleasant surprise," he said archly.

"Stop talking, Mordred, and fight," Gawain snarled.

It was Mordred who had dishonored his sister, not Lancelot—Mordred who was the cause of all the sorrow in Camelot. And if he could spare Arthur the pain of having to execute the monster that was his own son, Gawain would happily do it.

"I thought you might enjoy some light conversation before you die—but as you wish."

Gawain swung his sword before Mordred had finished speaking, but Mordred parried it with ease. His strength and speed were against nature, and in the space of a dozen blows he had battered the sword from Gawain's hands. Mordred tore off Gawain's helmet, holding the blade of his ax against Gawain's cheekbone, forcing Gawain to his knees as he bled from the wounds—none yet fatal—that Mordred had given him.

Why doesn't he finish me? Gawain wondered.

"Mordred!"

Lord Lot appeared out of the mists, roaring with fury as he ran to rescue his son.

It was what Mordred had been waiting for. He whipped the ax backward. A blade shot out of the back of its head, piercing Lot through the heart.

"Father!" Gawain screamed. He floundered forward on his knees, falling across Lot's body. Lot's eyes stared skyward, sightless in death. *Father . . .*

"Clever boy," Gawain heard Mordred say as consciousness left him.

Until Excalibur was carried into the Battle of Sarum against Mordred, the enchanted sword had never been raised in battle. Merlin had struck down Vortigern with its magic only, and Uther had never truly possessed Excalibur. Arthur had carried the sword for many years without ever drawing Excalibur in anger. Now everything changed.

The legend said that Excalibur could not be defeated, and today Arthur proved the legend true. The sword seemed to move of its own will, mowing down the men who faced it as though they were summer wheat.

But Arthur wielded more than a blade of steel. Excalibur was a blade of spirit as well, and the spirit of the sword cut through the spell that had bound Mordred's armies to him. Everywhere on that battlefield men came to their senses, the dark glamour that had seduced them vanishing as night vanishes before the dawn. They ran from the field in increasing numbers—or surrendered to Arthur's troops—and slowly, Arthur felt the tide of battle turning.

Slowly, he began to believe in the possibility of victory.

He'd lost Gawain in the mist and the trees. Looking for him, Arthur ran across Sir Boris, leaning against a tree, his sword resting upon the leaves. There was a footman beside him, leaning on his pike.

Sir Boris had been a warrior since Arthur's father was a child. Arthur had begged the old knight not to accompany the army on this campaign, but Sir Boris had refused to heed him, and in his heart Arthur could not blame him. In this war, there were no noncombatants.

"Are you all right, Sir Boris?"

"Just getting my second wind, Sire," the old knight said staunchly. "We have them on the run, I think."

"I do too," Arthur said, but he knew that wouldn't

matter if their commander managed to escape. "Where the devil is Mordred?"

"I saw him over there," the footman volunteered in a thin nasal voice. He pointed. Arthur ran in that direction, Excalibur at the ready.

Mordred was waiting for him. Even in the mist, there was no mistaking that figure in his bat-winged helmet. Mordred stood in the shadow of an enormous oak, leaning against its trunk nonchalantly. In his right hand was a long-handled black ax.

Arthur slowed to a walk at the sight of his son. The anger that he had expected to feel at this moment ebbed away, to be replaced by sorrow for all that had been lost. However sinful his birth, Mordred was Arthur's son, but Arthur had never been given a chance to love him.

Mordred . . . Guinevere . . . even Morgan. I've lost them all. Deep in his heart, Arthur mourned for the loss of what might have been. *I gave you life. Now, it seems, I have to give you death.*

"Mordred," he said.

"Father," Mordred answered, mocking his tone. He took a few steps forward.

"It's time to end it all," Arthur said, raising Excalibur.

"We agree on that, at least," Mordred said philosophically. "You know, Father—if you'd lived—I don't think we'd be very happy as a family." He raised his ax.

Arthur stepped forward.

In the Enchanted Forest, Merlin suddenly sat up.

"What is it, Merlin?" Nimue asked, sitting up as well.

"I heard a scream," Merlin said slowly.

He could still hear them—the screams of dying men and horses, the clash of battle. For an instant all the intervening years dissolved, and he was back on the ice near Winchester on a cold winter's morning, Excalibur in his hands, as Uther and Vortigern fought for the crown and men died all around them in the snow.

"No," Nimue said protestingly. "It's nothing to do with us," she said quickly, her hand on Merlin's shoulder. She kissed him and stroked his face, urging him to lie back once more, to give himself up to sleep, to dreams. . . .

"No," Merlin said, sighing as he lay back once more. *I suppose it isn't.*

There was something he must remember . . . if he could only concentrate. . . .

Mordred's black ax rang out as he parried the first blow, and in that moment, Arthur knew that strength and speed were not the only fairy gifts that Mab had given her catspaw. The ax met Arthur's blade unyieldingly, and the forest rang with the force of the impact. Magic fought magic, steel fought steel, strength fought strength in a battle of equals. Again and again the weapons clashed without disclosing a clear victor.

But while Mordred had only seven years of experience, Arthur had more than three times that.

They closed and grappled, their weapons useless for a moment. Arthur flung Mordred away with the strength of desperation, his boots skidding on the autumn leaves. Mordred fell, but sprang to his feet again cat-quickly, shrieking in fury as he ran at Arthur. Retreating, Arthur parried the ax blow and struck at Mordred with Excalibur, but the blade slid off Mordred's armor without wounding him.

He can only be slain by his own weapon! Arthur realized in a flash of inspiration. It must be true, if even Excalibur could not harm him.

Carefully Arthur laid his trap, circling and feinting until Mordred closed with him once more. This time when he flung Mordred to the ground, he followed up on his advantage, stamping down hard with his boot on the haft of the ax as it crossed Mordred's chest. The impact of the blow drove the spike at the back of the ax-head deep into Mordred's ribs.

Arthur reeled back, gasping with exertion.

As though it were only a practice bout, Mordred reached down and yanked the ax from his chest. He clutched at the wound, panting, and then raised his hand to pull off his helmet. There was blood about his mouth, but despite this, he seemed curiously unmoved. Slowly, painfully, he rolled over and got to his knees. He was gasping in torment, but his mouth was stretched in a murderous smile and his eyes never left Arthur's face.

The fight was over. All that remained was the execution. Arthur pulled off his helmet and cast it aside. When Mordred was dead his power would be broken, the battle ended.

"I'm sorry, Mordred," Arthur said in a ragged voice. He raised Excalibur to deliver the killing stroke.

"Tut-tut, Father," Mordred gasped weakly. "Another sin? You'd kill your own son?"

Arthur froze in horror. Only for a moment, but a moment was all that Mordred needed. He pulled the dagger concealed in his boot-top and thrust it into Arthur's chest.

The blade slipped through the plates of golden mail as though Arthur wore silk, not steel. He reeled back with the pain, his life's blood gushing like a hot waterfall from the wound.

Mordred gazed up at him, gloatingly.

And with his last ounce of strength, Arthur drove Excalibur forward into the wound Mordred's own blade had made in his black armor, and drove Excalibur into Mordred's heart. Mordred fell back against the autumn leaves, dying.

Pain rushed through Arthur's body like the flames of hell. He dropped to his knees and began to crawl away from Mordred, clutching Excalibur in his hand. He was dying, but the sword must be saved.

In the Land of Magic, Mab saw Mordred crumple to the ground, and for a moment she could not believe what she saw. Surely this was some trick, some feint?

But in her heart she knew it was not, and screamed a soundless wild scream of despair. Her world was crumbling away with his death, ebbing as his heart slowed. Mordred, the child of her black heart, her last love, was dying.

Excalibur!

Merlin fought his way painfully up out of sleep. It was Excalibur that drew him. In his dreams, he had seen Arthur fall. If Arthur died, who would wield Excalibur?

Then he was fully awake at last, the cries of the dying ringing in his ears, though Nimue still lay dreaming upon the leaves. Now Merlin could see the battle as well as hear it, see the two combatants—one as bright as the golden sun, the other as dark as death—battle until both of them fell.

Dying.

Arthur was dying.

Merlin struggled to rise. His senses were confused, but his course was clear at last.

Since the moment I reclaimed it for the world, Excalibur has brought about only suffering and pain. If magic's time is past, then Excalibur's time is over as well.

"Sir Rupert!" he called, staggering to his feet. His voice emerged as a weak croak.

Are we leaving? the horse asked, trotting up. The animal was saddled and bridled as always.

"Yes." Merlin said no more. He moved to mount, but it took him several tries to get into the saddle. His limbs were curiously weak. When he finally managed to mount, he looked back to see Nimue had wakened. She had gotten to her feet and was gazing toward him beseechingly. Her eyes were bright with tears at the sight of Sir Rupert.

"What is it, Merlin?"

"Arthur is dying." Admitting that was almost like admitting defeat. There was a heavy ache in Merlin's chest. "I must go to him."

She smiled, a smile of painful resignation.

"I'll be back very soon," Merlin said. *Just this one last task, Nimue. Then we will be together for always.*

"I'll be waiting for you. Always," she answered.

Merlin turned Sir Rupert's head toward the cave entrance. "Very soon," he repeated, as if reassuring himself. "I swear it." He rode toward the entrance of the cave.

Behind him, Nimue dissolved in tears.

The passage out of the cave was more oppressive than the journey in, and Sir Rupert, catching his rider's unease, was cantering by the time they reached the open air.

Merlin blinked at the brightness of true daylight after so much time spent in the Enchanted Forest. He had just reined Sir Rupert to a stop when suddenly there was a rumble behind him, and a tingle of magic over his skin. He turned, and stared in horrified disbelief as the rocks slid shut to seal the mouth of the cave.

He gestured, willing them to open again, but his magic had no effect. Though Sir Rupert tried to stop him, Merlin vaulted from the horse's back and ran toward the closing stones, as if mortal brawn could accomplish what wizardly magic could not.

But he strove in vain. The rocks came together, closing the Enchanted Forest away from the World of Men, and Nimue away from Merlin.

"Nimue! Nimue!" he shouted over and over, hammering his fists against the unyielding stone.

She had known that this would happen. All magic had rules and conditions that must be met. Mab would have explained them to Nimue before she brought her here. Merlin had sensed no trap when he had entered the cave, because there *was* no trap. It was Nimue herself who had been the trap. She had been supposed to bind him to stay within the cave through her love.

But she had not played the part that Mab had assigned to her. She had sacrificed herself so that Merlin could go free.

I will never see her again, Merlin realized with a pang of cold finality. The grief of his double bereavement—Arthur and Nimue, both lost to him in the same moment—was breathtakingly sharp. But he vowed that Nimue would not have sacrificed herself in vain.

"Sir Rupert!" Merlin shouted, turning back to his horse.

There was still time to reach Arthur and Excalibur.

Her robes—like her power—had faded to the soft grey of ancient dust, and streaks of bone-white swirled through her midnight hair. In the dirt and leaves of the forest floor, Mab knelt over the dying Mordred. Desperately she pressed her hands over the gaping wound in his chest, willing him to live.

It was useless. Once, long before the New Religion came to Britain, Mab had been Maiden and Mother as well as Warrior Queen. She had been able to grieve, and to love. But the power of life and death had never been Mab's to wield.

"I cannot save you," she complained, gathering Mordred into her arms.

Now all she had left was anger, and her voice was filled with a wild anger now as she commanded him. "Don't die, Mordred!"

Mordred gazed up into her face, and because he loved her, Mordred forced himself to smile. "Don't worry, Auntie Mab," he whispered, with a ghost of his old mockery. "That's the last thing I shall do."

And so it was. Mordred had never bothered to learn to lie, and he told the truth now. As he finished speaking, he gave a great sigh, and his body went limp.

He was dead. Mab's last, best, brightest hope. Her champion, her child, her love. Dead.

She looked up and saw Lord Idath, waiting to receive Mordred's soul.

"Save him!" she cried. "You are the Lord of Death— give him back to me!" Her fingers curved like claws. If Idath had been a mortal enemy, she would have fought him, but he was Death Itself, and her equal.

"Did I not tell you when you came for the Black Sword that Caliban was the last boon I would grant?" Lord Idath said inexorably. "You chose vengeance over love, Queen of the Old Ways. Be content with your choice."

Then he was gone, and Mordred's spirit with him.

Mordred had left her.

Mab was alone in a world that hated her.

But she no longer cared. Now Mab lived only to destroy.

She threw back her head and howled her vengeance.

There was a long trail of blood behind him in the leaves. Every inch was agony, but Arthur crawled doggedly onward. Excalibur must not fall into the hands of his enemies. He must reach water, so he could return Excalibur to the Lady of the Lake.

He could smell the lake ahead. At the edge of a steep

slope leading down to the water he stopped to rest for a moment. He could feel his strength ebbing with every heartbeat, and knew he was going to fail. One last failure, to set beside a lifetime of unmet expectations. Then a shadow fell across his face, and Arthur knew that he had been delivered from that final shame.

"Old friend," he whispered painfully, looking up at Merlin. "I knew you'd come."

Merlin smiled down at him, and if the old wizard's heart ached at the sight of Arthur's battered body, his face gave no sign of it.

"How goes the day, Arthur?" he asked quietly.

"I've seen better," Arthur whispered, and managed to smile.

Merlin knelt beside Arthur and put his arm around the dying man's shoulders, lending him the warmth and comfort of another human presence. He could do no more. The Old Ways dealt in illusion and trickery. Merlin had never learned any magic that could bring a man back from the gates of death.

"Take the sword to the lake. No one must have it . . ." Arthur said. He struggled to hand Excalibur to Merlin. Merlin stopped him, closing his hand over Arthur's. The King's flesh was as cold as rain beneath his palm.

"Go, Merlin," Arthur demanded in a whisper, his voice shaking with pain. "Now."

I can't let you die alone! a voice in Merlin's heart cried. But he knew he owed Arthur the peace of knowing Excalibur was safe.

"Rest easy, son. You were the right man to hold Excalibur," Merlin said as he took the sword.

Arthur smiled in triumph. His face was white with agony.

As gently as he could, Merlin laid Arthur back against the tree to rest. With Excalibur naked in his hand, he strode down the hillside to the lake.

Behind him, Arthur pulled himself up to watch Merlin go. The last effort was too much for him. With a soft sigh he toppled forward, his body rolling slightly along the slope in death.

Now that Arthur was not there to see them, the tears welled up in Merlin's eyes. He had held Arthur in his hands when the boy had been only a few hours old. Arthur had been the only son he would ever have, the crucible of all Merlin's hopes and dreams. No parent should ever have to watch the light of life fade from his child's eyes.

Merlin reached the water's edge.

"Take it back, Lady!" he shouted in grief. He flung the sword out over the water with all his strength, not certain of what would happen. The blade flashed as the sword spun, end over end, and finally began to fall toward the water.

An arm clad all in white samite thrust up out of the water to clasp the hilt of the blade and point it toward the sky. So Excalibur had flashed the first time he had seen it, and the ghost of the joy he had felt then was like a dagger in Merlin's heart.

The hand slowly sank below the surface of the lake, and Merlin heard Excalibur's magic song for the last time then as the Lady of the Lake drew the sword into her keeping once more.

But not forever. Excalibur was the sword of heroes. It would not rest forever. Someday, a new hero would wield it.

But not today. Camelot was broken and doomed. Lancelot—Guinevere—Arthur—Nimue—all were lost, all gone. Here on this very shore the Lady of the Lake had once promised Merlin a champion to protect Camelot. . . .

"You lied to me!" Merlin cried, sinking to his knees in an agony of grief.

"I didn't lie to you, Merlin."

He could see her out of the corner of his eye, swimming in the lake of air. She looked very much as she always had, silver as the lake itself and shining like the moon. She hovered in the air above the lake like a fish hovering in water and regarded him with distant kindliness.

"I told you the answer was at Joyous Gard," she said slowly.

"That's where I found Lancelot," Merlin said accusingly. *Lancelot who doomed us all.* But there had been no other warrior at Joyous Gard. Who else could Merlin have chosen as Guinevere's champion?

Suddenly Merlin realized the answer. He gazed up at the Lady of the Lake.

"It wasn't Lancelot, was it?" he said in a ragged voice.

"It was the boy," the Lady of the Lake said gently.

Galahad . . . who knows what would have changed if I had brought him to Camelot instead of Lancelot?

Merlin's face twisted with the bitterness of the realization. He had been wrong to blame Guinevere,

Lancelot, anyone but himself. The fault was his, and his alone. He had been so blind. . . .

"It's human to make mistakes, Merlin," the Lady of the Lake said in her slow, tidal voice. "And part of you is human . . . the best part. Good-bye, Merlin. My sister Mab was right about one thing. . . . When we are forgotten, we cease to exist."

Her last words were spoken with slow deliberation, as though she meant him to understand something beyond what she had said. But the day had been too long, too full of loss. Merlin stared numbly as the Lady of the Lake leaped high into the air and dove beneath the surface of the water once more, never to return. Then he turned his back upon the Enchanted Lake and trudged wearily away.

Frik crouched wearily at the base of a tree among a small group of the King's soldiers, staring at nothing as the baneful mist curled around them all. If the mist had been Mordred's spell, it had not vanished with him like all the others. If Frik looked up, he could still see the baleful red eye of the comet shining through the mist.

At least he was still alive, and Mordred wasn't. Frik supposed his being here meant that they must have won. That was something.

But Mab would want her vengeance for Mordred's death. Even without his magic, Frik had felt her screams of rage as they had reverberated through the forest. The Queen of the Old Ways no longer had anything left to lose.

Now you know what it's like to lose someone you

love, don't you, Mab? But I don't suppose it will make any difference. Compassion was never your strong suit.

Love had changed Frik, and this day had changed him even more. He was sickened by what he had done, caught up just as all of them had been in the wild joy of war. His armor was battered, his muscles ached, and his face was spattered with the blood of the slain.

Who would have thought mortals had so much blood in them? the gnome thought, shuddering. His mind was filled with the ghostly howls of the wounded, the phantom screams of the dying. He had seen pain and cruelty, malice and suffering, greater than anything he had ever imagined, and with his newly-human heart he had felt it all. After what he had seen today, Frik knew that he would never be able to go to war again, no matter how righteous the cause.

He felt as if he had bathed in the blood of men. Innocent men, for the most part, beguiled by Mordred. Now that the Black Prince was dead, the survivors of his army had fled, or surrendered, or gone mad and killed themselves. There was a rumor that Arthur was dead as well, but no one knew for certain.

The losses they knew about were bad enough: a few feet away Gawain stood leaning against a tree, weeping unashamedly for his father. Lord Lot had been killed by Mordred, along with so many others. Arthur's foster-father Sir Hector, his brother Kay . . . today the finest flower of Britain's chivalry had been ground down into the dust.

Frik heard the sound of a horse approaching. He looked up. Slowly the figure became visible through the mist. His eyes widened as he saw who it was. He got to his feet and faced Merlin.

So Mab didn't finish you after all, the gnome thought. *Well, I always said you were an apt pupil. A survivor, like me.*

"What are you doing here, Frik?" Merlin asked, dismounting from Sir Rupert's back. There was concern and caring in his voice.

"Betraying my principles, I'm afraid," Frik said, striving for his old ironic tone. It was strange to see his old pupil again under these circumstances, and warming to know that Merlin remembered him kindly. "Indeed, I've always believed it's better to be a coward for a second than dead for a lifetime. But here I am—fighting. And fighting on the side of right, which is worse." He smiled his old toothy smile.

"And Mab?" Merlin asked.

"As a matter of fact, I gave in my notice. If you're going after her, you'll need help."

Merlin smiled wearily. "All I can get, my friend." He clasped Frik warmly upon the shoulder, then walked past him to where Gawain stood.

"Gawain," Merlin said.

The Iceni prince looked up, his eyes slowly focusing upon Merlin. "So you came back," he said slowly.

"Arthur is dead," Merlin said, as gently as he could.

Gawain's face settled into lines of deeper grief. "I should have killed that little monster the moment he set foot in Camelot," he said raggedly. There was a moment of silence. "What of Excalibur?"

"Gone, back into the care of the Lady of the Lake," Merlin answered.

"Good. This isn't a world for magic swords—or for heroes." Gawain gazed at Merlin challengingly. "Arthur told me—if he should die—he wanted me to take the throne. I suppose I shall, now."

"I won't dispute your right. I don't suppose there is anyone now in all of Britain who has a better claim to the throne. Your aunt was Uther's sister, after all. You will make a good king, Gawain."

"I don't want the job," Gawain said, shaking his head in disbelief.

"All the best people don't," Merlin told him kindly. "I know you will do your best."

"I can begin now," Gawain said. "Show me where Arthur lies."

Merlin and Gawain brought Arthur's body back to their camp laid across Sir Rupert's saddle. The soldiers were straggling back toward the tents along with the most able of the wounded.

Gawain rallied the surviving troops, found horses, and sent men out with wagons to retrieve those who were so badly injured that they could not walk. Once that had been set in motion, he had Arthur's body laid out on a bier draped in scarlet samite, so that the men who had fought for him could pay their last respects to their beloved commander. Torches on long poles burned at each of the four corners of the bier, casting their wan illumination into the misty gloom.

"He will be buried at Avalon," Gawain said, standing

beside the bier. "Beneath the floor of the Grail Chapel, so that he can be as close as possible to the last earthly resting place of the Grail." He bowed his head in grief.

Merlin gazed down at the still face of the boy he'd loved and raised and relinquished to death. He had sacrificed everything for Arthur, but he did not feel bereft. What Arthur had striven for had been a worthy gamble, and the good that he had done would live on.

For a moment Merlin's mind was far away and long ago. Uther had been about Arthur's age when Merlin had gone to him to stop the greedy king's foolish war over Igraine. Standing in Uther's tent, Merlin had experienced a vision—of a golden King whose name would live for a thousand years. Despite all the grief, the pain, the loss, the betrayal that had come after, Merlin knew that his vision had not lied. Arthur would be remembered for as long as men sought the Light.

He watched beside Arthur's bier a few moments longer as the last of the day faded, and then went into the tent to rest.

"I've brought you a weapon," Frik said.

Merlin sat up, blinking owlishly.

The candles had burned low as he sat brooding over his wine. He must have dozed, for he had not heard Frik come in.

The gnome was still dressed as a soldier, his long pointed ears poking up from the sides of his plain bronze helmet and his shirt of scale mail gleaming dully in the dim light. As Merlin watched, he laid an object upon the table between them.

It was about as long as Merlin's forearm, white and curved like the twisted horn of a bull, but no bull had ever shed this particular horn. Its smooth surface gleamed with the translucent opalescence of mother of pearl, and as Merlin reached for it, he saw that its surface was covered with thousands of tiny runes, their strokes no thicker than a human hair.

The Horn's bell was rimmed in gold, and it had a gold band about its middle and a gold mouthpiece. Each of these three bands of gold was set with rubies and opals, and between and around them, the gold was carved with more faint symbols of magic. A strap of carved and gilded leather was attached to the Horn at two points, so that it could be slung over its owner's shoulder. The magic horn sparkled even in the faint candlelight, and even without touching it, Merlin's fingers tingled with the magic it radiated.

"What is this?" Merlin asked.

"I do hope you haven't forgotten all your lessons, Master Merlin," Frik said, simpering in his old schoolteacherish fashion. "This is one of the Thirteen Treasures of Britain, of course."

"The Horn of Idath," Merlin said, picking it up. The shock of its magic ran down his arm and through his chest as if it were alive.

He remembered his lessons well. The Horn of Idath had the power to strike terror into those who heard it, to suspend time, or to summon Lord Idath himself. It could not be used except by a Lord of Fairy or a wizard. Neither Frik nor Mordred, touched with magic though they both were, could have used its power.

"How did you get this?" Merlin asked.

"From an old friend of yours, as it turns out," Frik said. "My late employer turned him into a tree, but somehow she forgot to take this away with her. Careless of her. Perhaps she thought no one would notice it was there."

Merlin smiled grimly. A weapon, Frik had called this. But how was it to be used? He did not wish to summon Lord Idath, even if he could be certain the fairy Lord of Winter would help him in his battle against Mab. And its magic would not work against Mab directly. She had said it herself, when he had met her last near this very place: *"Magic only makes me stronger."*

Suddenly Merlin remembered something that the Lady of the Lake had said to him. It had not seemed important at the time, but now he thought it might hold the key: *" When we are forgotten, we cease to exist."*

He knew at last how to defeat Mab.

"Come, Frik," Merlin said, getting to his feet. "We can leave Gawain to deal with matters here. Tonight we must ride for Camelot."

He tucked the Horn carefully inside his cloak.

The two of them rode through the night and half of the following day to reach Camelot, but fast as they were, word of Arthur's death had already preceded them. The citizens of Camelot had fled the castle, the city, and the surrounding village, leaving not even a chicken behind.

But the city was not uninhabited.

Shadows of creatures that had once been the Bright Folk of Fairy slunk through its streets, hungering for human prey. Mab had created monsters in Mordred's honor, monsters enough to haunt the dreams of children for a thousand years.

The golden stone of Camelot had already begun to crumble, and black weeds had grown up through the blocks of stone. Broad patches of green scum already covered the surface of the shining lake, and the River Astolat had become choked with weeds. It had spread beyond its banks, turning the land around it to a stinking mire into which Camelot was slowly sinking. The city that Arthur and Lancelot had labored so long to build was crumbling away, and the wind wailed through its deserted towers with a sobbing sound that was nearly human. From this place Mab would spread the blackest of her magic, slaying what she could not subvert, until she had destroyed all of mortalkind on the Isle of Britain.

Unless someone stopped her.

"Here?" Merlin asked, looking down from the crest of the hill to the city of Camelot.

"Yes," Frik said, looking around. "This will do nicely."

"You know your part?" Merlin asked, for they had made their plans together on the long ride here.

"Perfectly," Frik answered. "I've always fancied that my skills lay in a literary direction, and I dare say this will be a perfect time to demonstrate them."

Merlin smiled bleakly and raised the Horn to his lips.

He blew the first note on the Horn, and it seemed as if he could see its magic, as if ripples moved out through the air at the sound as they would have from a stone thrown into water. The very fabric of reality rippled.

He blew the second note on the Horn, and the ripples

grew more pronounced, turning the world to concentric bands of light and dark, so that the vista around them seemed to form a dizzying spiral of ebony and gold, swirling like a whirlpool that pulled all into its depths.

He sounded the Horn for the last time, and now the ripples equalized. Everything became bright and still, glowing with the bright gold of summer.

As the last note of the Horn faded away, the Horn itself rippled in Merlin's fingers, crumbling away as if it were made of sand. He dropped it to the ground, brushing flecks of it from his fingers, and before it struck, the only parts left were the jewels and the three golden bands. Then the golden bands powdered away as well, and for an instant the jewels winked among the blades of grass until they melted like frost on an autumn morning.

The Horn had served its purpose.

Without another word, Frik and Merlin strode down the hillside into Camelot, to confront Mab.

CHAPTER NINE

THE BATTLE OF MAGIC

The two men, gnome and wizard, strode boldly through the crumbling halls of Camelot. Merlin knew exactly where Mab would be, in the one place in Britain that had been the seat of Arthur's pride and all his hopes.

As the two of them approached, the iron-bound, red-painted doors to the chamber in which the Round Table stood flew inward.

Mab was seated at Arthur's place at the table.

Mordred's death had aged her terribly, as if part of her magic had died with her last hope of victory. Her flowing hair was now more white than black, and where she had once worn glittering black, iridescent as crows' feathers, now her tattered raiment was the soft pale color of ancient dust.

"I knew I'd find you here, Mab," Merlin said as he

walked through the door. Frik strode beside him, his gnomish face pale but determined.

"So you've come to see my final triumph!" Mab whispered.

For the first time, Merlin felt a twinge of fear upon seeing her. The Queen of the Old Ways was truly dangerous now. Her magic was unraveling, and with it, the ancient bindings that had kept her from killing. The power she expended now she could not replace through her ancient earth magic, but even with her proud enchantments failing, Mab was still a thousand times more powerful than a mere half-human wizard who had not mastered the third stage of magic. In this moment, Mab was as deadly as a venomous serpent, and just as unpredictable.

But Merlin would not allow himself to care. Destroying her was too important.

"I've come to see your final defeat," Merlin answered implacably, standing across the table from her. How long had it been since he had stood in this very spot to tell Arthur good-bye for the last time?

"You were always a dreamer," Mab sneered. "Let me see," she said, ticking her words off on her fingers. "You've lost Arthur—the battle—your one true love—"

"The battle isn't over," Merlin said.

"She's weakened herself," Frik whispered in Merlin's ear.

It didn't really matter what he said. The point was that Mab see them together, both on the same side.

"All you have to do now, Master Merlin, is—"

"Why are you consulting with that traitor?" Mab demanded irrationally, for if Frik was a traitor to the Old

Ways, Merlin was just as much of one. She sprang to the top of the table and stalked across it, glowering down menacingly at the two men.

"Madame!" Frik protested, feigning outrage. "After all my years of faithful service! I mean, that's rather harsh."

"Not as harsh as I'm going to be," Mab growled. She raised her arms, preparing to hurl a lethal spell at her former servant.

"Sorry! Can't stay," Frik said briskly.

He turned and scurried from the room, slamming the doors behind him. A moment later, Mab and Merlin heard the sound of bolts being thrown. The room was sealed.

"Mordred's dead," Mab said, looking down at Merlin.

For a moment the inhuman rage in her features was replaced by grief. Merlin almost pitied her. To reach out so hungrily for love and to be so incapable of feeling it . . .

But that was no excuse for her crimes.

"So we both have nothing to lose," Merlin said, taking a step toward her. "The battle is just between you and me, Mab."

Merlin smiled faintly. He had never been her equal in wizardly power, and after the one attempt when he was a boy and another at Sarum, Merlin had known that he could never match her strength to strength. But now all the rules were changed.

The Queen of the Old Ways smiled as if to say she had expected nothing less from him. Then, in a heartbeat, she had put the width of the table between them once more, and with the tiniest of nods ripped it in half. The green-and-white table split down the center, its pieces flung to the walls, exposing the splintered ruin of its carved pedestal. Blue sparks of magic and the smoke of burning wood filled the chamber.

Merlin flinched back from the explosion, raising his arm to protect himself, but the destruction of the Round Table—a symbolic echo of an already-accomplished literal act—was not the real danger. As the dust began to settle, Mab leaned forward, her mouth stretched in the fearsome wail of the *bean-sidhé.*

Her soundless scream whipped itself around Merlin like the winds of a high gale, carrying splinters and small bits of debris with it. Slowly he was lifted off his feet, rising higher and higher until he was pressed against the timbered ceiling of the tower, a hundred feet above the flagstoned floor.

Quickly and carefully—for to fall would place Merlin wholly at Mab's mercy—he cupped his hands, feeling for the main thrust of the magic. When he was sure he had touched it, he turned it gently, not stopping it, but bending its force away from him. Slowly, he drifted safely back to the ground.

Mab glared at him, breathing hard with the effort the spell had taken. Merlin smiled to himself. Frik had spoken no more than the truth here a few moments ago. She was weak, her magic failing.

"I'll show you how weak I am!" Mab cried, as if she'd heard his thoughts.

She flung her hands out before her, fingers spread wide. Her nails became silvery dagger points, then arrowheads shooting outward on slender deadly shafts. With a shrug, Mab launched all ten of the deadly missiles straight at Merlin's heart.

In that instant Merlin achieved his apotheosis. He became a Wizard of Pure Thought, the highest stage of wizardry. He did not think. He did not plan. He simply raised his hands, knowing he must counter her attack. Knowing that failure was not an option. Knowing he must win.

In the twinkling of a thought, a shield grew in the air between his hand and the arrows, the central iron boss growing a fan of thick wooden planks that stopped all ten of Mab's missiles. It was white with a green band around the edge—the Round Table in miniature.

As the arrows thudded into it, Merlin straightened and flung the shield aside. He saw Mab snarl in disbelief. She had always mocked his weakness, his inability to master the highest grades of magic.

No more.

But Mab was far from being defeated. She reared back, and in her outflung hand grew a ball of pure brightness that danced there for a moment before she flung it, swift as a burning spear. Mab was no longer toying with Merlin. Now she was lashing out with the raw, untransformed power of magic itself, power that could unmake Merlin in an instant.

It took all of Merlin's power to deflect the elemental flame and send it careening about the room to spend itself against the carven beams of the roof, charring the praying angels fixed there.

On the heels of the first, Mab flung a second bolt, though she could little spare it, but Merlin brushed that one aside as well. She did not yet realize that Merlin was only countering her attacks, letting her expend her strength while he did nothing to fight back. Now he saw her draw deep upon her inner resources, holding her hands out before her and summoning up the biggest fire-bolt yet, an orb of flame a foot across that roiled darkly beneath its bright surface.

And outside the room, Frik was doing his part.

Merlin had blown Idath's Horn and summoned Idath's magic. Time had stopped in the chamber in Camelot where Merlin and Mab engaged in desperate battle, sealed away from the rest of the world while Mab, distracted from realizing what had been done, concentrated all her energies upon Merlin.

But it had not stopped elsewhere. Outside, the world went on without them.

Gawain was crowned on Christmas Day. He became King of Britain just as his father had once hoped, though the lands he ruled over were much diminished by the inroads of the Saxons to the east. Gawain married his childhood sweetheart, and they had a son named Constans who would come to rule Britain after him.

The Great Comet disappeared from the sky by the autumn of that year, and slowly the ravages of the wounded land began to heal. Some said it was because Galahad had found the Grail and returned it to Avalon Abbey. Those few who still followed the Old Ways said that Britain itself was the Grail, ever-renewing, ever-full.

And by the time Gawain died in a rich old age, people already thought Arthur was a myth, for King Gawain was the last of those who had known Arthur the man.

With his death, the last link to that age of marvels was broken, and slowly, as Merlin had once predicted, they came to believe that Arthur and all his companions were myths, tales from the morning of the world.

Frik helped that along, just as he had from the very beginning. He was first Gawain's court poet, then Constans's, then a traveling bard.

He told many tales of the wondrous King Arthur, who had defeated many foes, fought giants and dragons and enchanters, and brought peace and plenty to Britain by saying might must always be used in the service of right. He told of Arthur's beautiful wife Guinevere, who had loved Arthur's champion Lancelot. He told of Arthur's wizard, Merlin, the last of the great enchanters, who had gained the miraculous sword Excalibur and given it to Arthur so that he might prove himself the true King. He told of Herne and Morgan, of Uther and Igraine, of the Lady of the Lake and the Old Man of the Mountain, but in all his tales and stories, Frik wrote nothing of Mab. No one remembered her.

And others who followed him learned his songs and stories, and added stories of their own, of Mark and Tristan, of Iseult and Perceval. Years passed, and the wheel turned. Slowly the Saxons became Britons, as did the Normans who followed them into Britain.

Arthur's story lived on in all of their hearts, each generation telling it over afresh and adding new signs and wonders to it. They told of the wicked and beautiful enchantress Morgan le Fay, but there were no tales told of the Fairy Queen who had given Morgan her power.

No one remembered Mab at all.

And slowly the people came to settle on the river Astolat once more, and to build a new city there, though they no longer remembered that Camelot had once stood here. Camelot was not a real city. Camelot was a beautiful dream of a time long ago, before the end of magic.

But that was outside the room.

Inside it, Mab readied her last and most lethal attack. Merlin could have no hope of turning it aside.

And so he did not try. His purpose had not been to defeat Mab himself. The Lady of the Lake's words had taught him that she could not be defeated, for to make war upon her would only be to give her the power that came through remembering her name, and it was from fear and worship that all the Old Ones drew their power. And so Merlin had planned only to hold her here, to distract her while Frik made sure that the people of Britain forgot her completely.

And now they had.

The firebolt rolled through the air toward him, growing larger as it came. Merlin flung himself down and let it pass harmlessly above him.

It struck the door, and when it hit, it blew a great hole through the door, destroying the cocoon of magic in which the chamber had been wrapped for so many years. There were cries in the corridor beyond as the great glowing bolt of fairy-fire rolled through the people standing there, but it did not hurt them. They no longer believed in fairies or fairy magic, and thus it had no power over them.

Inside the chamber, when she saw that Merlin still lived, Mab snarled and hissed in pure animal fury. She was staggering with weakness—still dangerous, but only a shadow of her former self.

But in that instant, Mab thought she saw the path to victory. Through the open door she saw the people gathered in the hall. Frik must have summoned them, Mab decided, in order to try and rescue Merlin from her wrath. But the gnome had played right into her hands. The pain and suffering of the mortals gathered to gawk at her would fuel her waning powers, and their deaths would cause Merlin unspeakable agony.

"My strength may be fading," Mab hissed, "but I can still deal with these poor humans! What do you plan to do, use your puny swords and axes on me?"

"No," Merlin said, answering for them. "We're going to forget you, Mab."

He climbed through the smoking hole in the door, and walked out into the corridor. Frik was there waiting, and Merlin stood beside him. The people around him were puzzled at the disruption of their day, but already beginning to forget what had just happened. Everyone knew there was really no such thing as magic. And none of them had ever heard of Mab, or the Old Ways. All of them stood with their backs to the door. They knew there was no door there, just as there was no chamber behind it, and so they did not see either one.

"Merlin! What are you doing?" Mab cried imperiously. But of all those gathered in this hall, only Merlin and Frik could hear her.

Merlin half-turned to look back at her. "You can't fight us, or frighten us. You're just not important enough anymore. We forget you, Queen Mab. Go join your sister in the lake and be forgotten."

He turned away for the last time. He would always remember her, of course, and so would Frik, but two memories were not enough to sustain Mab's reality.

"Look at me!" she cried, and Merlin heard terror beginning to creep into her voice.

"Look at me!" she begged.

Of all things, Mab had most feared the oblivion that would come with being forgotten. The Lady of the Lake, the Lord of Winter, the Old Man of the Mountain, had all accepted their fates, and so their memories survived in Frik's stories, even though no one actually believed in their reality anymore.

The people in the corridor began to move away, back to their daily tasks.

But the Queen of the Old Ways had fought to stop time and the normal progression of things, and soon she would no longer be even a memory.

"Frik!" Mab cried desperately.

Merlin saw an expression of stubborn anger cross the gnome's face. Was it his imagination, or did Frik already look more human, less like a creature of the Old Ways? Frik walked away, ignoring his former mistress.

"Merlin!" Mab wailed. "Merlin!"

Merlin stayed where he was. He would not acknowledge her, but he owed one last duty to the people of Britain to watch over their greatest enemy until she vanished forever.

"Don't forget me, Merlin! I . . . love you," Mab croaked at last. "As a son!"

The Fair Folk could not lie. Perhaps what she said was the truth, or at least *a* truth. It did not matter. Mab had destroyed Merlin's ability to love her long ago. It was the greatest of the many injuries she had done him.

He began to walk away.

And then there was silence, and the faintest of whispered wailing. Merlin felt the last of Mab's magic thin out and fade away.

When he turned, all that he saw through the hole in the door was an empty room, and slowly the door faded, and the room beyond faded with it, and Merlin was alone.

He had won, but victory did not carry with it the joy and exultation that it ought, for his own losses were so very great. For the first time since his sixteenth year, Merlin found himself without a purpose in the world. The fight he had chosen—that had been his true destiny—was over.

But unlike the neat endings in the tales of bards, Merlin still had a life to live and a chance to live it. It seemed only days since he had lightly spoken those words to Arthur, but now Arthur was a myth and he, Merlin, the last wizard, was an anachronism, a creature out of time.

He left the castle. For months afterward Merlin searched for Nimue, for the cave, for the Enchanted Lake and the Door Into Magic. But he never found any of them again, and finally he gave up.

There was nothing now to tie him to Britain, and so he traveled, working at odd jobs along the way, always moving on when people became suspicious of him, as they nearly always did. For Merlin still carried Mab's blood in his veins. He was half-fairy, and though he aged, he did so far more slowly than mortal kind.

But age he did.

The Italian sun was a more generous overlord than the pale sun of Britain had ever been. Though it was barely March, the spring flowers were well established in the Tuscan hills, and the air was soft and gentle with warmth. It was a blessing for old bones. And Merlin was old, grey and bent with years of wandering.

The staff he had once carried for show and for power served now only as a support to his stiffness. The gnarled wood was still the same, but the wizard-crystal it had once borne was long gone. Merlin thought he had thrown it in the Tiber. Or perhaps the Danube. Whichever river it had been, it was a long time ago.

These days, everything seemed a long time ago.

Last night Merlin had dreamed. He'd stopped for the night in some country inn, where for a few coppers the landlord would give him a mug of beer and let him—an old man, with an old man's privileges—sit by the fire.

There he had dreamed, and in his dream Merlin had seen himself as he had been when he first came to the Land of Magic—so young! Frik and Mab were with him.

"This is you as you will be," he heard Mab say, *pointing at him as he drowsed by the fire in some country inn.*

The boy looked shocked. "Me? Will I grow that old?" *he blurted gracelessly.*

"Have a care, young Merlin!" he said, glaring at the

boy and tightening his grip on his stick. Had he really grown so old and grey that this young boy thought him unbelievable? This was his younger self. Perhaps he could help him, warn him about what was to come in his future: Arthur, Lancelot, Mordred. But what could he say that would help? "Try and always stay as young inside as you are now. And that's another thing. Don't start giving advice. It always ends badly."

"What—" the boy began, but Mab gestured, and Merlin awoke, the dream fading.

He knew it was a dream. Mab had been gone for many years, and Frik . . . well, Merlin didn't quite know where Frik was. He hadn't seen him since that day they had stood shoulder to shoulder in the halls of Camelot to put an end to Mab forever. Perhaps the gnome was dead, for Mab had taken away his magic, and without it Frik was as mortal as anyone else.

As mortal as Merlin.

It was time, the old wizard thought to himself, to go home. He had traveled enough, seen all that the world had to offer, fulfilled all the boyhood dreams that the years had left him. It was time to go back to the place where he had begun.

It was a bright autumn day in Nottingham, the day of the fair, and Marian had wandered away from her nurse to see the delights the fair had to offer *all by her self.* Marian was eight years old, and the daughter of the *shire reeve*—or as the Normans said it, *sheriff*—who was a very important man in these parts. Her father had given her a whole silver penny to spend on whatever she chose, and Marian wandered among the booths of the fair, trying to make up her mind what she would buy.

Here were bright ribbons tied in knots that fluttered against the wind, but she had ribbons a-plenty at home, and she had never had a silver penny of her own. There were slabs of gilded gingerbread and barley-sugar candy painted red, but still, the girl did not feel that such treats were special enough to spend her money upon.

Then she heard the voice.

Marian had always loved to listen to the bards that traveled through the land performing at weddings and other great occasions. It was said that King John had minstrels in attendance at his fine London court all the year around and so could listen to their songs any time he wished. Marian thought it was a great thing to be king, but even more than she loved the songs they sang, Marian loved the stories the bards sometimes told—old stories, of the days of heroes and marvels. When she heard the man's voice, she moved toward it as the bee moves toward the flower.

She reached the edge of the crowd and pushed through them until she had reached a place where she could see and hear clearly.

The storyteller was an old, old man. His white hair and beard flowed down over his shoulders, and he was dressed in a long raggedy robe that looked as if it had sticks and burrs caught in its weave. As he spoke, he leaned on a staff that seemed to be made from an old gnarled tree-branch. He was shabby and not very prepossessing, but Marian did not care. He was telling her favorite story of all, the story of Arthur the boy-king and how he had defeated the wicked sorceress Morgan le Fay and her evil son Mordred.

The storyteller told of the great battle Merlin fought as if he had really been there. Marian listened, enchanted, spellbound by his words until at last they drew to a close.

"I had won. I was trying to smile, but it was the smile of desolation. Inside I felt only the pity of the terror and the waste of it all. Everyone I ever loved, and who ever loved me, all gone, all gone down.

"But then Galahad returned, and brought with him the Holy Grail, and Spring, and the land became fertile again, and the cycle of death and darkness ended, and so does my story."

He turned aside and lay down his staff, and picked up a box, getting slowly and painfully to his feet.

"And now, if my story entertained or enchanted, you may show your appreciation in any way you think fit . . . but particularly with money." He set the box down on a tree stump and looked expectantly at the audience.

"Master Merlin!" Marian asked, clutching her penny. "Did you ever find Nimue?"

The old storyteller shook his head. "No, I never found Nimue, or even the cave again." He shook his head sadly.

Marian came forward and shyly dropped her silver penny into the box. The story had been worth it. And maybe he really was Merlin the wizard.

"Maid Marian!" her nurse called, and Marian, guilty, ran toward the familiar cry.

"What about the magic? Can you still do magic?" a man's voice called out.

Merlin sighed. He loved to tell the stories, but he hated the questions that inevitably followed. So often they were questions he had asked himself, over and over. This question was an easy one, though. They always asked about the magic.

"No," he said tolerantly. "I got out of the habit—and besides, nobody believes in it any more."

The audience that had gathered to hear him was drifting away, back to the other delights of the fair. Merlin looked down into the box. Two or three bronze groats, and among them, one shining silver penny. He wondered who had been so generous. He scooped the coins up and tucked them into a pocket, then glanced up. One of the townsfolk was still sitting on the bench, as if hoping Merlin would continue.

"It's all over, friend," Merlin said gruffly. "There is no more."

"It's not exactly the way I remember it, Master Merlin," a familiar voice drawled.

Merlin stared. "Frik?" he whispered in disbelief, peering toward the stranger. "Frik, is it you?"

The old man on the end of the bench drew back his cowl to reveal the long pointed ears and bulging eyes of a very old gnome—though he did not look quite as old as Merlin.

"Yes," Frik said simply, "it's me."

Frik's hair was white and wispy with age, but he was unmistakably Merlin's old teacher. He chuckled with delight at the expression of astonishment on Merlin's face, and Merlin joined him, more lighthearted than he had felt in many years.

They came together and embraced, two creatures of magic who had survived into a world that no longer believed in their existence.

"I must say," Frik said, "you do tell a good tale—terribly exciting and all—but I was intrigued that you chose to omit certain . . ."

"Well, that's how they like it," Merlin said philosophically. "Besides, I don't think they'd believe me if I told them how it really was." He held Frik at arm's length and studied him. "And how are you doing in this world, Master Frik?"

The elderly gnome simpered self-deprecatingly. "Well, I mean there will always be a need for the perfect gentleman's gentleman, and I was and always will be one of the best," he said with simple pride.

Together they walked away from the storyteller's circle. Merlin jingled the coins in his pocket.

"Meager pickings, Frik. Meager pickings," Merlin said with a sigh.

"You'd do better if you gave them some magic," Frik said judiciously. "Even if they don't believe in it any more, that's what they're always hoping for."

Merlin shook his head. "The time for magic is done. It would bring back too many sad memories." Of Nimue, and all that he had lost. Merlin sighed sorrowfully.

"As a matter of fact," Frik said, "that's why I'm here."

He led Merlin around a corner, to where an ancient

horse stood patiently waiting. Merlin stared in astonishment.

"It can't be—it is!" Merlin whispered as Frik chuckled in glee at the success of his surprise.

"Sir Rupert!" Merlin moved forward to stroke the old horse's satiny nose.

"I found him grazing in a field and we got to reminiscing," Frik said offhandedly.

Merlin found a bit of bread in one of the pockets of his tattered robe and held it out for the horse to take.

"Dear old boy! Shouldn't you be dead by now?" he asked, still stunned by seeing his old companion from the days of the Wild Hunt once more.

No, no . . . there's a little magic in me, too, Sir Rupert said fondly.

"Oh yes," Frik said casually. "I almost forgot. Nimue."

"What about her?" Merlin said levelly, for the memory of losing her still brought him pain, even after all these years. It always would.

"Oh, nothing, really," Frik rattled on in those too-casual tones. "Other than that she was inquiring about you when I saw her last month."

It took a moment for Frik's words to penetrate Merlin's senses. He turned slowly away from Sir Rupert to stare at Frik.

"I don't understand," Merlin said. He and Frik and Sir Rupert were all touched with magic, but Nimue was only mortal. Even if she had managed to escape the magic that Mab had set around her, she should still have died long ago.

Frik took pity on his bewilderment and explained.

"Sometime after Mab disappeared, her spells began to lose their power, and Nimue was set free."

Now Merlin understood. Nimue had been cocooned and protected by the last of the Old Magic on her passage down through the years. She was alive! Alive!

"Where is she, Frik?" Merlin asked eagerly.

"Sir Rupert knows," Frik said, with a touch of his old mysteriousness.

"Thank you, my old friend. For everything," Merlin said unfeignedly.

"Oh, no need to thank me," Frik said, raising his hands in protest as he began to walk away. "I just love happy endings."

And we've had too few of them in our lives, haven't we, Master Frik? Merlin watched for a moment longer as the gnome strode purposefully away, then turned back to the horse. Sir Rupert regarded him with a sparkling gaze.

"Well now," Merlin said. "Shall we see if either of us has anything left of our youth in us?" With the aid of a nearby bench, Merlin managed to mount his old companion, and old horse and ancient rider left the fair at a gentle walk.

Sir Rupert's leisurely ramble took them north, out of the town and toward the vast forests now claimed by the King as a hunting preserve. Merlin struggled to remain calm, but inwardly he was breathless with anticipation. To see Nimue again after so many years, to hear her voice . . . !

Slowly the landscape they traveled through began to seem familiar. It had changed greatly with the years, but

Merlin still recognized the trees of the forest through which he had roamed as a boy.

We're here, Sir Rupert said, stopping. *And now I'll leave you, Master Merlin. You won't need me again,* the horse said confidently.

Carefully, Merlin slid down from the saddle. Sir Rupert tossed his head and began to trot away, growing younger and more vibrant with each step. At last he gave a great leap into the air and disappeared.

Merlin hardly noticed. There, up ahead in the clearing, was Ambrosia's old cottage.

It had been much mended, and showed the wear of the passage of many seasons. But there was firewood stacked outside it in neat piles, and a curl of smoke wafting upward from the hole in the roof.

Barely able to breathe, Merlin began walking across the clearing. When he had covered about half the distance, a woman came out of the hut.

Her hair was as white as his own, and she wore coarse peasant clothing, but Merlin would have known her anywhere. It was Nimue. She smiled delightedly to see him and walked sedately toward him, moving with the carefulness of age. Though her face was seamed and lined with the tracks of age—and bore, once more, the scars of dragon-fire—she was more beautiful to him than she had been in her long-ago girlhood.

"Oh, my dearest," Merlin whispered, taking her gently in his arms. They kissed, as gently and companionably as the old lovers they were.

"Frik found you," Nimue said. Tears glittered in her eyes, and Merlin could feel her body trembling. Like him, Nimue had not dared to hope that Fate would allow them to be together once more.

"I never believed I would ever see you again," Merlin said quaveringly. "So many years lost."

Nimue nodded, her eyes growing sad. "You've grown older," she said, inspecting his white hair and fierce wrinkles.

"You too," Merlin said, wagging a finger at her and then touching her lightly on the tip of her nose. For some reason the simple remark struck them both as terribly funny, and they laughed together like schoolchildren. He hugged her tightly, and they began to walk toward the hut.

"Does it hurt?" Nimue asked.

Merlin knew what she meant. All the loss, all the failure, all the loneliness of his life . . .

"No," Merlin answered, still chuckling in the wheezy way of the very old. "Not anymore."

They stopped before the door of the hut. Nimue turned to face him.

"But . . . I think I still have one trick left," he said.

Merlin reached deep inside himself, calling upon his true magic, his heart magic. Not the illusions Mab had wanted him to learn, but the true transformation that he had once used to turn himself from a boy into a hawk—to bring the green of the spring. He reached out, stretching one hand toward Nimue's face, turning the other toward himself.

The magic kindled slowly. Nimue gasped as it raced over her, erasing the marks and scars of age, doing for her in truth what he had once tried to do for her in illusion: making her whole, young, beautiful.

Unscarred.

She stared at him in wonder as Merlin was transformed in turn: the white hair melting away to leaf-brown, the gnarled fingers and stooped back of age straightening into youthful vitality. Time ran backward as it filled his veins with the hot fire of youth.

Nimue cried out in wonder, reaching to feel her own smooth skin and to run her hand over his beardless face. Merlin kissed her again, this time with the passion of youth, and as he did Merlin felt the last of Mab's gift fade from his bones. His fairy heritage melted away, leaving him wholly mortal at long last.

He gazed down at Nimue. They had long lives before them now, lives to spend as they had always dreamed: together, at peace, in love. Not a princess and a wizard, but a husband and wife. It was all either of them had ever wanted.

"There's no more. That's the end of magic," Merlin said, smiling down at her.

And so it was.

APPENDIX A

THE CAMELOT COMET

There's a good reason to write about a comet coming to Britain at the time of Arthur's death: there probably was one. Though we have no definitive records from the chroniclers of the period, we have other ways of determining what was happening in sixth-century Britain, the period most commonly associated with King Arthur and the Matter of Britain.

Dendrochronology is the study of tree rings to provide evidence of ancient environmental conditions. Good years produce wide growth rings, while bad years appear as narrow ones. In western Europe in the past two millennia, one particular dendrochronological pattern stands out. Between A.D. 536 and 545, the weather in Britain wasn't good at all. In fact, this period is characterized by crop failures and famines worldwide, and constant references in contemporary records to a "dry fog" or "dust veil."

The relevance of this to the Arthurian mythos is twofold. First, Arthur's death traditionally heralds the beginning of a time of famine and drought in Britain. Second, the Arthurian mythos is inextricably intertwined with that of the Grail, which is also associated with famine. Now we have scientific evidence to indicate a widespread famine at precisely the period history has assigned to Arthur and the Grail.

Famine—drought—darkness—what could have caused them? Since we're able to rule out volcanic eruption, the likeliest answer is the close approach of a comet. Passing through its tail could load Earth's atmosphere with enough cometary debris to produce the same "little winter" that occurred on a much smaller scale in Tunguska in 1908. Records of heavy meteor showers beginning around A.D. 400 and extending for the next two centuries suggest that Earth was at increased risk from cosmic interlopers during this period, and a comet would fit the few facts we have.

Roger of Wendover actually reports that a comet passed near the Earth somewhere in the 540s. He reports that it could be seen from Gaul and that it was "so vast that the whole sky seemed on fire." Roger also says that in the same year "there dropped real blood from the clouds . . . and a dreadful mortality ensued." In *The Ruin of Britain,* written circa 540, the monk Gildas cites a long series of extracts from the Old Testament as being similar to contemporary catastrophes. Among other things, Gildas specifically mentions that the land was made a wilderness, the stars were dimmed, the sun and the moon were shadowed, and that there were clouds, fog, and plagues.

Though Science can only speculate, the novelist is more fortunate. What could be more fitting than that Arthur should die at the appearance of a red dragon that blazed through the sky in a time of war and destruction, the death of which heralded the beginning of a dark age of famine and plague?

A comet.

APPENDIX B

The Matter of Britain

Camelot wasn't built in a day, and neither was Arthur's legend. Here are some key dates from British history and the flowering of the Matter of Britain.

63 C.E.   Joseph of Arimathea comes to Glastonbury on the first Christian mission to Britain, bringing with him (according to legend) the Holy Grail.

184 C.E.   Lucius Artorius Castus, commander of a detachment of Sarmatian conscripts stationed in Britain, leads his troops to Gaul to quell a rebellion. This is the first appearance of the name Artorius in history. Some believe that this Roman military man is the basis for the Arthurian legend.

383   Magnus Maximus (Macsen Wledig) of Spain is proclaimed Emperor in Britain by

the island's Roman garrison. With an army of British volunteers, he quickly conquers Gaul, Spain, and Italy.

388   Maximus occupies Rome itself. Theodosius, the eastern Emperor, defeats him in battle and beheads him in July. The net result to Britain is the loss of many valuable troops needed for the island's defense.

396   The Roman general Stilicho reorganizes British defenses decimated by Magnus Maximus. Transfer begins of military authority from Roman commanders to local British chieftains.

406   In early January a combined barbarian force sweeps into central Gaul, severing contact between Rome and Britain. That autumn, the remaining Roman army in Britain mutinies, and the last legion withdraws from Britain the following year.

410   Britain gains "independence" from Rome, expelling weak Roman officials and fighting for itself against barbarian incursions.

c. 438   Probable birth of Ambrosius Aurelianus, scion of the leading Romano-British family on the island.

c. 445   Vortigern comes to power in Britain.

c. 446   Vortigern authorizes the use of Saxon mercenaries to defend the north against barbarian attack.

c. 457   Death of Vortigern.

c. 458–60   Full-scale migration of British aristocrats and city dwellers across the English Channel to Brittany, led by Riothamus (perhaps a title rather than a name), another candidate for the original figure behind the legends of Arthur.

c. 469 — Roman emperor Anthemius appeals to Britons for military help against the Visigoths. Reliable accounts name Riothamus as the leader of the British force. The bulk of the British force, including Riothamus, is wiped out in battle against Euric near Avallon in Gaul.

c. 470 — Ambrosius assumes high kingship of Britain.

c. 496 — Britons, under overall command of Ambrosius and possibly the battlefield command of the "war leader" Arthur, defeat Saxons at the Siege of Mount Badon.

c. 496–550 — Following the victory at Mount Badon, the Saxon advance is halted, with the invaders returning to their own enclaves.

c. 501 — The Battle of Llongborth. Arthur is mentioned in a Welsh poem commemorating the battle.

c. 540 — Probable writing of Gildas's *De Excidio Britanniae.*

c. 570 — Probable death of Gildas.

c. 600 — Aneirin, a Welsh bard, writes *Y Gododdin,* alluding to Arthur's prowess as a warrior.

c. 830 — Nennius compiles *Historia Brittonum.*

c. 970 — *Annales Cambriae* compiled. It dates the Battle of Camlann to 542. Geoffrey of Monmouth follows this dating when writing in 1136, and adds the death (or unspecified other disappearance) of Arthur to the end of the battle.

c. 1019   Earliest possible date of composition for *The Legend of Saint Goeznovius,* a Breton legend that mentions Arthur and calls him the King of the Britons.

c. 1090   Professional hagiographers write various saints' lives, some of which include mentions of Arthur and his exploits

1125   William of Malmesbury completes *Gesta Regum Anglorum,* which states, "This is that Arthur of whom the trifling of the Britons talks such nonsense, even today; a man clearly worthy not to be dreamed of in fallacious fables, but to be proclaimed in veracious histories as one who long sustained his tottering country and gave the shattered minds of his fellow citizens an edge for war."

1129   Henry of Huntingdon writes *Historia Anglorum.* Ten years later, in a letter to Warinus, Henry describes Arthur's last battle and mentions that the Bretons say that he didn't die and are still waiting for his return.

1136   Geoffrey of Monmouth publishes *Historia Regum Britanniae.*

1155   Master (Robert) Wace completes *Roman de Brut,* a version of Geoffrey's "History" in French. He is the first writer to introduce the concept of the Round Table to the Arthurian cycle.

Of Arthur, Wace says,

"I know not if you have heard tell the marvellous gestes and errant deeds related so often of King Arthur. They have been noised about this mighty realm for so great a space that the truth has turned to fable and an idle song. Such rhymes are neither sheer bare lies, nor gospel truths. They should not be considered either an idiot's tale, or given by inspiration. The minstrel has sung his ballad, the storyteller told over his tale so frequently, little by little he has decked and painted, till by reason of his embellishment the truth stands hid in the trappings of a tale. Thus to make a delectable tune to your ear, history goes masking as fable."

c. 1160–90	During this period, Chretien de Troyes makes his contributions to the Arthurian cycle, including the first mention of Lancelot, Camelot, and the Holy Grail.
1184	A great fire ravages Glastonbury Abbey, destroying the Old Church. "Arthur's Grave" is discovered at the Abbey six years later.
c. 1190	Layamon publishes *Brut,* an English translation of Wace into alliterative verse. His work marks the first appearance of the Arthurian story in English.

And so on, to the present day . . .

FURTHER READING

If you want to delve deeper into the story of Merlin, King Arthur, and the Matter of Britain, here are some places to start:

For Young Readers

King Arthur, by Howard Pyle and Jerry Tirtitilli (Troll Books, 1989). Adapted for readers ages 4–8 from the Howard Pyle original.

The Story of King Arthur and His Knights (1903; reprint, Atheneum, 1991). The classic 1903 retelling of the Arthurian legends for ages 9–12, excellent for reading aloud.

For Older Readers

The Acts of King Arthur and His Noble Knights, by John

Steinbeck. A retelling of the Arthurian legend, with much of the original language preserved.

The Once and Future King, by T. H. White (19th reprint, Ace Books, 1996). The classic modern retelling of the Arthurian legend, basis of the musical *Camelot.*

Further Research

The Arthurian Handbook, by Norris J. Lacy and Geoffrey Ashe (Garland Publishing, 1988). A critical survey of the Arthurian legend from the fifth century to modern times.

The Arthurian Encyclopedia, edited by Norris J. Lacy et al. (Garland Publishing, 1986). As the title says, an encyclopedia of things Arthurian, with substantial entries on modern Arthurian writers.

The Discovery of King Arthur, by Geoffrey Ashe (Henry Holt, 1987). The first of the recent books to discuss the evidence for a "historical" King Arthur.

On the Internet

HTTP://WWW.LINKFINDER.COM/ARTHUR.HTML is a resource for links to various Arthurian sites on the Internet.

HTTP://DC.SMU.EDU/ARTHURIANA is the website of the International Arthurian Society. Links, membership information, and subscription information to *Arthuriana,* their quarterly journal, can be found here.

About the Author

James Mallory attended schools in California and the Midwest before moving to New York to pursue a career in writing. From an early age Mallory has been fascinated both with the Arthurian legends and their historical evolution, an avocation which also triggered a lifelong interest in fantasy literature. Mallory's interests include hiking, comparative religion, and cinema.

Royal Assassin

Book Two of The Farseer Trilogy

Robin Hobb

The legend continues . . .

Regal's treasonous attempt to usurp the Six Duchies throne from his half-brother Verity has been foiled; but Fitz has been left prone to bouts of trembling and faintness as a result of the foul poison administered to him.

One night, Fitz has a dream: of Red-Ship Raiders sacking a coastal village, leaving not a single man, woman or child alive or unForged, including, it seems, a familiar dark-haired woman sheltering two children in a fisherman's cottage. Was it Molly he saw in his dream? Is she still alive; or worse, has she been Forged? Tortured by this terrible vision and by his physical traumas, Fitz returns to the Six Duchies court. Where all is far from well . . .

'Robin Hobb writes achingly well'   *SFX*

ISBN 0 00 648010 1

Assassin's Apprentice

Book One of The Farseer Trilogy

Robin Hobb

A new legend begins . . .

In a faraway land in which members of the royal family are Named for the virtues they embody, one young boy will become a walking enigma.

Born on the wrong side of the sheets, Fitz, son of Chivalry, is a royal bastard, cast out into the world, friendless and lonely. Only his magical link with animals – that old art known as the Wit – gives him solace and companionship. But the Wit, if used too often, is a perilous magic, and one abhorred by the nobility.

So when Fitz is taken from his warm stable and finally adopted into the royal household, he must give up his old ways and learn a new life: weaponry, scribing, courtly manners; and how to kill a man secretly, as he trains to become a royal assassin.

'Refreshingly original'   JANNY WURTS

'I couldn't put this book down'   *Starburst*

ISBN 0 00 648009 8

Assassin's Quest
Book Three of The Farseer Trilogy
Robin Hobb

'*Keystone. Gate. Crossroads. Catalyst.*'

Fitz is about to discover the truth of the Fool's prophecy. Having been resurrected from his fatal tortures in Regal's dungeons by channelling his spirit into the body of his wolf Nighteyes, Fitz has once more foiled the evil prince's attempts to be rid of him.

Now, back in his own body, and after months of rehabilitation, Fitz must begin the painful and slow process of learning the ways of a man again. Under the watchful eye of Burrich, old King Shrewd's Stablemaster, Fitz must learn to cast off the ways of the wolf and enter the human world once more: a world beset ever more viciously by the relentless Red Ship Raiders who are now left free to plunder any coastal town they please. But more immediately, a world in which Fitz finds himself utterly alone . . .

'Achieves a bittersweet, powerful complexity rare in fantasy'
Locus

'An enthralling conclusion to this superb trilogy'
Kirkus Reviews

ISBN 0 00 648011 X

WIN A TRIP TO NASA

worth over £2,000 with *Voyager*Direct

The book you're holding now is just one of the many fantastic titles you could be getting direct to your door. What's more, order our new catalogue today and you could be heading for Florida.

Exclusive offers, big savings, signed copies and free books! *Voyager*Direct – A whole new world direct to your door

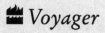 *Voyager*

www.voyager-books.com